GLACIER MURDER

GLACIER MURDER

A PHILIPPA BARNES MYSTERY

TRISH MCCORMACK

Glacier Press

Published by
Glacier Press
Wellington
New Zealand
glacierpress@gmail.com
2016

Cover Design: Jared Davidson garage.collective@gmail.com

ISBN: 978-0-473-35379-7

Typesetting services by BOOKOW.COM

To Paul for believing in my writing, to Ghosty for being there for the whole ride and to Annie for keeping things real.

Acknowledgments

My first thanks go to my parents, Elizabeth and Peter McCormack, who gave my sister Annie and me the Franz Josef Glacier as our playground. From an early age we scrambled all over the glacier; its icy surfaces were as familiar as our back garden. Cecilia Edwards has been as much of a friend to my writing as she has to me. She knows the Coast and its people and was able to give valuable comment on Glacier Murder as it evolved. Many thanks to Anne Couper for her great editing. Glacier Murder is vastly improved as a result. Anne gave me a lot of work to do and made me laugh. Honourable mention to Andrew and Steph as well. Thanks to Bev Robitai for copy editing and for reading Glacier Murder from the perspective of a fellow crime writer. Her feedback has been invaluable - not to mention all the work she has done getting my crime novels into the digital age as ebooks. My mother took the photo of the glacier that has been used for the cover. Jared Davidson, colleague and fellow author, transformed a 1950s Kodak slide into a creative and beautiful book cover. It fits the story brilliantly. I've had a lot of support but any mistakes and all thoughts of murder are my own.

Prologue

'THE jury's coming back – and they have a verdict!' The words rang out from the tangle of television cables, cameras and reporters clustered outside the High Court.

I had walked past a few times already that day, and found the reporters looking bored as they waited on the street, cameras and microphones ready for action that never seemed to come. Two blonde women television reporters were glamorous in bright jackets and tight skirts. They looked cold. The camera crews were warmly dressed in puffer jackets and beanies. A cool wind whipped down the street.

The jury had been out for two days. And now they were back. The media pack scrambled for their camera equipment. My heart rate sped up and I started to run.

It was a long way from the busy city street to the icefall of the Franz Josef Glacier where this story had begun. A long way and a long time. I still couldn't really believe that it had come to this. People were filing into the public gallery of the court and I followed.

The silence was total.

Reporters were setting up their equipment on the press benches. The public gallery was almost full. I sat next to an old woman who seemed to be having breathing difficulties and it served as a useful distraction.

'Are you okay?' I whispered.

She nodded. 'I'll be fine in a minute. Aren't we lucky to be here?'

It wasn't a word I would have used. We stood up as the judge came in. I looked at the jury. Eight women and four men. They looked tense. I looked at the back view of the person in the dock and felt nothing but sadness. How must it feel? Would there be any feelings left after all that had happened? I had been so sure of what the verdict would be – but suddenly I was full of doubt. My hands were shaking and I squeezed them together.

'Have you reached a verdict?'

'We have,' the foreman replied.

'And is this the verdict of you all?'

'It is.' 'How do you find the accused – guilty or not guilty?'

I stared at the person in the dock and held my breath.

Chapter 1

One year earlier

It was not a day for death. My life in Franz Josef had settled into a comfortable groove. The glacier was a brilliant place to lose oneself. Once up in its white silence there was plenty of space to think and be free.

The trouble was that there didn't seem to be a lot to think about. Futility, my old companion, had been stalking me for weeks. I wasn't unhappy but there didn't seem to be anything worth striving for any more. Once upon a time this would have frightened me. I knew it was bad to be in a place where nothing mattered and you couldn't summon up the energy to care.

Things were too easy, that was part of the problem. My young sister Kate and I were getting along well now that the intensity had gone. You could only grieve for so long and this was a good thing. Our parents had been killed in a climbing accident over a year ago. The whole thing had been unspeakable and horrific but we were past the worst of the pain, free to get on with our lives.

Now I was bored. It was getting to the stage where I almost wanted Kate to do something I couldn't cope with just to make things interesting again.

There was something else on my mind that day. Tim Wallace, my perennially single boss, had met someone and was off to spend six months with her in Canada. And he had asked me to run his glacier guiding company while he was away. That meant managing the guides, running the glacier operation, and keeping onside with the Department of Conservation.

DOC, as everyone called it, administered the national park, and this included Tim's glacier guiding concession. The relationship between tourism operators and DOC was often difficult. Tim was much more tactful than me and had good political savvy which served him well when dealing with bureaucracy. I wasn't sure I was up to the task. But Tim had been good to me and this would be a way for me to help him. I was the most experienced guide but I wasn't at all sure what I'd be like at looking after a team of disparate personalities and keeping the changeable beast that was glacier guiding on track. Chances were Tim would come back from overseas and find his thriving business in tatters.

I tried not to think about it as I approached the terminal face of the glacier. I strapped on my crampons and stood up abruptly, feeling a rush of blood to my head which reminded me I hadn't eaten anything for hours. The ice was crystalline and wet. I crunched my way upwards with ease, feeling my body in tune with this much-loved cold place. I tried to empty my mind, walking with the terrain – a side step here to avoid a pinnacle, a leap there to avoid a crevasse. This was good. It was real and fresh and free.

Jumping over a small crevasse I glanced down and saw a strange-looking rock perched on an ice hummock just under my feet. At first I didn't know what I was looking at. It was a weathered brown colour and its shape was familiar. It was – it couldn't be – but it was.

Oh God It was a human hand, twisted and leathery yet still recognisable.

I stepped back sharply, forgetting I was on crampons, nearly impaling my left leg with the spikes on my right foot. After a second I moved forward again to the edge of the crevasse, knowing what I was about to see even before I looked in.

There was a body down there, curled away from the light in this coldest of wombs. Blue ice and brown flesh.

I rocked back from the edge, disturbed but not really puzzled. Lots of climbers died in the mountains and their bodies were not always found. There had been a strange guy in town a few years back who'd gone climbing up the glacier alone and never returned. The chances were it was him, but I knew it could be anyone really. It was incredible that something as soft as a human body could survive the pressure of a ride through what amounted to an ice wringer, but this wasn't the first time such a thing had happened.

I recalled a story told by an old mountain guide. He'd been walking down the Hooker Valley at Mount Cook one day when he'd noticed something that didn't looked like tussock. It had turned out to be the remains of someone's head, complete with a vigorous tuft of red hair. It had survived decades being thrown around by a glacier after its owner lost his life on Mount Cook.

This particular body looked too small to be human but ice could compress that which it couldn't destroy.

This was a good antidote to boredom. There was stuff for me to do now. The search and rescue guys would need to come up and dig the body out of the crevasse and the police would have to be advised. And somewhere out there in the world a family would find out what had happened to their lost son or grandmother – or whoever. It was sad, but when you lived in the mountains it was the kind of thing that happened.

I glanced again at the hand. It must have been torn free as the body was mangled by the ice, and I wondered at the chance that had cast it up on the surface for me to find. I'd have never seen the rest of the body if I hadn't seen the hand. Another day and the ice would have moved again and the hand would have plunged back down to join its body and the whole thing would have disappeared as the crevasse reshaped itself around it

That's when I saw it. There was a ring on the middle finger made of some kind of metal. It was elaborate and shaped like tendrils on a vine. In the centre a black opal glowed from its bed of metal. It was a strange and rather sinister-looking ring. And I'd seen it before. Back when I was Kate's age and the world was an easy place to live in.

...

Vivien Revell had a gift. She brought vitality and meaning to the smallest actions and everyone wanted a part of her, this young woman who could make life glow. She had long black curly hair and unusual dark green eyes. She dressed like a gypsy in flowing dresses in primary colours when everyone else wore casual tops and body-hugging pants. She laughed at the world and everyone in it. She was clever. She had gone away to university but unlike most who'd left the glacier village forever, she had come back.

She'd come to the local school to talk about the mountains and their history.

'You,' she'd said, pointing to a random boy at the back of the classroom, 'when did you last go on the glacier?'

'I haven't,' was his answer.

'Then shame on you and all you other children that live in this magic place and never go there,' she had said with a laugh in her voice that took the sting from the reproach. And she'd gone on to tell us just why the village we lived in was unique, how it drew mountaineers from all over the world, how there were stories galore and that people who lived here should show more interest in them.

'I'm writing a book about Patrick Blake,' she had told the class. 'Who can tell me about him?'

The boy who had never been on the glacier had put up a hand, obviously trying to make up for his deficiency. 'He was one of New Zealand's greatest mountaineers – he could've been better than Hillary if he'd had the chance.'

Yes!' Vivien had replied. 'That's what a lot of people said but you know, if he was that good, what stopped him?

My classmate didn't know.

'We make myths about people,' she explained. 'Patrick Blake was lucky – he was a hero back in this village when your parents were at school, so he had everyone on his side. Not everyone has that advantage. Maybe he could have been another Hillary but he didn't achieve that. It's not about chance, it's about choice. Some of you will leave this place and never look back and some of you will stay. The thing to remember is to let it be about choice. If you choose, you win.'

I had never forgotten the vibrant young woman who stood in front of our class that day. Sometimes when I was in one of my bored spaces I remembered the energy and life that had been Vivien and felt dull and ashamed. Of course no one that brilliant stays in one place for long and Vivien had spun out of the village one day and had never come back. I'd imagined her having a life of adventure, pausing only to gather people and experiences around her before she flew on to the next thing and left them all behind. Vivien Revell inspired and then she fled, leaving energy and colour in her wake.

It was inconceivable that she had gone nowhere after all. That her life had been crushed by a glacier, her body ground to pieces, and then thrown into the harsh late summer sun for me to find.

Chapter 2

I jumped off the glacier, stripped my crampons from my boots, and set off down the moraine as if the devils were after me.

All was normal down here in the valley where the tourists swarmed. Solitude? You could forget it. That was what made the glacier itself so special; it was rare to be disturbed in the places I climbed and this made it harder to cope with the sudden onrush of people once you descended to riverbed level.

Today I saw a young couple arguing, a young man talking loudly into his mobile phone and a family group posing for a photograph dangerously close to an ice cave. I jogged down the valley, my crampons bouncing noisily against my pack as my thoughts whirled. My car was old and I flooded the engine in my haste to start it. This was silly. There was no hurry.

I recalled the story of a small plane that had crashed high in the icefall decades before. The locals had salvaged wheels, seats and virtually everything else that could be taken off the fuselage, but the skeletal frame of the plane had been left to make its own way down, borne by ice currents to reach the terminal – or front face – of the glacier many years later.

Vivien had disappeared from Franz nearly twenty years ago, so she must have been high on the glacier when she'd had her accident. If she had fallen lower down on the ice her body would have reappeared at the terminal years ago.

I frowned, trying to think about what must have happened. Although Vivien had been so enthusiastic about the glacier and the mountain history of the area, she'd been a novice climber. My father had taken her on the ice a couple of times, I seemed to remember. What had possessed her to go up there on her own? And why had no one gone looking for her?

There'd been no mystery about her disappearance from the village – I'd have remembered if there had been. Her mother, Rose, had told everyone her daughter had got sick of researching and had gone overseas. This was just what you'd have expected someone as adventurous as Vivien to do. But she hadn't. She'd come up here to die, her body pulled every which way by a slowly moving glacier.

I drove into the village and pulled in to the guides' office. The main street was teeming with people. The billboards were out in force as were the café tables. The sky throbbed with tourist helicopters, a sound I hated.

'Philippa! Philippa!' I turned towards the sound and smiled at Jem Brown and Angie Bennett, two locals with time on their hands, who spent a lot of time hanging out in the village. They were seated at a café table, each with a pint of beer, and I dropped into a seat grateful for their company. These two were Franz Josef's answer to MI5. They had an unerring instinct for news and knew just how to uncover the best seams of village gossip. They were wasted here; they'd have made great tabloid journalists. People underestimated them and told them stuff they shouldn't. They made an incongruous pair. Angie was tiny with a pointed face and very short black hair. She cultivated an "après-climbing" look, always dressed in the most fashionable outdoor casual gear even though I knew for a fact she never went near the mountains. Jem, old enough to be her grandfather, sported the dissolute look. His sparse grey hair framed a drinker's face, red and lined, while his ancient corduroys and work shirts were so old and worn they looked painted on in places. The only hint that life wasn't completely on the skids for this old man was his eyes – shrewd, bright and eternally interested.

He and Angie were mates, drawn together by an insatiable interest in the goings-on in the village. They scored well today.

I looked at them for a moment, then spoke, my voice shaky: 'You'll never guess what I've just found – Vivien – you know Vivien Revell. She didn't leave – I've just found her body on the glacier!'

They stared and then with the skill of a pair of surgeons drawing shattered glass from an open wound they were in, asking all the right questions as I poured out every detail of my discovery.

'Well!' Jem leaned back in his chair and sipped his beer. 'I always thought it was damned odd the way Vivien up and left like that.'

'She was always up and leaving,' Angie objected. 'I didn't think anything of it.'

'You were busy back then, lass,' he said.

Angie grimaced. 'Yes... Mum was dying. I wasn't out much. Funny though – I did think of her on and off down the years. Rose never talked but I put that down to a falling-out.'

Rose Revell was an artist. She'd arrived in Franz one day, trailing a young daughter and a host of unusual friends. Franz had never experienced anything like it. There had been the woman who appeared in the village store to buy cigarettes clad in nothing but a large towel. Then there was the man in the kilt...

'Remember that odd bugger in tartan,' Jem said as if he had been reading my thoughts. 'Standing in the middle of the road singing.'

He'd been Franz Josef's first busker, that long-ago visitor of Rose's, and it had caused a sensation in Franz. It had all been put down to drugs and immorality, and as a result of all the Revells' unusual visitors, many of the locals hadn't exactly encouraged their children to make friends with Vivien.

There had been one exception. Julia McLoughlin had been the same age but from a very different world. Her father had left her mother, Ann, years before and she and Julia lived in a cold old farmhouse and eked out a living somehow. Ann worked as a housemaid at the tourist hotels in season and did other odd jobs but there was never a lot of money around. Ann and Rose might have been the village's only solo mothers but there any similarity ended. Ann was hard working and lived a simple life while Rose didn't seem to work at all but oozed flamboyance and style.

Their daughters should have had nothing in common either. Julia was sensible. That was the best way I could describe her. She planned a future that didn't involve menial hard work and went for it, fully encouraged by her mother who wanted to see her girl educated with options in life. Julia was a jeans-and-jersey person. She was attractive, but made no effort to enhance her looks, looked on rather than leaped into social situations, and worked hard. She was in Wellington these days, working for some government department. Doing what, I had no idea. But she came home often and had gradually made her mother's life more comfortable, renovating the farmhouse so that it no longer seemed cold and miserable. Her mother visited her in Wellington often too. They were close.

Vivien and Julia had been inseparable right through childhood – and beyond into university even though they must have had many other opportunities to find friends by then. I wondered if Julia had ever challenged Rose's explanation that her daughter had gone overseas and never come back.

'So what now?' Angie interrupted my thoughts. 'You're going to have to tell the police.'

'And search and rescue. It's going to be a job getting her body out of that crevasse. It looked embedded,' I said with a shiver.

As I spoke, the glacier excursion bus pulled up and Tim leaped out. There were no tourists on board. I ran to meet him and told my story all over again.

Tim looked concerned. He hadn't known Vivien but it wasn't every day you found a body in a crevasse.

He frowned to himself as he thought it through. He is good looking if you're into outdoor macho – which I was. But for some reason there'd never been a spark between us. He had been single until very recently, but for me he'd always been more of an older brother than a love interest. This was good. I was notoriously hopeless with men and Tim was one friend I wanted to keep.

'We need to get the police up there as soon as we can. And the search team … Do you want to give Stu a call, Philippa? I'll get some gear together and we can go up now.'

'Ok. I'd better tell Jem and Angie to keep things quiet till we tell Rose.' I had a sudden thought. 'Hell, I hope I've got it right. I'm basing an awful lot on that ring. I didn't see her face.'

Tim looked alarmed. 'Yeah – you know what this place is like – especially when those two are involved.' I ran back to Jem and Angie and swore them to silence, then went into the guides' office and rang our local cop. Stu Adams had come to Franz Josef thinking it was going to be a cruisy rural lifestyle change. It hadn't proved that way and he had to deal with plenty of rural crime as well as mountain accidents and aircraft crashes. He sounded hassled as I told him what had happened and he said he would meet Tim and me at the guides' office in ten minutes.

Jem and Angie had abandoned their pints and were both perched outside the office watching Tim loading gear into his pack. Further down the street tourist billboards were being taken in for the night. I looked around me and sighed. Franz was getting so commercial. The village was wedged between rainforest and the glacier-fed Waiho River. It had been a quiet place once and during floods you could sometimes hear the grinding of chunks of glacier ice being borne down the river. Now it was noisy and the only thing you heard was the sound of tourist helicopters. When I was a child there was nothing like that in our skies and the few tourism operators lived in apparent harmony. Now the competition for the tourist dollar was fierce. It was always a relief to look past the commerce-cluttered main street to the mountains high above the village. At least they hadn't changed.

Tim appeared. 'I've rung DOC. Callum's on his way.' I pulled a face. Callum Jackson was the head of DOC in Franz - and as far as I could see he'd been chosen for his mountaineering skills not his personality. A good man to have on a search and rescue – and he had street cred with the locals because he was more rugged than any of them, which made a change from some of the city-bred rangers that had lived here over the years. Callum was a village mystery. He'd come here to climb and lived in a dilapidated gold miner's hut while he built himself a house. I didn't particularly like the guy but I admired what he's done with his section. He'd left most of the bush intact and built a two storey cottage with a pitched roof, dormer windows and lots of stained glass. Very few people got inside his front door. He'd been here a couple of years when the job he now occupied became vacant and we'd all been surprised when he was appointed. Callum didn't do politics and he suffered no fools. Not good qualities for the average public servant. I should have liked the guy. He was so damned ornery; we should have got on well. But we didn't. He was one of the reasons I didn't really want to manage Tim's guiding business. It would mean regular meetings with Callum, something I was already dreading.

Callum was good to look at. He was tall with untidy fair hair which he wore longish. He had a determined face and great physique and a total lack of interest in his appearance. He wore his DOC uniform carelessly. His shirt often hung out, his clothes were never ironed and he slouched round the village in boots that were never laced up. His looks were a problem for him. If he'd been short and fat with bad eyesight all the locals would have been happy to leave him alone and make up stories about him. Instead women tried to salvage him and they were all rebuffed. Except Vivien. *She* had got herself in that front door of his, so Angie had once told me.

'What was the story with Callum and Vivien?' I asked her.

Angie shrugged. 'Who knows? She did all the running, I re-member that much. She never looked happy when she was with him.'

'And the next thing you know she vanished,' Jem said. 'You have to wonder.'

'Wonder what?' Angie looked disbelieving. 'You're not suggest-ing he did her in are you?'

'Could've. He doesn't like encumbrances, that one.'

'You're being ridiculous.' Tim gave Jem an irritated glance. 'I don't know why everyone is so critical of Callum. He's not a bad guy. And there's no way Vivien was murdered. It must have been an accident. Any other suggestion is mad.'

'We'll see.' Jem looked pleased to have provoked a reaction, something Tim noticed too late.

I was distracted by the sudden appearance of my sister Kate and her best friend Sally Stuart, who skidded in front of the guides' office and leapt off their bikes. Sally looked ordinary with a thick mop of brown hair, freckles and a round face but she was possessed with a crazy imagination, something my sister wasn't lacking either. I frowned, remembering something. My discovery of Vivien had driven it out of my mind but my sister had been missing from her bed that morning then had arrived for breakfast announcing that she and Sally had things to see to. She seemed to be trying to bait me so I'd ignored her but I was worried. What were they up to? They looked ready to ask me the same thing. Sally picked up the atmosphere in seconds.

'Something's wrong isn't it?' she said, her face excited.

Kate looked scared.

'Nothing to do with any of us,' I told them. 'I've just got to go back up the glacier with Tim and show him something.' To my relief they accepted this lame offering. 'I won't be too long Kate. There's leftover lasagne in the fridge – just throw it in the microwave.'

'Fine,' my sister said. She turned back to her bike but not before I caught her expression. She looked relieved. I had no idea why, nor any time to question her. I watched as she and Sally disappeared on their bikes. Something to worry about another day. I forgot them the moment they disappeared from sight. A mistake.

...

'It was over here,' I huddled closer into my polar fleece jacket and kicked a fresh foothold in the ice with my cramponed boot. None of us had talked much as we'd made our way up the shadowy valley. Many of the rescue team had known Vivien Revell and it was always hard when a body recovery involved one of our own. Tim peered down into the crevasse. 'This isn't going to be easy. 'She's well and truly embedded. And I don't think that's the whole body.'

'I thought it was just curled up,' I said.

'Don't think so. I reckon this is only the torso. I just hope the rest of her body's not too far away or this whole thing's going to be beyond gruesome. It won't surprise me if things have got spread out.'

'Thanks for that thought Tim.' Callum looked towards us from a perch above us where he'd been frowning down into the crevasse.

'Mangled pieces spread over miles,' commented one of the search and rescue guys.

'We'll work with what we have,' said Stu Adams the policeman.

'Let's get it out now,' Tim said. 'You know what this place is like; it'll be all over the village by now and we need to beat the sightseers. We've got a good couple of hours of light left.'

We began work chopping open the crevasse and eventually an icy pathway emerged that was large enough to accommodate a couple of the search guys. They made their way to the body which was predictably stuck fast. Someone swore. They worked skilfully around the body, chipping away at the ice until they could roll it free.

I wasn't the only one to gasp in shock. Tim was partially right. There were no limbs to be seen but the head was still there, bent sharply and unnaturally against the still-clad body so you couldn't see the face. There was plenty of thick dark hair which dispelled any doubt in my mind. First the ring, now the hair. It was Vivien Revell all right.

'Good job she's frozen,' said Matt, one of Tim's guides. 'I wouldn't want to be round when she starts to thaw.'

'The undertaker's in for a fun ride tomorrow,' his climbing mate Ian agreed. 'Unless we keep her on ice. Anyone got room in their freezer?'

They were both young guys and they had probably never seen a dead body before. I wasn't fooled by their flippant tone, recognising it for the coping mechanism it was. I recalled one of Tim's stories about a night the rescue team spent in a broken plane fuselage with dead victims. They'd been flown in to the crash site but before they could do anything about body recovery a whiteout had come in and they were stuck in the only shelter, the crashed plane with the dead. All of the corpses' watches were still going and the team had joked about what a great advert it would be for Swatch.

I was getting seriously cold, as were the others who had been watching rather than chipping away at the ice, and I could hardly make my limbs cooperate as I rolled out the body bag on a flat piece of ice.

It had taken longer than we had expected to get the body out. It was getting dark and too late for a helicopter to pick it up. Which meant we'd have to stretcher it out.

I shivered as Stu picked up the hand from the edge and stowed it in there beside the body. Everyone was relieved when it was zipped up and strapped onto the stretcher and we began our descent. It was cumbersome and slippery. I cursed as I tripped, then started paying more attention to my feet. We all took turns with the stretcher and eventually we were at the terminal and lifting it down the steep ice slope onto the moraine.

Everyone was concentrating on getting the stretcher off the ice and we didn't notice the woman arrive until she was right in front of us, panting and distressed. I flashed my torch in her direction. She was wearing a scarlet polar fleece and dark trousers and her face glowed from the exercise. Her long black hair trailed behind her. Vivien's mother.

'It's Viv. Isn't it?' her voice was shrill.

'We don't know, Rose. We can't tell who it is.' Stu took a step towards her but she pushed him away.

'Jem Brown's telling people you saw her ring, Philippa!' I cursed him. And myself. 'I think so,' I said. 'But I could be wrong, Rose.'

'Well let me see for myself,' Rose pushed past me and bent towards the stretcher.

'Don't Rose!' Stu looked appalled. 'It's better you don't look.'

'Leave me alone! It's my daughter for God's sake!' She tore at the zip of the body bag and trained her torch onto the mangled remains inside

Then she stood on the side of the glacier and screamed and screamed.

Chapter 3

Tim paced around the boot room as the guiding team gathered that morning. Matt didn't look quite as blasé as he had the night before. He was slumped forward on his seat and was staring at his hands. Matt was the outgoing type – quick and cheeky with his comments, and a favourite with the tourists. They never seemed to notice he never focused on anything they said. He had a script, he adapted it to the people of the day and he did it well considering he had little interest in anything outside his own world. It was clever. I admired the way he kept himself apart while making his tourists laugh and enjoy their day on the glacier.

Sara on the other hand never laughed at anything. She was slight with short dark hair and she climbed like she was born to it. It was hard to believe she was city-bred. She had come to Franz on a climbing trip a couple of years ago and had never left. She'd got talking to Tim and had been hired as a guide. And she was brilliant at it. She was tuned to every level of fitness and skill in our customers in a way I'd never seen before. It was Sara who got an old blind man on the ice one day and made him experience the whole thing as if he could see. I'd never forgotten his radiant face as he put increasingly confident crampon-shod boots onto the ice and lifted his face to the glacier breeze.

Sara had so much talent but she gave herself no credit for it. She never talked of herself or where she had come from, but had one day told me there was no way back to her old life. She didn't say why and I didn't like to ask. But of course I was curious.

I watched her as she took armloads of socks from the huge industrial drier and lined them on the bench to sort into pairs. She frowned and looked at Matt.

'What?' his voice was defensive.

She lifted a sock to her face and sniffed. 'You didn't wash these, did you?'

Matt shrugged, easing himself from his seat and moving over to her side. He ran a couple of socks though his hand. 'Who's going to know?' he said. 'If you give them a quick spin in the drier they feel clean.'

'You can't keep doing this, Matt! People will get veruccas.'

Tim came back from whatever planet he'd been on. 'Matt I've told you about this before …'

Matt lifted a hand. 'Yeah, I know. Sorry boss. I was in a hurry last night. There was someone I met on the glacier yesterday and we were off for drinks if you get my meaning.'

'Bad timing finding Vivien then,' I commented.

He grinned at me. 'It just delayed things a couple of hours, that's all.'

'Oh stop it,' Sara snapped.

'Okay guys,' Tim said. 'We're going to have to work out a strategy for today. We have ten people for the icefall this morning. I want you to take them, Sara. Philippa, Matt and I can join up with the DOC guys and have a look round for the rest of the body.'

We all knew without saying that body recovery work would not be good for Sara. Even Matt had no argument with that. Sara had never asked for it but we all looked out for her where we could. 'And Philippa?' Tim said as I turned to leave the boot room. 'You and I need to go and talk to Callum about you filling in for me while I'm away. I pulled a face. 'I didn't realise I'd said yes!'

'You'll be brilliant,' Matt told me. 'You won't take any shit from DOC – it'll be a blast.' Tim didn't hear this remark which was a shame as it might have made him change his mind about leaving me in charge.

...

We searched but we found nothing. It was a brilliant summer day and it was good being up on the glacier – even if we were looking for the legs and arms of a person some of us had known. I watched Callum walking loosely across the ice, hands in pockets, kicking the occasional stone into crevasses. He was apart from us all. His own staff didn't seem to have a lot to say to him or him to them.

We called a halt after a few futile hours. Tim took an apple from his pack and crunched on it, his face frustrated. 'It could be down the river by now and no one will ever find it – or my tourist party could fall over it tomorrow,' he said.

'Yeah well we got the most important part,' Callum said tipping a hand to his forehead and squinting up the glacier.

'Enough for a funeral,' said Matt. No one said anything for a while,

Tim sighed. 'We might as well go back and see if it's hit the media yet. This must be awful for Rose.'

After we got back Matt and I finished a painting a wall round the back of the guides' office, something we had been meaning to do for a long time, then repaired to a local café for a drink. There was no sign of Sara and her tourist party but that wasn't surprising. The weather was brilliant and they had all looked fit – they'd be making the most of their day. Tim appeared just as we were washing our paintbrushes. Sara and her tourist party returned soon after. We cleaned up and headed for the pub, relaxing over our drinks and giving Tim a hard time about his new love. We didn't refer to Vivien at all. There would be a flurry of media interest, a funeral with Rose in a starring role, and then life would go back to normal again. None of us had a clue.

...

Kate was at home before me. She had nuked herself some two minute noodles and was scoffing them on the sofa. Spree our giant schnauzer lounged at her feet waiting for donations which were being liberally splattered in front of him.

I reached for the remote and the news came on. Franz Josef was in the headlines complete with a reporter on the scene dressed for the occasion in climbing gear which I'd be willing to bet she'd never used for the real thing.

'A search and rescue team last night recovered the body of Franz Josef woman Vivien Revell from the glacier,' she said. 'Ms Revell was last seen in the village seventeen years ago and was believed to have left to go overseas. At the time there was no concern for her safety.'

Constable Stu Adams appeared on screen. 'Vivien Revell must have been high up on the glacier when the accident happened given how long it has taken her body to make its way down. She was not an experienced climber and should never have attempted such an expedition alone.'

Then the reporter was back on screen. 'Ms Revell's body was found by glacier guide Philippa Barnes who is no stranger to tragedy in the mountains. She lost her own parents in a climbing fatality,' she announced.

'Shit!' I jumped to my feet tripping over Spree as I did so. He howled with indignation. 'What's that got to do with anything?'

'You're connected to a lot of death,' my sister told me. I scowled at her. This quality time was interrupted by the phone. I didn't recognise the voice of the caller and was about to hang up, thinking it might be a reporter, when she said her name. Julia McLoughlin. Vivien's friend. Ringing me because I was the one who'd found the body. And because she was sure there was something strange about Vivien's death.

...

Julia McLoughlin was flying down from Wellington to Hokitika the next day and would pick up a rental car and drive down to Franz. She wanted to talk to me and I wasn't sure why. I'd told her what I'd found; I'd been a child when Vivien disappeared. There was nothing more to tell her.

And in the meantime there was my reluctant promotion to think about. Tim had arranged a meeting with Callum Jackson and wanted me to come along. I wasn't keen – on any of it. Ours wasn't the biggest game in town when it came to glacier guiding. There was a big company that did the lion's share; our Glacier Climbers was a fringe company that specialised in day trips for small groups. We weren't even on the web yet and most of our business came from word-of-mouth. But we were still thwarted with the same rules as our much larger opposition. And it never ceased to annoy me that my life could be affected by salaried bureaucrats who were paid whatever happened. Their decision to close off access when they deemed the glacier valley dangerous affected how much money Tim had to put into his company.

'And they do it over nothing,' I grumbled as Tim and I made our way to the national park headquarters.

'You have to admit Callum keeps things real,' Tim said. 'He knows what he's talking about; he's a mountaineer himself.'

'Yeah, yeah,' I said childishly.

Callum looked as if he'd had a hard night. His eyes were red and he hadn't shaved. He seemed in serious need himself of the coffee he served us in his office. I looked around me as I waited for the talks to begin, taking in the uncluttered space. Callum didn't appear to do paper and there was little on his desk other than a laptop with an iPod plugged into the back of it. There was a huge black and white photograph on the wall of an ice-bound mountain hut, but there was nothing personal anywhere. No photographs of family. No ornaments. His ice axe, battered pack and a well-worn climbing rope were stashed in the corner.

Tim was right. He was no office bureaucrat. And yet, I did not trust him.

'So Callum, as you know Philippa's taking over for me while I'm away. Not the admin – I'll hire someone else to do the bookwork. She'll manage the guides and keep you in the loop if there's anything you need to know about.'

'There's the small but puzzling issue of our disappearing signs, Tim,' Callum said, his voice neutral.

I hid a smile. The glacier valley needed danger signs, we all knew that. It was fair enough to have them right by the terminal – the high mass of ice at the front of the glacier where large chunks of ice frequently fell off. People had been killed trying to get up close to the glacier only to have a piece of it fall on their heads. But DOC had overreacted, placing the signs well down valley as well – in places where there was no danger at all. Tourists were mystified and reluctant to trust us as we led them carelessly past these imprecations of doom. Matt often joked that there was a rogue mountain lion, an escapee from a circus, living in the valley. This didn't always help the tourists' nerves.

Then the signs had started disappearing and reappearing in the village propped against tourist flight operators' offices or local cafés. *Extreme Danger. Do Not Proceed.* I had thought Matt was responsible but he'd sworn he wasn't.

'I hope you aren't suggesting we're doing this, Callum?' Tim asked.

He stared across his desk at us. 'I don't know who's doing it. But you have to admit the concessionaires are the most likely ones.'

'Well you don't make our job any easier, you have to admit.' I couldn't help myself. 'Every day we have to persuade our tourist parties to ignore those ridiculous signs. They think we're going to get them killed.'

Callum smiled. 'I don't think it's quite that bad, Philippa.

Sexist pig. I scowled but said nothing.

'You have to admit they're overkill,' Tim said.

'They are over the top,' Callum admitted. 'But we have our own hassles with management you know. I don't get to make all the decisions.'

But you get to collect your salary whatever happens, I thought, giving him a cold look. Yes, this was all going to work really well.

My doubts were only increased with the next comment from Callum.

'What about reporting?' he asked as he took a long sip of his coffee.

I raised my eyebrows at Tim.

'Yeah,' he said. 'I hadn't actually talked about that. No big deal, Philippa – you just email Callum a report every month – just a summary of the operation – numbers of tourists, any issues with access, that kind of thing.'

'And what happens then?' I asked.

'Nothing if it's routine. But if there are any problems you and I will need to talk,' Callum said.

His tone was neutral. So why was I taking it as a threat? Get a grip, I told myself. I looked from Callum to Tim trying to think of something to say. Like, I'm not doing this. But I said nothing.

...

'There was no way she would have gone up the glacier on her own.'

Julia had arrived just as I got home that night and she was still here an hour later drinking my red wine and getting herself more and more wound up.

I was trying to find something edible in the fridge for dinner and I wasn't really in the mood for visitors but short of throwing her out of the house there was no way I was going to get rid of her. Sighing, I gave up on dinner and joined her at the table.

Julia was a slim redhead with a pale complexion. She was much as I remembered her – casually dressed in jeans and a grey Guernsey jersey. The skin round her eyes looked smudged with tiredness. Julia was someone I'd known since childhood yet not really known. She always came across as tense and somewhat troubled. I had a vague recollection of her spending time with my mother, Susan, years before. Susan had never said what it was all about, but she had been helping Julia through some crisis or other. I recalled that much.

I looked at her now, at the uncompromisingly short haircut which only heightened her anxious appearance. It was a hairstyle that had been fashionable ten years or so ago when women went for the sharp chic look. I was no arbiter of style myself. I wore my thick dark hair long because it was easy to look after that way and when it needed a trim I took to it myself with kitchen scissors. But even I had noticed that women were letting their hair grow longer these days. Not Julia though.

'So – what are you suggesting?' I asked.

'I think someone killed her.'

I stared at her. I hadn't seen this coming 'What? Who could possibly have wanted to kill her?'

'If I knew that, I'd know who did it.' She stared at me and I was puzzled by the flare of anger in her expression. Then it was gone and I wondered if I'd imagined it. 'Viv would never have gone up the glacier on her own,' she said again. 'She was scared of it.'

'It does seem weird, I agree. But if she went with someone, that person has known all that time that she never made it home. I can't believe it.'

'It's the only explanation.' Julia's face was stubborn. I suppressed a surge of irritation. I had no reason to feel this way but Julia was getting to me. It was probably because back in the days when my mother was still alive Julia had intruded into the edges of my life and I hadn't liked it. It was childish to be reacting the same way now but here she was again, needing something – and it was setting my teeth on edge.

We both jumped as Kate and Spree erupted into the room. I looked at my sister wishing I wasn't feeling so distracted. There was something I needed to do. Talk to her. But I couldn't focus on that right now.

'How badly was she smashed up?' my sister asked cheerfully.

'She was in bits,' I snapped. 'What do you expect, Kate? She'd been in the glacier nearly twenty years!'

I knew the score. Kate would have been in demand at school that day as all the kids examined the choice offering from Kate's big sister who'd just dug a body out of the glacier. I didn't need any of this but that was not going to stop Kate.

'Was she dead when she went into the crevasse?' she asked.

'I hope so,' Julia shivered and took a large mouthful of wine.

'Why did no one find her?' Kate asked.

I pulled myself together with an effort and put my voice in neutral. 'It must have happened right up in the icefall. The crevasses change every day. One day they're open, next day they're gone. The ice would have closed over her and pulled her down.'

'And she's only just come up now?' Kate looked like she didn't believe me.

'Who knows? She could've come up and down a hundred times for all I know! She's up now, anyway. Most of her, that is.'

'Didn't they get all of her?'

I sighed. 'She's minus her legs and arms if you must know. And don't go quoting me at school, all right, Kate! I don't want another summons to your teacher.'

'Can I tell Sally?'

'Oh, all right. Now please can we stop talking about it?'

'Maybe I should go too,' Julia said as we watched Kate slam out of the room.

'It's okay. Why do you want to talk to me?'

'Philippa, I know you think I'm mad. But I'm as sure as I'm sitting here that someone killed Vivien. It's not just her going that far up the glacier on her own. There was other stuff going on with her that summer. There was something seriously wrong in her life.'

'What do you mean?' Despite myself I was interested.

Julia got up and walked to the window. She peered out over the garden for a minute, then turned to me. She looked defiant but pleading as well. 'Something was wrong between her and Rose. Something big. Viv was hurt – and angry. Rose was amused by it. Viv said that was the worst thing of all. That her mother thought the whole thing was a joke.'

'What thing?'

'That's the problem. I don't know. I never found out.'

'Was it to do with Callum Jackson?'

Julia shook her head. 'I don't think so. Philippa, what do you know about Luke Riley?'

Luke ran a mountain bike touring business in the village. He was an easygoing guy who, according to Angie and Jem, was heading for the skids fast due to his lack of business acumen. He had a much younger wife and a little girl. He was always friendly and I liked him. All the more because he wasn't a sharp businessman.

'What's he got to do with anything?' I asked.

Julia hesitated. 'He and Viv had a thing going. But then she got involved with Callum. Luke was away so she thought she could get away with it. But he came back unexpectedly and found out. She was pretty upset – she wanted Luke to be there for her. I think she always knew Callum was a road to nowhere.'

'So maybe that's why she told no one she was going up the glacier. Because she was going with Callum. But if that's the case…'

'Yeah. If that's the case he knew she was dead. Even if he didn't kill her, he must have just walked away and left her there. But why would he? He was calling all the shots. If he was sick of her, he would have just dumped her. And if she'd gone with him, she'd have told me. I had a thriving role as confidante that summer.' Julia's voice was bitter.

'What were you doing back then?' I asked.

'I was working in Christchurch. I'd just finished my degree and I'd managed to get a job in an office - admin and stuff. Boring, but I was broke. I didn't want to come back to Franz that summer. But then Viv put the pressure on and so I did. She told me she'd found out something that had changed her life. That she needed to talk about it.'

It was uncanny. Julia was sitting right beside me but she seemed to disappear before my eyes. Into a place that wasn't fun to be in, judging by the strained look on her face.

'So what was it?' I asked after a long silence.

'I never found out. Once she'd got me back here she wouldn't talk about it. Said it was more complicated than she had thought and that it might even be dangerous. I was angry but that made no difference. Viv wasn't worried about putting me out.'

'Who else might she have told?'

'I don't know. Maybe Callum. Or even Penelope Blake.' Penelope was the widow of Patrick Blake the mountaineer. She was as cool as he'd been gregarious. A remote woman who cleaned the church and did good works. Remedial reading. Collections for the blind. Someone who wasn't fobbed off with weak excuses such as having no cash on hand. She also organised tramping trips for local children. But she was a person no one warmed to. It wasn't fair really. She had done more for people in the village than her late husband had ever done, yet he was the hero and she was the outsider.

'I can't imagine Viv confiding in her,' I said.

'I know,' Julia agreed. 'She didn't like Penelope all that much but she knew she had to keep on side with her if she wanted access to Patrick's papers. They hadn't been put in an archive – Penelope was holding on to them.'

'So are you saying that you think someone killed Vivien because of the thing she wouldn't tell you?'

'Look I know it sounds unlikely, but it's a possibility isn't it! Everyone thinks Viv's death was an accident. They're ignoring the fact she wouldn't – couldn't! – have got that far up the glacier on her own. And they're just going to close the books on her. I can't let that happen. You can help me, Philippa.'

'How?' I crossed my arms across my chest feeling defensive. I knew what was coming and I didn't like it.

'Because of the murder at Lake Kaniere. You were the one to find the killer. You could do the same now. You know all these people. You see them all the time. What's to stop you trying to find out what happened that summer?'

Suddenly I was furious. It came out of nowhere. All that had happened back then was over. It had been horrible. People had died. People I knew. Someone I really cared about. I'd got in the way of a lot of stuff that had nothing to do with me and it had nearly taken me down with it. It had taken me a year to get my head back together and now this woman I hardly knew was trying to cash in on it.

'I am a glacier guide, not a private detective,' I said. Deceptively quietly.

Julia didn't notice a thing. 'You're going to be seeing a bit of Callum this year now you're running the Glacier Climbers. All I ask is that you get to know him, try to get him to confide in you ...'

'Have sex with him?' I interrupted. 'Would that do the trick do you think? And he's just going to crumple and tell me everything of course. Then what, Julia? How do you think I'm going to get to Penelope Blake? And Rose Revell? And all this is on top of a fucking busy job and looking after my sister! You don't ask a lot!'

Kate reappeared just in time for this outburst. She glared at Julia. Then she amazed me. 'Leave my sister alone!' she screamed at her. 'Everyone expects her to do things for them. She never asks anyone to do anything for her. Get out of our house!'

Julia left. Fast. Kate and I stared at each other then we started to laugh. It took us a long time to stop.

...

I woke up feeling guilty. It had been satisfying at the time, the loss of control, the telling the world – as represented by Julia – to go to hell. But now all I could think of was her white strained face and the way my defensiveness had created a lightning rod for Kate's anger.

We'd moved on, Kate and me. Life was relatively normal now. We were no longer defined by tragedy. And yet ... we could go back into the darkness just like that. Nothing to laugh at in fact. So why had we?

'Spree,' I said to our errant schnauzer who had appeared in my room with a pork chop in his mouth, 'you've picked a great family to live with, d'you know that?' He ignored me, intent on downing his stolen treat before I could take it from him. I left him blissed out and went and picked up the phone.

I stared at it a moment before I made the call. 'Julia? I'm sorry about last night. Do you still want to talk?'

She sighed. 'I'm sorry too – I was totally insensitive to what you'd been through. Kate was quite right.'

'Yes and no. We're supposed to be coping and over it all. I shouldn't have got so angry and I don't even know where it came from. Look Julia – can we meet for a coffee this morning in the village? I'm learning about report writing from my boss so I'll be in serious need of a caffeine hit in a couple of hours.'

'If you're sure? Yes, that'd be great. Where do you want to go?'

'Ice Rocks? Do you know it? It's just round the corner from the Glacier Climbers' office. It does the best coffee in town. How's 10.30 for you?'

'Good. See you there. And thanks, Philippa.'

'Don't thank me – I doubt that I can do anything,' I warned. But Julia had hung up.

...

I had been right about one thing. I was in serious need of coffee. I could do a whole day up on the ice without thinking of it but two hours in the office and the need was strong. It couldn't be caffeine addiction as it only struck when I was bored or worried. And I was worried today. What had possessed me to agree to Tim's request? How was I going to keep on side with Callum and the Conservation Department when my default reaction to them was defensiveness and anger? Well I was going to have to get that under control for a start. Play the game. Write their crazy reports. Consult them every time something went wrong in the glacier valley. It happened a lot, which was the problem. Nature was in full command here – anyone human was kidding themselves if they didn't acknowledge this Those bloody signs. The river had been on the move lately. Having spent months flowing innocuously in a bed on the far side of the valley, it had decided it was time for a change and headed straight for our track. Then, once it had done its damage, it had gone back again and everything had been fine until DOC had started putting up their *Extreme Danger* signs in the most harmless places. The river wasn't going to leap out of its bed on a fine day and head straight for us. Bad weather had to be involved for this to happen and DOC's signs were overkill. But judging by our conversation with Callum there was no chance of getting rid of them any time soon. Even if someone was having a damned good go at getting rid of them by stealth.

And if I didn't watch myself, I'd be in the frame for that. DOC didn't know how ornery I was as they had never had to deal with me directly – until now. So what should I do? Go along with the stupidity? Or say what I thought? I knew what I wanted to do. But I was going to have to get that impulse under control.

Julia was there before me, sitting at a café table and reading the newspaper. She smiled at me, and then crossed over to the counter. 'I'm buying,' she said. 'I insist. Do you want something to eat as well?'

I eyed the carrot cake, suddenly feeling starving. 'Go on, then,' I said. 'I don't know why I'm hungry. I've done nothing all day.'

'That'll be why,' she said.

We chatted about nothing as we waited for our coffee. I looked around. There were a few people around a large table down the back but apart from that we had the place to ourselves. The woman who served us was plugged in to an iPod. I didn't blame her.

'I've been thinking about what you said. You're right. It is unbelievable that Vivien went that high on the glacier on her own. But the alternative is even more unlikely.' I sipped my coffee and looked at Julia.

'I know,' she said. 'But I still think I'm right.'

'Have you talked to the police?'

'No. I can't prove anything. I've been waiting to see if they say anything. You know, that the death was suspicious or something like that. But they haven't.'

The story was dying with nothing more to feed it and there were no reporters left in town. Julia was right.

'Do you think Callum could have killed her? I hope you're right. It would get him out of my hair for the next six months,' I said.

Julia looked appalled. 'Are you involved with him?'

I laughed. 'Kind of – but not in the way you think.' I proceeded to fill her in on my move into tourism concession management.

'You'll do a great job,' she said. 'You know that glacier and all its quirks.'

'It's not the glacier I'm worried about,' I told her. 'Julia, I don't quite see why this matters so much to you. Vivien didn't sound like she was much of a friend to you. Why don't you leave it the way it is?'

'I just can't! I need to know. It's been torturing me for years. You'd think it would get better but it hasn't!'

'What hasn't?'

Julia crashed her cup into its saucer and stared past me. I was reminded of the previous night when she had sat in front of me but disappeared into her head, into her thoughts. It didn't seem to be a happy place. In fact…

I leaned towards her. 'What are you frightened of, Julia?'

'Nothing! I'm not frightened of anything! I just need to know.'

We were interrupted by my cellphone. I cursed. I hadn't been aware the damned thing was even on. Things didn't get better when I heard the caller's voice. It was Kim Patterson, Kate's teacher. Kate, it seemed, was sick and needed to be collected.

'What's wrong with her?' I asked.

'Nothing serious. She has a headache.'

I'd heard that one before and I didn't believe it for a moment. But I couldn't ignore the call.

'I'll be there in ten minutes.' I clicked the off button with unnecessary force. 'Kate,' I explained. 'Pulling a sick day. I have to go and get her.'

'How is she coping with everything? It must have been hell for her losing her parents when she was so young.' Julia said. She seemed glad of the distraction.

I sighed. 'Okay on the whole. We're over the worst of it.'

'Did Tom never come home?'

I didn't feel like discussing my brother. 'No – there was no point.'

'He should have helped you.'

'Susan and Liam were dead. There was nothing anyone could do.'

'He's like your father.'

I would have resented this from most people but for some reason I didn't mind Julia saying it. She was right after all.

'He wouldn't have been any use and I had enough to deal with getting Kate and me through it all. I encouraged him to stay away.'

'Why do you think he's like that?'

I stirred the remains of my flat white. 'I don't know. He is a good guy. Kind – he'd give you anything. But if something bad happens he's not there. He withdraws. He might have come back but it wouldn't have been any help, believe me. He didn't need it. *We* didn't need it.'

'He really loved your mother,' Julia said.

'Yeah. And a lot of good that did them both.'

I was silent for a few minutes, thinking about my family. Julia had known them better than I had realised and I wondered just how much she and my mother Susan had talked about things.

I stood up. 'I guess I'd better go and find out what Kate's playing at. And Julia, I will ask around. I'll try to find out what was going on the summer Vivien disappeared.'

Julia stared across the table at me. She didn't look happy. For a brief moment I again sensed her fear but it was gone in a flash. 'I'll deal with it better if I know the truth,' she said.

...

Kate was waiting for me in the staff room and she really did look unwell. I felt guilty for doubting her. Kim was bustling around offering her cold drinks but she wasn't responding.

'What's wrong?' I asked squatting down by her chair.

'I just feel sick,' she whispered.

'OK – let's get you home.'

Before we could move the door opened and Penelope Blake walked in. I was surprised then remembered that she did remedial reading with some of the children. Kim looked pleased to see her.

'I was going to ask if I could use this room for our session,' she said to Kim. 'But I can see you are busy. How are you, Philippa?'

'I'm fine – and we're just leaving. Kate's sick.'

Penelope considered my sister. 'You don't look well.'

Kate stared at her without responding. Penelope gave a small smile and bent to touch her forehead. 'Hot,' she murmured. 'There's a bug going round, I understand.'

Penelope was tall and strongly built. She wore dark wool trousers and an ivory blouse which was tucked in, emphasising her slim waist. Her face was a near perfect oval but there was discord there somehow as well. Something in her expression that I couldn't define. Her skin was tanned, her hair long and silver, wound into a coil against the back of her head and secured by two wooden combs.

'Would you like some books to read?' she asked Kate. 'I have some new ones I think you might enjoy.'

'That would be great,' I answered for my sister. 'She's running out. I could come and collect them later today if that suits you?'

'Certainly,' Penelope said.

And that would give me a perfect chance to talk about Vivien Revell.

...

I spent the afternoon cleaning the house, keeping an eye on Kate. She went straight to bed and to sleep. If I hadn't known better I'd have said she was just tired, but she didn't have anything to be tired about. I was grateful she wasn't throwing up and soon forgot about her as I finished my work and retreated to the conservatory with coffee and a book. An hour or so later I got to my feet and stretched. It was 4 o'clock. Time to head over to Penelope's and collect the books she'd promised Kate.

I glanced into Kate's room. She was still asleep. Spree looked up but didn't show any sign of following me and I was glad to know Kate had him there beside her. Slipping out of the house quietly, I got my bike out of the shed and headed off into the sunny late afternoon. I passed the neighbour's farm, glancing above the green paddocks to the sculptured beauty of Mt Elie de Beaumont. The sky behind was a dark blue and the contrasting white flanks of the mountain sparked light into the atmosphere. The air was still and there were no cars on the road.

Penelope lived near the glacier valley road in a small weatherboard house screened from the road by large rhododendrons. None were in flower at the moment but when they were it was an impressive sight – the wall of scarlet contrasting with the dark green of the native bush in the glacier valley.

When Kate was little she was convinced that Penelope's house was a witch's cottage. Penelope often rode an old black bike with her grey hair loose and streaming out behind her so she looked the part.

Sally Stuart, Kate's over-imaginative best friend, had many theories on the subject. Her most lurid had Penelope biking up the glacier valley by night to light fires under the glacier to bring dead goats back to life. What she did this for, Sally never made clear.

Penelope met me at the door looking nothing like a witch. She led me though to a book-lined living room and left me while she went to make coffee. Sunlight spilled in through the long French windows making the polished wood floorboards glow. I browsed her shelves while I waited. Contemporary fiction and classics shared space not broken up into any discernible order. She also had a large shelf of children's fiction and I was pleased to see some old favourites – Famous Five in abundance, all of the *Anne of Green Gables* series, lots of Angela Brazil, Gene Stratton Porter's *A Girl of the Limberlost* and many others. There were a lot of shiny new books by authors I were not familiar with.

'These were the ones I was thinking of.'

Penelope placed a tray containing coffee plunger, mugs and a jug of milk on the table then handed me three books. Eva Ibbotson. Not an author I knew. *Journey to the River Sea, The Dragonfly Pool* and *The Star of Kazan*.

'She's a marvellous writer,' Penelope was saying. 'A great storyteller but there's some down-to-earth humour in her work too. Things children latch onto. I've only just discovered her and I love her work. I think Kate will too.'

'Thanks so much,' I said picking up *Journey to the River Sea* and glancing through it. 'I'll read them as well. They look great.'

Penelope depressed the plunger and poured coffee into the mugs. I helped myself to milk.

'I've been meaning to call in and see you,' Penelope said, leaning back in her chair and taking a sip of coffee. 'You have had a terrible time, both of you. How are you coping with it all?'

'Better now,' I said. 'But it's been pretty awful. It's much worse for Kate than me. I always knew that Susan and Liam weren't there for me – and I don't mean that in a self-pitying way. It's a fact. They were like that. But Kate was so young when they died. She didn't understand that.'

'She's learned a hard lesson at a very young age. You can't rely on anyone but yourself in life. Most of us don't make that discovery till we're a lot older.'

'Yes. That's certainly true.'

'Once you realise you're on your own there's a freedom in that. Need is the most crippling thing.' Penelope's voice was suddenly hard.

I sipped my coffee in silence wondering about her. All the work she'd done for others over the years yet her personality was like a polished stone. There was no real warmth there. Except when it came to children. I'd seen the way she could connect with them a couple of years ago when I'd gone along as an extra adult on one of her school tramping trips. The kids had loved it. They were right there with her, gathering wood for the fire, asking her for stories as they lay in their sleeping bags. Penelope was much warmer than usual, and had got right down to their level. It was strange she had never had children of her own.

'I heard that you found Vivien Revell's body,' she said, giving me a perfect opening. I'd been wondering how I was going to work this into the conversation.

'Yes. It was strange that I recognized that ring, but for some reason I remembered it. Even though I was only a child when I last saw her.'

'It was a very distinctive ring – and Vivien was a very distinctive person.' Penelope's tone was dry.

'Apparently so. Penelope, do you remember Julia McLoughlin?'

'Yes of course. She was Vivien's friend – even if Vivien had no real understanding of friendship. She was very careless about Julia's feelings.'

'Julia's here now – in Franz. She came back when she heard about Vivien.'

Penelope sighed. 'She was a loyal girl – loyal to the point of stupidity when it came to Vivien Revell. I'm not surprised she's here but I don't know how she thinks coming back is going to help her.'

'She doesn't believe Vivien's death was an accident.'

Penelope looked at me, her face impassive. 'So what does she think happened? Surely she doesn't think that Vivien killed herself?'

'No - she thinks someone killed her.'

'That's ridiculous. Why would anyone do such a thing?' Penelope put her mug back on the table and looked at me, her expression disbelieving.

'Julia doesn't seem to know. But she's convinced Vivien wouldn't have gone that far up on the glacier on her own.'

'She must have had her reasons. She was writing my husband's biography, did you know that? Vivien was meticulous in her research. That's one of the reasons I asked her to write the book. She used to say that the only way to understand someone properly was to walk in their footsteps. She was fascinated by one of Patrick's stories. He used to tell people that he'd gone on the glacier alone as a boy with a woodsman's axe and with nails in his boots that he'd hammered in himself. That he'd got right up to the icefall with this unsuitable equipment. I think she must have decided to try that herself. Not with that kind of primitive equipment of course – she would have had crampons and a proper ice axe. But to go up there alone.'

It was a plausible suggestion. And much more likely than the scenario Julia had suggested.

'Why did she get interested in writing about your husband?'

'I was never sure,' Penelope said. 'She was doing her MA and needed a thesis topic but mountaineering seemed such an unlikely choice. She had the brain for something of much greater depth. There's a limit to how much analysis you can do on the subject of mountaineering.'

'So she approached you? How did you feel about it?'

Penelope smiled. 'Patrick was the last of the great mountaineers of his era. Various people wanted to write his story but he would never agree. Planned to do it himself. I told him that would be a mistake, that he'd never have been objective enough. Then he died and I was left with all his papers. I wanted to clear them out of my life. So when Vivien told me she was writing a thesis on 20th century mountaineering I asked her to write Patrick's biography.'

'How did she feel about that?'

'Not entirely keen. But she needed his papers for her thesis and I wouldn't have agreed to one without the other.'

'You obviously thought a lot of her?'

'I thought a lot of her brain. She was extremely clever.'

'So her disappearance must have been quite a blow to you?'

'I was angry. I wasn't at all sure that she would honour our book agreement once she'd used Patrick's papers for her thesis so I formalised it through a solicitor. She had signed up to it and she couldn't get out of it. So when she disappeared – overseas as we all thought – I was convinced that she'd done so to escape our agreement. She'd got an MA with Distinction and there was no reason for her to stay any longer in Franz for except for a legal obligation she had no intention of keeping.'

'I don't blame you for being angry,' I said.

She made a dismissive gesture with her hands. 'I'm over it now. I really don't care if Patrick disappears into obscurity. Most of us do, after all.'

'What brought you to Franz?'

'I met Patrick in Auckland. My father and I had gone to the ballet and there he was with one of my father's friends. A handsome mountaineer. Someone from a different world yet with a fine eye for culture. I'd had a sheltered upbringing. It was an easy conquest. I had looks, my father had money. Patrick appreciated both. I was in love.' Her final words were acidic.

'So – you lived to regret coming here?'

'I lived to regret marrying him. Don't throw your mind and life away on a man, Philippa. Women of your generation don't have to make such final choices and you are very lucky. There was no going back for me.'

'That's really awful. I've made some mistakes with men myself but I've been able to walk away from them. Vivien Revell could have had it all,' I said in a clumsy attempt to get back on topic.

'She made her choices.'

'You don't seem to have liked her much.'

'I didn't. She had no compassion for others. And she lacked humility. Traits that would have served her well in life if she hadn't taken got herself killed.'

'You must have been one of the first people to notice she was missing?'

'Yes I suppose I was. She'd actually been based in my house working in my office but she told me she was taking a break the day she disappeared. I didn't think anything of it until she failed to reappear the following day.'

'Can you remember what you did the day Vivien disappeared?'

'I went up the glacier myself. But I didn't go very far onto the ice and I saw no sign of Vivien. I do remember one thing. The ice was very hard that day. You know how slippery it can get. So it's no wonder she ran into trouble. The conditions weren't good for a novice ice climber. You know – if Julia is right and Vivien was murdered, she is the one with the motive.'

In an instant I recalled Julia's fear, the feeling I'd had that she was holding something back from me.

'What motive?'

'The usual one. A man. Luke Riley was Julia's lover until Vivien stole him from her.'

I stared at Penelope, amazed. 'No one has ever mentioned that. Least of all Julia! I thought she was teflon when it came to men. She is so self-sufficient.'

'She's had nearly 20 years to work on it.'

'Yes but she can't have murdered Vivien. The police are treating it as an accident. Why dig it up if she did it herself?'

'I know,' Penelope agreed. 'It's a ridiculous idea anyway – that Vivien was murdered I mean.'

I stood up and walked across the room to stare out at the garden. Then I turned back to Penelope. 'There's another thing Julia told me. She said that Vivien discovered some secret just before she disappeared.'

Penelope stiffened and some of the colour seemed to leach from her face. 'What secret?' Her voice was harsh.

I stared at her. 'No one seems to know but it was about herself. That's why Julia came home that summer. Vivien said she needed to talk to her but then when she came rushing back to Franz, Vivien wouldn't discuss it.'

'I see. Well Vivien and I weren't close enough to discuss personal secrets so I can't help you there.'

I wondered if I'd imagined the shocked expression on her face. There was no sign of it now. Penelope's mask was back but I was sure of one thing. If she knew something that she didn't want me to find out she would never tell. Not now. Not ever.

Chapter 4

IT was party time.

It was Tim's last night in Franz and he was shouting drinks for his team – and introducing us to Helen, the woman who'd persuaded him to leave his glacier. I was looking forward to a night out. Kate was looking forward to seeing the back of me. I was running out the door as Sally arrived, several DVDs in her hands, and a look of innocence on her face that made me instantly suspicious.

'What's the plan, girls?' I asked.

'Nothing,' they chorused.

I gave them a dubious look and left them to it. There was no point in my saying anything. Spree pushed his way past me into the house and the door slammed behind him. I forgot about them almost instantly, responsible elder sister that I was.

Ice Rocks was buzzing. The night trade was much livelier than that of the day and the place was full. Pausing at the bar for a glass of red wine I glanced over towards the guides' table. Matt was holding forth about something and Tim was smiling and relaxed. There was a slim blonde woman at Tim's side who looked highly amused by Matt's story. This must be Helen, I thought. Her hair was fine and straight hanging to chin level. Her face was alive with humour.

'So I said to her, "if you want to stay up here for the night there'll be nothing to eat. And I'm a really bad snorer",' Matt was saying. 'That didn't faze her one bit. She was up for it, big time. Turned out her boyfriend had done the dirty on her at Queenstown and she wanted to pay him back with me. That might have been ok but she was forty at least – and she had a moustache. I tried to get Philippa to stay instead of me but she was hell bent on getting back to the village with the rest of the party and they all buggered off and left us to it.'

'It never occurred to me that you might need protection, Matt!' I said 'Remind me - why were you staying the night up there?' There was a hut part way up the glacier that was used occasionally by our glacier parties for an overnight stopover.

'Well it certainly wasn't my idea! It was her – said she was exhausted and couldn't go on,' Matt said. 'Then she kept me awake half the night telling me her life story. Thought I wouldn't sleep a wink but I must've dropped off. Woke up to this horrible smell. She was trying to get into my sleeping bag, and her breath! Yuck. I had a hell of a job rolling her off me!'

'So what did you do?' Tim asked.

'Went to sleep – eventually. It scarred me, I'm telling you.'

'It probably scarred her more,' Sara said.

The banter continued but my mind drifted. Attraction. It was such an uncontrollable force and one that in my experience you kept on paying for long after the pleasure had ended. My mind went back to Julia and the strange vibe I'd noticed when she talked to me about Vivien. It had seemed like fear. The more I thought about it, the surer I was. If Penelope was right and she had reason to hate Vivien, she could have killed her up on the glacier that day. All it would have taken would have been one hard push. But if she had, there was no reason at all for her to try and stir things up when the police and everyone else were sure it had been an accident.

There was one other possibility though. She had been in love with Luke Riley. He'd left her for Vivien only to get the same treatment himself when Vivien had a fling with Callum Jackson. What if he was the jealous type? What if he had killed Vivien? And what if this was the thing Julia was afraid of?

No. This was ridiculous. No one could hold a torch for someone for nearly twenty years. Could they? If someone ditched me there was no way I'd be worrying about their welfare one year later, let alone twenty! Love had never burned me that badly and I couldn't imagine it.

'Penny for them, Philippa?' Tim said.

I laughed. 'I was thinking about love.'

'As in?' Sara looked interested. 'Are you …?'

'No, not me – after my last relationship debacle I'm sworn off. I was just thinking about a friend who seems to still care about this worthless guy twenty years after he ditched her for someone else. I don't get it. How could anyone feel that way for so long?'

'You could under some circumstances.' Helen leaned forward in her chair, cupping her wine glass in both hands. 'How old was she, your friend, when she was with this guy?'

'Early twenties,' I said. 'But from what I can gather he was her first boyfriend.'

'Well then. It could easily happen. Those first relationships – they're lethal. You give them your all, you're messed up with hormones and everything hurts so much! Don't you remember?'

'No,' I said flatly.

'Well you are lucky in some ways. It's something you feel so acutely and it can take you years to get over it. Is your friend in a relationship now?'

'No, she's a real career woman.'

'Even more dangerous! The lost possibilities would just intensify as the years went on.'

'Hmmm.' I took a large sip of wine. 'It sounds awful. I suppose it could grow like a cancer – no good old reality to bring the whole thing back down where it belongs.'

'Trust you to compare love to cancer, Philippa!' Tim looked amused but concerned too. 'It's not healthy.'

'It's a lot healthier than love, if you ask me,' I replied.

'Love is fine if you keep things under control,' Matt said.

'Something you'll never have a problem with,' Sara snapped. 'You deserved that woman – even if she didn't deserve you.'

Matt looked hurt then spoiled the impression by winking at Helen. 'So what's your secret?' he asked her. 'I've worked with Tim for two years now and the only thing I've seen him eyeing up is the glacier. Then you come along and it's true love. What's it all about?'

'I don't think it's something you're ever going to find out,' she laughed. 'Not so long as you treat women the way you do.'

'I treat them well,' he protested. 'I just don't want to keep them long term, that's all.'

This was too much for Sara. 'I am so over you!' she snapped, pushing back her chair as if to leave. Tim and Helen both moved to soothe her and I wondered as I had often done what had gone on in her past. She was always so tense, so quick to anger yet with strangers – tourists – she was wonderful.

I looked around the room and saw Callum Jackson at the bar. I wasn't best pleased when he joined us but Tim made him welcome. He settled himself in next to Helen and to my amazement started chatting to her as if he'd known her for years. There was no reticence or sarcasm. He was a different person. I settled back and listened, intrigued. Helen, it turned out, had done a lot of mountaineering. She had been whisked off to a city lifestyle when she was young by an ambitious mother whose career took her family on restless circuits all over the country. As soon as Helen could leave home, she'd come back to the mountains. They gave her life meaning; she would never live away from them again.

'So why this decision to take Tim away from Franz?' Callum asked.

She laughed. 'I'm taking him away from Franz, not away from the mountains. We're going to spend most of our time climbing overseas. Didn't he tell you?'

'Tim's been too busy trying to make Callum and me like one another,' I said.

'And good luck with that,' Matt grinned at me.

'I don't think it'll be all bad,' Callum sounded almost as if he meant it.

I relaxed. Maybe we could get on with one another. Angie Bennett joined us half an hour or so later. She looked strangely incomplete without her gossip-loving sidekick Jem Brown. Tim had hired her to be the front woman for the Glacier Climbers – doing the bookings, dealing with enquiries. She was also going to do all the other administration for which I was eternally grateful. I had originally expected that I was going to have to do all that as well. I was pleased that Angie was joining us for other reasons as well. She was fun and cynical – two of my favourite traits.

She didn't look all that happy as she flung herself down and took a large sip of wine. 'Bloody Alan,' was her opening remark. She rarely referred to her husband without this endearing preface to his name and no one reacted except me. I always enjoyed the stories.

'What's he done now?' I asked.

She sighed. He had one – one – small job to do tonight. I was bringing the kids back from sports in Whataroa. We're running late and I wanted dinner early because I was going out tonight. So I texted him to fry the bacon. And he couldn't even get that right! Got home to find him on the internet – googling how to dry bacon! Loser!'

'How did he get that wrong?' asked Tim when the laughter subsided. 'Well I hit "d" instead of "f" in my text,' she said, 'but he should have been able to work it out.'

'He's a man,' I said darkly. Everyone laughed – except Callum.

'Rose is back,' Angie said, changing the subject abruptly. 'I saw her in the shop just before.'

This was news. Rose Revell had left Franz the day after Vivien's body had been found, telling no one where she had gone. I could understand her need to get away from a village full of questions but we'd all been puzzled that there had been no talk of a funeral for Vivien.

'I asked her why she hadn't had a funeral.' Angie seemed to be reading my thoughts. 'She told me it was between her and her daughter – no one else. She's had her cremated and has brought her ashes back.'

'I think that's a bit sad,' Tim said. 'People need the chance to say goodbye.'

'Not when someone's buggered off years ago without a backwards glance,' Callum said.

'But she didn't,' I said. 'She's been here all the time.'

'Philippa I've been meaning to ask you,' Angie put her drink on the table and leaned towards me. 'I saw you and Julia McLoughlin here yesterday. Is she back in Franz because of Vivien being found? They were close.'

I had not seen Angie but I wasn't a bit surprised she had seen me. It occurred to me that this was an opportunity to find out a few things from Callum. With a few drinks inside him, he was as relaxed as he was ever going to be.

'Julia is pretty gutted about it all,' I said. 'She is convinced that Vivien couldn't have gone up the glacier on her own.'

'I know it seems odd – but she must have. There's no other explanation,' Tim frowned.

'Julia thinks someone killed her,' I announced. There was a silence around the table.

'Why would anyone want to do that?' Callum asked.

I shrugged. 'From everything I've heard there was a lot bad feeling around Vivien the summer she left. Relationship trouble. Work trouble. Julia is convinced something was wrong in her life.

'If you are referring to what I think you are, put your mind at rest. There was no "relationship trouble" between Vivien and me,' Callum told me, looking slightly amused.

'I've always wondered what went on that summer,' Angie said. 'Vivien was with Luke Riley one minute and with you the next. Neither of you seemed to be making her all that happy.'

'I wasn't in the business of making girls happy,' Callum said with a smile. 'Vivien knew the score. We had a fling, that was all. The only problem was that her real boyfriend came home too early and caught us at it.'

'And you think that kind of thing is okay, do you?' Sara had been quietly watching and now she erupted like a fury.

Callum gave an unamused laugh. 'It was more than okay – for both of us. I wasn't into commitment and you can bet your life she wasn't either.'

'We only have your word for that, don't we?' she snapped. 'Maybe it wasn't an accident. Maybe Vivien killed herself.'

'No way.' Callum sounded sure – and bored.

'There was something else that Julia told me,' I said. 'Apparently Vivien had made some really important discovery just before she disappeared. Something she had to keep secret. She asked Julia to come home because she wanted to talk about it but then she wouldn't tell her what it was.'

Callum gave me a swift glance. I saw something in his expression that suggested he already knew about this. But the look had gone so quickly I wondered if I'd imagined it.

'I get it – you're looking for a mystery to solve aren't you Philippa? Our very own glacier Miss Marple.' His tone was mocking.

'I'm not looking for anything.' With a huge effort I kept my voice light but I didn't fool him.

'A body on the glacier. Of course it couldn't be an accident. That'd be far too boring!'

'Far too convenient for someone more like,' I said. 'There was a secret. Julia didn't make that up. Something had happened to Vivien just before she died. And Julia's not the only one who knows about it. I was talking to Penelope Blake yesterday and whatever it is, she knows about it and she's damned scared about it too.'

I don't know why I said that – I didn't even really think it. Until I saw Callum's face. His detached manner was gone. He was angry. 'Play your detective games if you have to Philippa. But leave Penelope Blake right out of it. She has nothing – nothing – to do with any sordid secret in Vivien Revell's life.'

That seemed to be the end of the party. We all went our separate ways. Callum and I now disliked each other more than ever so that was going to be helpful in our new working relationship. But I wasn't going to think about that.

Instead I lay awake thinking about Vivien Revell. Had she been murdered? And if so, had it been over this secret? Julia had known about it and so, I was sure, had Callum. His reaction had only confirmed the impression I'd had that Penelope not only knew what it was but feared its exposure. Vivien had been going to tell Julia but had then changed her mind. So who else might she have told? Her mother Rose?

...

If Rose Revell had known Vivien's secret maybe she also believed someone had killed her daughter. In which case she had a lot to deal with. She would probably not welcome visitors like me. But I went to see her anyway.

I was starting to think that Julia might be right. If someone had killed Vivien ... This person would have had to persuade her to go up the glacier, search for the perfect crevasse to push her into, then, having made sure she was dead, walk away and leave her. She hadn't been found but all it would have taken was for someone else to come along the same route in the next day or so and she would have been. It would have taken a very bold and confident person.

And I could think of one. Callum Jackson.

But there was no reason for him to have done it. I believed him when he said he'd been having a no-strings fling with Vivien Revell because that was the way the guy lived his whole life. He didn't let anyone get close to him.

I paused outside Rose's house looking through the tangle of shrubbery to her dark red front door. The plants were exuberant, crawling over each other and crowding out the narrow pathway. On a wet day you'd need a scuba mask to get to the door.

Rose opened it almost as soon as I knocked and looked surprised to see me as well she might. But she invited me in and offered coffee without any apparent reluctance. She looked tired and sad. Her dark hair was in need of a wash and she was dressed carelessly in old jeans and a white blouse that had been liberally splashed with paint. She had appeared youthful in the forgiving evening light in the glacier valley but she looked her age now. Her neck and face were deeply scored with lines, her hair was grey at the roots and her eyes were tired.

'You've caught me working,' she said as she handed me a mug of coffee. 'It's the only way I can deal with all this.'

'Did it help going away?' I asked.

'Yes – because no one knew me. I didn't have to put up with all the sympathy – and all the curiosity.'

'I know how that feels,' I said. 'After Susan and Liam were killed everyone wanted to help and there was nothing I wanted them to do. The best night was the one when I got to watch the whole TV news without anyone turning up to tell me how sorry they were.'

Rose laughed. 'I can relate to that.' I looked around her large airy living room. The walls were white and liberally covered with bright abstract paintings. The furniture was worn but almost as colourful as the art work.

I noticed the grubbiness after a while. The dirty plates and wine glasses, dust on the art magazines stacked on the low glass coffee table.

I told Rose what I was trying to do.

'Julia McLoughlin thinks Vivien could have been murdered. She's asked me to keep my eyes open, to see if I can find out what happened. I don't see how I possibly can after all this time but I said I would.'

'Julia?' Rose sounded as if she was struggling to remember who she was. Then she sighed. 'She could never let go, that girl. It's not healthy.'

'So you think she's wrong?'

'No. Actually I think she could be right.'

'Did you think that someone had killed Vivien when she disappeared?'

Rose drew her legs under her as she sat on the sofa. 'No! God, no! Do you think I'd have sat back and done nothing if I had? I really did think she had gone overseas. Things had got a bit hot for her that summer here in Franz and she'd always planned to go to Europe one day. And she had got her first passport.' Rose smiled to herself but she didn't look happy.

'But weren't you puzzled when she didn't write to you?'

'Not really. Viv and I were nomads before we came to Franz. And after. We did our own thing. Out of sight, out of mind. That's what I thought and it would have been right in character as well. I didn't hold it against her. She'd got into that ridiculous tangle with Callum Jackson and Luke Riley. And she'd signed her life away to Penelope Blake. More than enough reason to take off overseas; I'd have done the same myself.'

'But she didn't,' I said. 'So what makes you think she could have been murdered?'

'I just don't see what else could have happened. There's no damned way Vivien would have gone up that glacier alone.'

'Penelope Blake thinks she would have. Her theory is that Vivien was trying to emulate Patrick Blake's first solo trip on the ice to try and get under his skin.'

Rose laughed. 'That woman's something else isn't she? What a ridiculous idea.'

It had sounded plausible to me but I didn't say so.

'No. She went with someone,' Rose sounded certain.

'Callum Jackson?'

'The most likely person, I'd have to say.'

'We were talking about it in the pub the other night,' I told her. 'Callum was at pains to tell us that it was nothing more than a fling – for both of them. So what possible motive could he have?'

'We've only got his word for it that he didn't care. I admit he seems like a heartless bastard but when those ones get burnt they're sometimes more affected than they expect.' Rose's voice was bitter and I had the feeling that she wasn't just talking about Callum Jackson.

'Well it would make my life easier if he was taken off to prison,' I said in a none-too-tactful attempt to lighten the atmosphere. 'Tim's left me in charge of the Glacier Climbers and that means meeting Callum every time something goes wrong in the valley.'

Rose looked amused. 'Is someone still stealing DOC's signs?'

'You heard about that?' I was surprised.

'I don't spend my whole life in my studio you know. I was in the village the day the sign was on display outside the church. Very appropriate. *Extreme Danger Do Not Go Past This Point.* Hilarious! The sign thief has a sense of humour.'

I laughed. 'Yes that was a particularly good one. But I've got a nasty feeling the joke's going to be on me soon. Callum would love to pin it on me.'

'I wouldn't be surprised if it was your fellow guide Matt.'

'Neither would I – but he's admitting nothing. Rose, what do you think of Penelope Blake.'

'Mrs Good Works. Not my type. Why?'

I told her of the hints of a secret Vivien had supposedly uncovered – and about Penelope's reaction to it, adding that I wondered if Vivien could have found out something incriminating about Penelope's husband.

To my surprise Rose burst out laughing. 'Oh I'm sure she could have but if she had Penelope Blake wouldn't have cared. Under that cultivated persona she expects the world to admire, that woman is a realist. She knows just what her precious husband was like even if she'll never admit it.'

'But even if that's true surely she'd have wanted any scandal about him to remain secret?'

'Possibly.' Rose still sounded amused. 'Though from what Vivien told me, Penelope actually wanted her to write something controversial about the great man. A kind of posthumous revenge for all the wasted years.'

'Did Patrick treat her that badly?'

'You could say so, but she invited it. I couldn't have handled her life of pointless self-sacrifice. Patrick never thanked her for it.'

'So you don't know what this secret might have been?' I asked.

'Unfortunately I do. And I know something else. Viv would never have told Penelope. She'd have been the last person ...'

'You know?' I interrupted. 'Why haven't you told the police?'

'Because it's got nothing to do with her death! Vivien was pregnant to Callum when she disappeared.'

'So is *that* why she wanted Julia to come back to Franz?'

'I suppose it must have been. Not that Julia would have been much help. She was so conventional, so narrow – she'd have been horrified.'

'But don't you think that gives Callum a motive after all? He didn't want to be tied down. But to kill someone for that reason ...'

'This was the 1990s, Philippa – not the fifties! But anyway he never knew a thing about it. Viv didn't tell him.'

'Why not?'

Rose didn't answer for a minute and when she did she sounded reluctant. 'Because by then she'd decided there was something strange about Callum Jackson. Something off.'

'What did she mean?'

'She never really said.'

'So she wouldn't have been pleased about the baby?'

'What do you think?'

'I know I said that Vivien had discovered some secret – but her words were more along the lines that she'd discovered something that had changed her life. Is that the way you'd talk about an unplanned pregnancy?'

'I don't see why not,' Rose said.

'I may have got the wrong impression from Julia but I thought she meant that Vivien had found out something that was complicated but ultimately a positive thing in her life. Being pregnant to a guy she thought was unstable doesn't seem to fit.'

'Julia must have misread the whole thing.' Rose's tone was dismissive. 'Vivien certainly didn't want a baby, especially not to a man she had serious concerns about. She was only 24, she had a brilliant life ahead of her – motherhood was never going to be part of the deal. She was going to get rid of the baby. Another good reason for her sudden exit from Franz – or so I thought.'

'And you still weren't worried?'

'She wasn't going to a back street abortionist. She was going to a clinic in Christchurch. I'd have heard at once if anything had gone wrong. She had no reason to contact me. You've probably heard this already but Vivien and I didn't part on good terms.'

'I had heard that,' I said carefully. 'But I didn't know if it was true.'

Rose sighed. 'It was true all right. Now would you like a glass of wine? It must be after five somewhere in the world.'

'I'd love one.'

While I waited for Rose to come back I wondered if it was going to be this simple. Was she really going to tell me?

Of course she wasn't. When we'd had a few sips of wine she looked at me and smiled.

'You're too polite to ask, Philippa, so I'll give you my answer anyway. No, I'm not going to tell you what Vivien and I fought about. It was over something personal. And it had nothing to do with her death. Vivien thought she was so sophisticated but she still had a lot of growing up to do.'

Rose stood up. 'Come up to my studio. I want to show you something. You haven't really got Vivien, Philippa – and you need to know her if you are going to have any hope of knowing who killed her.'

Rose's studio was light and high above the village. She'd have been able to see almost everything from these windows.

'I see all I need of village life from up here.' She seemed to have read my thoughts. 'Now. You remember Vivien as the vibrant fun person who made life seems like a huge adventure – am I right?'

'Yes.' I was startled by her acuity.

'Well here's the Vivien you remember.' Rose pulled a cloth from a painting on an easel and I took a step backwards.

And there she was. Standing outside somewhere with a breeze tossing her tangly dark hair around her head. Talking with a hand up to make a point but a spark in the eye that told you that it was fun, whatever it was. She wore a red top which complemented the vibrancy in her face. She looked happy and full of life.

'I painted that one about a month before she died. She never sat for me in the conventional sense – she didn't have the patience. I had to work from photographs but if I got stuck she would come and sit for an hour or so and we'd talk. We did our best talking then.' Rose seemed to forget I was there for a moment as her mind drifted but she came back to the present quickly with no prompting from me.

'And over here,' she moved towards another easel, looked at me with something challenging in her expression and pulled off the cover. I gasped. This was a different person. The same trademark wild hair, the same sense of strong personality in the tilt of her jaw, but something was very different. It was her mouth and her eyes. The eyes no longer sparked – they gleamed. The mouth was set in a line. The effect was a look of utter contempt. I felt she was staring straight at me, judging me.

'My daughter didn't suffer fools,' Rose said. 'And the world is full of them, don't you find? This was a look I saw often but Vivien hid it from most people. When she saw this painting she wanted me to burn it. I told her she could do that when I died and that I'd never show it publicly. And I never have.'

'It's amazing.' Inadequate words, I know.

'But no one would want to live with this painting on their wall, would they?' Rose laughed. 'I can't handle it myself. It's always covered. And now, lastly ...' She moved to a third easel and pulled away the cover.

Vivien was backing away from something terrible. Her face was white and her eyes were wide. Lines were etched strongly at the sides of her eyes and her mouth was slightly open. She looked tormented. 'This is the last face my daughter ever showed me,' Rose said. 'I've lived with it for all these years, thinking she was out there somewhere. Now I have to live with it knowing she'd been dead all this time, that this was one of the last things she ever saw. This is how my daughter looked at me one day. So when she walked out of my life for good I wasn't all that surprised.'

'What was it that upset her?'

'It had absolutely nothing to do with her death. It was between Vivien and me.'

'But you do think you might know why Vivien died. Won't you tell someone? Not me – the police.'

'No Philippa – I won't. There's no proof of anything. I'm going to deal with this my way. I owe it to Vivien and you can be sure I'm not going to let her down – not again. In the meantime I have a memorial service to organize. I couldn't face a funeral ... but I'm ready now.'

'Where were you the day Vivien disappeared?' I asked, suddenly curious.

To my surprise Rose coloured. Then she smiled. 'Right here – in this very room for most of the day. Her eyes strayed to the large day bed on the side of the room. 'I can't tell you any more than that. It would be a little indiscreet – even after all this time.'

Well this didn't surprise me. From what I'd heard Rose had many lovers and I guessed she'd take a particular pleasure in a man who was off limits. She would enjoy the challenge and, if I read her right, her lover's discomfort would add spice to the whole thing. She might take a similar pleasure in settling a score with her daughter's killer. In which case she'd be playing a dangerous game.

Chapter 5

M{Y first day as manager of The Glacier Climbers was marked by one of the best downpours we'd had in weeks. The rain had started in the early hours of the morning and by the time Kate and I got up, waterfalls were pouring from the guttering making me wonder if the whole system was blocked by sticks and leaves. House maintenance was something I never did until something went wrong.

I made coffee while Kate towed an unwilling Spree out into the rain for his toilet stop, slamming the door in his face to stop him coming straight back in. He was only gone a matter of seconds but came in saturated and shook his woolly coat violently all over the kitchen.

'Spree!' I yelled. He gave me a hurt look and retreated to his purple bean bag.

'I'll drive you to school,' I said to my sister. 'You can't bike in that.'

'Ok.' She hesitated then said: 'I might stay home actually. I'm really tired again.'

'Tired? How can you be tired?'

'I just am.' She looked mutinous.

'Well you're not staying home - sleep at your desk if you need to.'

We left in silence. Despite my light words I was getting a bit worried about Kate. Who ever heard of twelve year olds suffering from tiredness? I should probably take her to the doctor.

Matt and Sara were relaxing in the office, he on Facebook and she reading the paper. There was no sign of our tourist party which didn't surprise me. 'I'll go up and check out the track in a bit, Philippa,' Matt said.

'Good idea. I hope the river stays where it is.' I stood at the window looking out through the teeming rain to the mist enshrouded trees on the other side of the road. The last thing we needed was problems with the access to the glacier. I tried to look through some of the reports Tim had written but it was hard to concentrate. After a while I pushed myself back in my chair.

'Coffee break – does anyone feel like running for it over to Ice Rocks?

Matt and Sara were both keen. There were a lot of others with the same idea and business was humming in the cafe. I was half way through my flat white when I spotted Luke Riley chatting to the woman at the counter. This was too good a chance to pass up. I wandered over and ordered another coffee, trying to look casual.

'Hi Luke,' I said. 'Any cyclists out today?'

'Jenny's dropping a group at Haast, can you believe?' he said. 'I tried to persuade them to leave it a day. They'll be drowned.'

'Sooner them than me. Do you feel like joining us? We've run out of work.'

'Sure.'

Luke followed me to our table and chatted easily with Matt about some cricket match they were both interested in. Sara and I didn't have a lot to say to one another. I watched Luke, trying to put him together with Julia. It was a stretch. Julia was ambitious and organised. Luke was neither. It was obvious to anyone. He was often to be seen drifting round the village chatting when he should have been working. He was always available to help with any community project that was going. He was generous with time and money. A couple of year ago some people I knew had hired bikes from him for a few days and he had tried to refuse payment because they were my friends. They'd insisted on paying which I was pleased about. It was little wonder his business was in trouble.

I looked at him today, trying to imagine him as Vivien's distraught and hurt lover. And as the man Julia still held a torch for despite what he'd done to her. It was hard to see the man fatale in the middle-aged guy sitting drinking coffee now. Luke was tall, fair-haired and tanned. He might have once had a good physique but he was running to fat. Too much beer and rich food – according to Angie who had radar for everyone's eating and drinking habits in this village. From the look of him she was right.

After a while Matt got up, stretched and looked out the rain shrouded window.

'Time to check out the damage in the valley,' he said. 'D'you want to come along, Sara?'

'Sure,' she replied.

I got up to leave as well when, to my surprise, Luke asked me to stay.

'Just if you've got a minute? There's something I need to ask you.'

It was as good an opportunity as I was ever going to get. I sat back down.

'I was talking to Angie yesterday,' he said. 'She tells me Julia McLoughlin's back in town. And that she's been seeing a bit of you? I know it's none of my business, but how is she?'

'She's very upset about Vivien.'

'Yes … It's been an awful shock. Is that why Julia's here?'

'I think so. She felt she had to come home. She and Vivien were good friends, so she tells me.'

'Yeah. They were.' He looked troubled. 'Did she tell you about me?'

'*She* didn't. Not about your relationship with her, anyway. But others haven't been so reticent. Your name has come up a few times.'

Luke smiled but there was no humour in it. 'I'll bet it has. Not one of my prouder memories. I treated Julia very badly. I thought it was all behind me but now it's right in my face again. Philippa – how is she?'

'She's upset about Vivien – but she's also very worried about the effect all of this must be having on you.'

'Not a good one. I'd never told Jenny about Vivien. It was all so long ago and there didn't seem to be any need. But now her body's been found the whole village is talking about it – and about my starring role in the whole thing. Jem Browne took it upon himself to tell Jenny the story the other day – before I got round to it. She's not happy, to put it mildly.'

'Well it's not like you were cheating on Jenny,' I said. 'It's ancient history. Or it would have been if Viv's body hadn't turned up in the glacier.'

'Yeah.' He looked gloomy.

'Luke, what was Vivien really like? I thought I had a good feel for her personality but after talking to her mother I don't think I knew her at all.'

'What did Rose tell you?' His voice was sharp.

'Nothing specific. Just that the persona she showed the world was not the whole Vivien. That she was cynical and unhappy. Things I'd never have imagined. I know I was only a child when she disappeared but everyone says the same – that Vivien was confident, happy, strong, and charismatic. After talking to Rose I'm not so sure.'

Luke stirred the remnants of his coffee, frowning. 'She was all of those things – but she had a really dark side as well. You saw the image she wanted the world to see and I thought that was the real her myself. It's only now that I can see how unhappy she actually was.'

'How do you mean?'

Luke shrugged. 'Some of it was about her relationship with Rose. It was bloody unhealthy – Rose liked scoring points off her. I don't know what it was about but it was toxic whatever it was.'

'What happened to Vivien's father?'

'She never mentioned him to me – it was kind of like she'd never had one.' Luke frowned. 'And that's pretty weird in itself. Since I've had Emma – well it's made me realise just how important being a father actually is.'

'To you maybe – but obviously not to everyone. You don't sound as if you like Rose all that much,' I said.

'That woman is pure poison.' His tone was flat but he looked angry.

'What do you mean?'

He shrugged. 'You know her, don't you?'

'How did you find out about Callum Jackson?' I asked, expecting Luke to tell me to mind my own business. But he didn't seem to find the question intrusive.

'I'd been away. I went to see Viv when I got home. She wasn't expecting me of course. And I wasn't expecting what I found that night either. They were together – and let's just say there was no doubt as to the nature of their relationship.'

'What did you do?'

'There wasn't much I could do. The only person I wanted to talk to was Julia but I didn't think she'd be all that keen to see me after what I'd done to her. After Vivien left town – as we thought – I did try to make things up with Julia but she froze me out. Hardly surprising. The thing is – I'd really like to talk to her now. Do you think she'd see me?'

'I think she would. Luke, there's one thing I should tell you. Julia doesn't believe Vivien's death was an accident.'

He looked puzzled. 'Surely she doesn't think she killed herself?'

'No. She thinks someone killed her.'

Unless Luke was a world-class actor, which I doubted, I could have sworn this idea had never occurred to him.

'No way,' he said, then a look of fear washed over his face. 'She's not saying … No! That's ridiculous!'

'Saying what?'

'She's not trying to tell you that she killed Vivien? There's no way.'

'Not exactly. I think she's more worried about you.'

'Me? She doesn't think that I killed Viv does she? I guess I had a motive but I could never kill anyone.' His reaction was mild which I found a little surprising. 'If Julia is coming out with theories like that she needs help. I don't care about Vivien – even now when I know she's been dead all this time. But I do care about Julia. I want to help her.'

'The best way you could help her is to tell her everything you know,' I said, ruthlessly trying to take advantage of his guilt.

'But I don't know anything.'

'Julia told me that Vivien had found out something really important just before she disappeared. She wouldn't tell Julia what it was and she wonders if it had something to do with her death. Did she tell you?'

'I was the last person Vivien would have confided in.'

Before I could respond the café door was flung open admitting a gust of rain. A child's voice called 'Daddy! Daddy!' and a small figure hurtled across the room and into Luke's arms. His wife Jenny stood watching, her expression cold. She looked young enough to be Luke's daughter herself. She was short and thickset with long brown hair tied back off her face. She wore jeans and a green jersey. Emma took after her father, her hair the same bleached marram grass colour as his.

'How's my girl?' he was asking her. Then he threw her in the air several times as she shrieked with laughter.

'Give it a break, Luke. Don't get her so excited.' Jenny looked annoyed. She ignored me. 'I've just been home. The fire's out and you're up here socialising.'

'I lit the fire before I left,' he protested.

'With wet wood. It's smouldering and cold.'

'I used the wood under the eaves. It was closer,' he said.

'Story of your life. So long as it's nice and easy for you that's all that matters. I'm going back to the office now and I want the fire sorted by the time I get home. And the washing needs doing too.' Jenny turned and walked out of the café without a second look, leaving Luke in possession of their daughter.

'Sorry about that,' Luke looked hassled. 'Philippa, please don't mention anything I've told you to Jenny.'

I laughed. 'You think I have a death wish? Luke, there's just one more thing. Where were you the day Vivien disappeared.'

He didn't look at me. 'Well, actually I was in Hokitika. I – I um – I had a dentist appointment. A root canal job.'

And that's a lie, I thought as I ran back to the guide's office.

...

'You've talked to him?' Julia looked tense. 'What did he say?'

'If you'll let me get in out of the rain I'll tell you.'

Julia and I had met outside my house. I hadn't been expecting her and I wasn't thrilled to see her. I'd have liked a bit more time to process my thoughts about Luke. I made coffee and carried the plunger pot and mugs through to the living room where Julia was perched on the sofa trying to look as if she was enjoying Spree's enthusiastic reception.

'Get down!' I told him and he did although he gave me a hurt look.

'Julia,' I said as I poured the coffee. 'I'm a little annoyed with you. Why didn't you tell me about your involvement with Luke Riley? I don't see how you expect me to find out things for you if you hold out on me.'

She looked upset. 'I'm really sorry Philippa. I was going to tell you, but it was hard. It still hurts so much even after all this time.'

'This is what you're scared of isn't it? That Luke killed Vivien?' This isn't really about Vivien being dead. It's about you being afraid that Luke killed her.'

'Yes – you're right. I still care about him. Can you understand that?'

'Not really. But I'm very shallow when it comes to relationships. I don't do devotion and from the look of you I'm glad of it. Well if it's any comfort to you Julia, I'm almost sure Luke hasn't killed anyone. The idea of murder hadn't occurred to him – I'd put money on that. Although now it has, the first suspect he came up with was you!'

'Are you serious?'

'Yes. He wasn't accusing you – just scared that someone else will. He wants to see you, by the way. But good luck getting past his wife. She's the boss in that relationship, I can tell you. Luke has not found perfect happiness, Julia – if it's any consolation.'

She ignored this.

'You're right. I was scared that Luke might have killed Vivien. He was obsessed with her – and when he found out about Callum I saw a side to him I'd never imagined.' She shivered. 'He's such a happy easy-going guy – I think that's why I fell for him. He's uncomplicated. I'm anxious about everything and he could make all the worries go away. But he's got a temper. I saw him just after he found out about Callum and Vivien. He was in his back yard – he didn't see me. He was smashing up a little rimu tree with an axe and he looked like he wanted to kill someone!'

'Hmmm. That is a bit scary – but it could be worse. If he'd done that to a dog or cat I'd be worried. Still, you're right. It's a side to him I can't imagine either.'

I filled Julia in on our conversation and she listened without interrupting. Then I told her about my talks with Rose, Penelope and Callum. Somewhere along the way I got out the red wine. Kate arrived, having been dropped off by one of her friends, but she ignored us, holing up in the kitchen with Spree to raid the fridge.

'So there's just one more thing to tell you. Rose told me something about Vivien that might explain her summons to you to come home. She was pregnant to Callum – and she had planned to have an abortion.'

Julia stared at me. 'So that's what it was! No. It can't have been. I mean she may have been pregnant – Rose wouldn't make that up. But it wasn't the thing she was going to tell me. I've been going through a lot of my old stuff today. I wish Mum hadn't kept most of it – it's pretty depressing exhuming your past. Anyway, I found the letter Vivien sent me.'

She pulled two worn sheets of paper from her pocket. 'It's lucky this was before the days of email!'

I took it from her and smoothed out the pages on my knee, glancing at the bold strokes of the letters. It was a minute before I started to read.

*Julia, how's the summer going? Mine's been exciting, interesting –
and quite full on! I've got so much to tell you. Look – can you come
home for a few days? I need to talk to you about something – you're
the only person I can tell. I have a day away from the dragon Penelope
on Sunday, so why don't you come home on Saturday. I'll even make a
cheesecake! Julia, something's happened. I've found out something that's
more important than anything that's happened in my life before. It's
wonderful but in some ways futile. It's made me think about things I've
refused to consider before and I'm amazed to realise just how strongly
I feel about them all. But secrets can be dangerous and that's why I
need to talk to you. I need a dose of your common sense – my head's
out of control right now. By the way I have a new man in my life.
Callum Jackson, remember him – that reclusive mountaineer. Not so
self-sufficient as he pretends, I can tell you. He's not into commitment
but neither am I! I haven't told Luke. Didn't think I'd have to as he was
supposed to be away for the summer but now he's turned up unexpectedly
and caught me out. Between that and Penelope it's all a bit much. I'm
convinced she wants me out of her house but she needs me to finish the
work on her husband so she's stuck with me – and me with her! She is
one very buttoned up woman but she won't be my problem for much
longer. See you soon! Love, Viv xxx*

Wonderful. Dangerous. Futile. Julia was right; it didn't sound
like the way one would describe an unwanted pregnancy. The tone
of the letter was happy.

'I don't think she knew she was pregnant when she wrote this,'
Julia said. 'But she must have found out before I got home. That's
why she was so strung up and strange.'

'Do you believe what Rose said – that she wouldn't have told
Callum about the pregnancy?'

'I don't know.' Julia stood up and paced round the room. 'Viv
never hinted to me that there was anything that disturbed her about
Callum. She seemed very keen on him and if she'd wanted to wring
a commitment out of him the pregnancy would have been one way
to do it.'

'Or it could have broken them up,' I pointed out. 'Julia you're not going to like me saying this but the more I hear about Vivien the more I think that she didn't deserve your friendship. She was using you – the letter says it all. It was all about her – she expected you to drop everything. I'm having trouble understanding why you stayed friends with her after what she did.'

Julia sipped her wine in silence for a minute. The she gave herself a small shake and looked at me.

'It's hard to explain. She was such an extrovert, so popular, so successful. At first I was flattered that someone like that wanted me as a friend. I was none of those things. But as I got to know her, I realised she wasn't really like that at all. Underneath there was nothing holding her together. She was actually very lonely, I think – and sometimes really worried about where she was going in life. But she hid it so well that no one who knew her would believe me.'

'Why was she like that do you think?'

Julia snorted. 'One reason. Rose. When we were children I envied their relationship. They teased each other, seemed comfortable together – they were like friends or sisters. My own relationship with my mother was so different. My mother was strict, undemonstrative, and not always easy to be around. But there was one thing I knew for sure – that she loved me and was there for me. Vivien had none of that security. But of course I didn't see any of that when I was young.'

I thought of Rose's cool analysis of her daughter's character as expressed in her paintings. I especially thought of the last one she'd shown me, of Vivien's anguished face – over something that Rose herself had done.

'Those paintings ...'

'Exactly,' Julia interrupted. 'Rose is cruel. She probes for weakness and when she finds it, she's bloody merciless.'

'You were right about one thing. It was Rose who upset Vivien just before she disappeared. She admitted it – but she wouldn't tell me what she'd done. Said it was personal and had nothing to do with Vivien's death.'

'I hate to think what it was. Because Viv became pretty impervious to Rose. She had to be.'

'Not this time, apparently. Julia, do you think Rose could have killed Vivien?'

'I doubt it. What possible reason would she have had? Philippa, you need to understand - Vivien wasn't like her mother. She was troubled and making some pretty selfish choices but fundamentally she was a good person.'

'Penelope told me Vivien lacked compassion and humility. She said her life had been so easy that she had no empathy for other people.'

'Well that is how she came across. Penelope hardly knew her. She was there working on an academic project; they never became friends. I sometimes wonder if I'm the only person who really knew Vivien. I cared about her a lot – and she cared about me.'

'She had a funny way of showing it,' I said. 'Getting back to her letter, I know it looks like it was about something personal to her. But what if it wasn't? What if she'd found out something about Patrick Blake that had the potential to turn an obscure biography into a bestseller? Something criminal or at least scandalous? It would have been a way of winning fame for herself – and money. That could be wonderful – but futile or even dangerous if Penelope tried to censor it.'

'That's possible – but I still think it was about something personal. I suppose I could be wrong.'

But Julia didn't look even slightly persuaded. Neither was I. After she left I made omelettes for our dinner, reflecting on my day.

Only Julia and Rose believed Vivien had been murdered. There was not a shred of evidence. Despite what Rose had said, I still thought Penelope's theory as to why Vivien might have gone on the glacier alone was plausible. There was no doubt there had been a lot going on in Vivien's life around the time she disappeared – and much of it wasn't good. But no compelling motives for murder had emerged. I might have given up on it then and there. But that night something happened to make me change my mind.

...

It was just after midnight and I was suddenly wide awake.

I sat up in bed, looking towards my window. I'd seen a light but there was no sign of it now. I crept across the room and tweaked my roman blind slightly to one side to give myself a peephole. The rain had cleared away and it was moonlight outside.

I had a clear view across the yard. There was no one there but someone had been. My bedroom was at the back of the house right away from the road. There was no way a light could have got there without someone behind it. This had been no passing car.

I crept out of my room and padded down the corridor, pushing Kate's door open. She and our wonderful watchdog Spree slept soundly, two heads on one pillow. They didn't stir and I crept away again.

After a search of the whole house and a check of the doors and windows I breathed more easily. There was no one but us inside and we were locked in.

My parents' bedroom looked out onto the road. I edged my way in, taking care not to stand in front of the uncovered windows.

I froze.

There was someone standing out there.

I could see no more than a silhouette and it was impossible to tell if it was male or female. As I watched a hand came up and I ducked behind the bed just as a shaft of torch light flashed into the room.

I crouched by the bed, heart pounding, and after a minute the light went out.

I peered out.

The person was striding away, off our property, and into the night. I peered cautiously out the front door and after scrabbling round in the dark for a few minutes found the reason for the visit.

Slipped under the mat was a crude picture of a dog.

With his throat cut.

Chapter 6

I was on the glacier.

The ice was covered in a thick layer of snow. There were people everywhere sliding down the uneven slopes on sheets of plastic, laughing and calling to one another. It was cold and fine. In some places the snow was melting and sparkling beads of water were splashing down into crevasses. I slid down in a whirl of powder, crashed off my plastic sheet and fell face down into the snow. Laughing, I raised my face, listening to the sound of water flowing among ice rivulets far below. I got up and ran over the glacier, across surfaces that would usually be treacherous, now made safe by the thick blanket of snow. I scooped snow in my hands and rubbed it over the back of my neck and face, luxuriating in the cold shock as the sun burnt my skin dry.

Then someone called my name and I followed the sound, vaguely aware that I was moving into the pinnacles and away from the rest of the group.

I was busy getting over a crevasse and I didn't see the figure in the dark coat until it grabbed me by the arm, forcing me round to look at – him? – her?

I couldn't tell for a second then as I looked into the person's face recognition came only to be torn away from me in a swirl of snow.

I flew downwards into a deep blue crevasse, choking on snow as I fell. After a while I knew I was no longer moving but I was too sleepy to care. I knew there was no way out even before a face appeared high above me over the rim of the crevasse. I heard laughter and I knew I had to work it out before my whole world went white. I just wanted to sleep, cushioned by hard blue ice. I curled up my body and started to close my eyes.

Then I saw my hands.

They were covered in silver vines which were growing out of nowhere to wrap themselves round my arms and legs and reach for my hair.

I saw a huge black opal beside me and struggled wildly, knowing that if it touched me I would die.

...

'Philippa! Philippa!' I struggled out of unsciouness, relieved to discover I was in my own bed fighting the duvet - not in a crevasse fighting snow.

Kate and Spree stood at the foot of my bed looking concerned.

'What's wrong?' my sister asked.

'Nothing.' I sat up. 'Just a nightmare that's all. Shit. What time is it?'

'Nine o'clock.'

'Nine oclock! Why didn't you wake me up?'

'I've only just woken up myself,' Kate said, looking offended.

'Okay – sorry. Just get some toast on, would you. I'll drive you to school. It's too late for you to bike.'

I jumped out of bed, remembering what had happened the night before. It seemed to have blended into the dream I'd just had and I wondered if any of it was real.

I caught my breath. The picture was still there. Lying face downward on my bedside table.

Thank God Kate hadn't seen it.

I gathered a surprised Spree in a clumsy hug. If anyone hurt my amiable badly behaved friend I'd kill them myself. Spree was a disaster zone some days, uprooting plants from the garden, shredding sheets he'd pulled off the line or just disappearing for hours at a time. A giant schnauzer AWOL in a national park wasn't a good look, but so far we'd got away with it.

His eruption into our lives had been the one bright thing that had kept us together in the wake of our parents' deaths. He'd made us laugh; he wanted to be with us. Kate and I were totally united in this one thing – we both loved our dog and if any harm came to him it would wreck the fragile recovery we had made in the months following our parents' death.

If I thought he was seriously at risk, I should stop this investigation now. I cared a lot more about him than I did about what might or might not have happened to Vivien Revell all those years ago.

After flying round uncoordinatedly for a few minutes, I told myself to chill out. Kate was going to be late for school and I was going to be late for work. The damage was done so I might as well have a coffee and relax for a few minutes. There was no way I was going to leave Spree alone today. I often took him to work anyway. There was usually someone in the guides' office and he was a popular addition. On fine days he spent a lot of his time sprawled in the sun on the front deck and he was great for business. Tourists would come over to talk to him, and would often then decide to book in for one of our glacier trips.

Maybe last night's events had nothing to do with Vivien Revell. Maybe someone from the opposition glacier guiding company had had enough of Spree's impromptu marketing?

No. That was mad.

But so was the other option.

Angie was doing the accounts when we arrived.

'You've got the monster,' she said as Spree hurtled into the office and launched himself on a pile of socks. She looked at him fondly.

'Angie, can I leave him here for the day? We've got a full day trip up into the icefall.'

'You know you can. I'll be glad of the company. Are you all going?'

'Just Matt and me. Sara's having the morning off but she'll be in this afternoon. She's keen to do some work on our website.'

'It's about time someone thought of that. Tim is hopeless at promoting his business.'

'Yes – and I don't think I'll be much better. Lucky we have Sara to think of things like that.'

Matt arrived back from the local store loaded up with lunch provisions for our party and we got to work assembling filled rolls and packaging them up with muesli bars and fruit. Soon after that our tourist group arrived and the office was busy as they tried on boots and were equipped with coats, crampons and daypacks.

Spree wandered amiably around making new friends and slowing down the operation but at last we were on the road and up the glacier valley, Matt at the wheel of our ancient bus.

Tim had bought a bus so old it looked like something from the 1940s. He'd had it painted red and white and decorated with paintings of ice climbers. The tourists loved it but it was a beast to drive and cost a fortune in fuel. I was only too happy to relinquish the wheel to Matt who drove as if he was leading an army assault into a war zone.

I did a running commentary, acquainting the tourists with the glacier and its history. They were young and looked fit. It should be a good day. We walked in single file along the short bush track then down onto the riverbed to be confronted by the usual DOC sign warning all comers as to the extreme danger ahead. Several people in our group were staring at it, looking worried.

'It's fine,' I said quickly before Matt could get in with his mountain lion story. 'It's to do with the river. When it's in flood it can be pretty dangerous but it's absolutely safe today.' I pointed towards the insignificant grey thread issuing from the glacier. The Waiho River was running low and far away, looking completely innocuous.

'That river is dangerous?' asked one of them, a French woman. For the hundredth time I cursed DOC in my head. We were the ones left to explain these bloody signs. If they had to do it, they'd have them down in a week. Matt made some lighthearted remark about bureaucrats and our party moved on, apparently mollified.

Later as we paused for a chocolate stop high above the glacier terminal I told Matt about my night visitor. For once he didn't have a careless riposte. He looked shocked.

'Do you think it might be Henry's crew? I asked, referring to the other guiding company.

'No way. None of them would do a thing like that. They all like Spree.'

'That's what I think too.'

I didn't tell Matt about Vivien – and the other theory I had, that someone was trying to stop me investigating her death. There wasn't time and it would have sounded ridiculous. I dug the shaft of my axe into the ice and watched the tourists exploring the glacier. They moved cautiously but well. It was hard to believe none of them had worn crampons before. It was a warm day and most of them had stripped down to t-shirts.

I glanced past the crusty white ice down to the grey rock in the valley and the silver twist of the river on the gravel below. My worries receded slightly as I enjoyed the atmosphere. I watched amused as Matt reeled the group in, talking about some of the early exploration of the glacier with his usual effortless gift for bringing the past to life. He would have at least one girl to go drinking with tonight if he so chose.

I zoned out as my mind returned to what had happened in the night. Whoever had left that horrible sketch had wanted to be seen. He or she could have slipped it under the door while we slept and we wouldn't have known a thing about it until next day. But they had wanted to scare us as well, shining lights through the windows.

And they had succeeded. I still felt shocked. So who had done it? The sketch was crude but clever. It was recognizable as a giant schnauzer. Rose was an artist. She could have done a much better job but if she had it would be obvious that it was her work. So had she dumbed her talent down to create a work that any amateur could have done? It was possible, but why? She had talked to me. She knew how little I knew. What possible reason could she have for trying to intimidate me?

But who else could have done it? Julia? No way. She was the one who wanted me to investigate this mystery.

Luke? I couldn't imagine him having the energy to get out of bed in the middle of the night for a little bit of recreational stalking.

Penelope? I couldn't see that either – let alone come up with a motive.

Callum? Now he was a possibility. He would be hard-hearted enough. But then I was biased. I didn't like him. And what possible reason could he have? No one had any motive that I could see. But someone had done it. I walked up a steep ice slope and buried the shaft of my axe in a sink hole to test its depth. Then I walked back to the rest of the group. It was a relief to fall back into my role as a glacier guide and stop thinking about anything else. We climbed higher, pushing ourselves and filling our lungs with glacier air. Everyone was enjoying the day. I refused to think of death. This was a day for the living.

...

I stood in the doorway to my parents' bedroom. When they had died I had plundered my mother's wardrobe. She'd had some brilliant outdoor gear and we were of a similar size. But everything else was still there – lots of clothes I would never wear, not to mention my father Liam's whole wardrobe. Their books were on the bedside tables where they'd left them; Susan's hair still clung to the brush on her dressing table. If we left it like this for much longer it would turn into a museum. I didn't want this. It wasn't healthy.

Kate was off somewhere with Sally. I'd just come back from a run with Spree when I made my decision. It was time to sort this out.

Taking out some large black bin liners I began work, piling everything from the wardrobe and drawers into them. There was some good stuff here and the Salvation Army would be able to put it to use. That part was easy. Susan's jewellery wasn't something I felt able to throw away even though none of it was particularly valuable. Neither Kate nor I would wear any of it.

I left it in situ and moved on to the boxes in the bottom of the wardrobe, flinching as I uncovered yellowed letters and packets of photographs. I wasn't ready for any of this either. I turned back to the dressing table, scooped the jewellery into my hands and poured it into one of these boxes. Then I shoved it to the back of the wardrobe and slammed the door. It was out of sight. That was the main thing.

I opened a new bag and threw in worn out clothing, the hair brush, old packets of medicine and other junk. This lot would go straight to the dump.

As I packed away the last remnants of their lives, I replayed scenes from the past in my head. Susan, slightly embarrassed, telling Tom and me she was pregnant with Kate. We'd been teenagers and neither of us had welcomed the news. No one of that age wants hard evidence of their parents' sexuality. Neither of us wanted a baby in the house either and I was ashamed to remember just how resentful I'd been when Kate had been born – and for a long time afterwards.

I remembered my grandfather arriving in a fury one day, sitting in the kitchen and telling Susan and Liam just what he thought of their lifestyle. Telling them how he'd worked his guts out to support his family, how children needed security, how he'd heard the bank was refusing them credit and how they needed to take stock of their lives.

I had silently applauded him. I'd seen the accounts arrive stamped with red "final demand" notices. I'd seen my father toss them carelessly into the old roll-top desk in the living room.

They ignored my grandfather's words and when he died they started spending the money he'd left them like there was no tomorrow. They took us on trips all over the country tramping and camping. And they renovated our house so you could see the mountains from most of the windows.

One day I'd flown into a rage and asked them how they planned to educate Kate. Amazingly they'd listened to me and put the rest of the inheritance into a savings account. It was there now. I could afford to send Kate to boarding school next year – even if it crippled us both emotionally.

I threw open all of the windows and stripped the bed. When I was finished it felt good. The room was bare and anonymous. No one lived here any more and it was no longer a sanctuary for the dead. I hoped Kate wouldn't be upset.

I gave Spree his dinner, had a long hot shower, poured myself a large glass of red wine and retreated to the conservatory with my book. The mountains were clear and the day was still light.

I relaxed and let my mind drift. Before long I was thinking of Vivien Revell. Had someone really killed her? It was hard to believe. They'd all been in their early twenties – Julia, Vivien and Luke. Callum was a good ten years older than them which meant he must be in his fifties now. I had to admit he was wearing well. I didn't understand how Julia could still feel so strongly about Luke. It had all been so long ago. Sure, I'd been burnt by relationships but I'd got over them.

It defied belief that Julia could still be tortured by the fear that Luke had killed Vivien. Why should she care given how badly he had treated her?

I sipped my wine and sighed. I liked Julia. And I respected the way she'd gone out and made an independent life for herself. But to my mind her feelings for Luke pulled her down and made her weak. This was not something I enjoyed seeing. Luke had hurt Julia and he had in turn been hurt by Vivien.

But could he really have killed her because of what had happened? Luke gave every appearance of being laidback and ineffectual. The prospect of his having lured Vivien up the glacier to kill her was so unlikely as to be laughable. Yet Julia, who knew him far better than I did, could imagine it happening. And maybe it had.

But when I had talked to Luke I could have sworn that the idea of murder had never previously occurred to him. Surely he wasn't that good an actor?

There was one thing though – he had not liked me asking where he was the day Vivien had disappeared. And he had lied about it. Why?

Rose also believed her daughter had been murdered. It wasn't just Julia who thought so. I needed to remember that. What was she up to? And what had been wrong between Rose and Vivien the summer she disappeared? Was it related to Vivien's death? Their relationship was obviously difficult but that didn't prove anything. From what Rose had told me she didn't only believe her daughter had been murdered – she also believed she knew who was responsible.

I could understand her not confiding in me. Why should she? But if she knew anything she should go to the police. Playing games with a killer was not all that smart.

Rose had been positive that Callum had not known that Vivien was pregnant, but even if he had there was no reason to kill her over that. One thing had occurred to me though. He was obviously close to Penelope. Had he killed Vivien to protect Penelope from something?

No. That was ridiculous. And from what? If Penelope hadn't seemed worried when I'd mentioned Vivien's secret I'd have never even considered her as a suspect. But I knew I hadn't imagined her reaction.

It was funny how wrong you could be about people. I'd never forgotten Vivien Revell, the young woman who'd walked into our classroom all those years before and made the world seem magic and exciting. She'd seemed to have it all. I could see why Penelope thought Vivien's life had been so easy and that she had no empathy and compassion for others.

Yet Vivien's life had been full of problems and she had died before she could sort them out. She had inspired others but had ultimately not been able to save herself.

I shivered, sipping my wine and staring out over the darkening paddock to the mountains.

My thoughts returned to Susan and Liam. They may have been irresponsible but they'd given us so much. The outdoors had been our home and they had taught us to know and respect it in all its moods. In a village where people gossiped about their neighbours and mortgaged their souls to pay for possessions, our parents had stood out. They had taught us to value the mountains and the glacier, to be secure with ourselves in the wilderness. They'd also taught us the power of books to transport us to other worlds.

Everyone thought I was so different to them, sensible and pragmatic, but it wasn't really true There was a part of me that longed to be as mad and unfazed by life as my parents had been.

I thought often of their free spirits. And missed them like hell.

My little bout of nostalgia dulled my wits. I forgot that there could be a killer out there who had made one threat already – and who was capable of more. Against anyone who was looking too closely at Vivien Revell's untimely death.

Chapter 7

I woke up. My light was on and my book was splayed across my chest. It was midnight and it felt as if I'd been asleep for hours. I had no clear recollection of going to bed but I did recall one glass too many of red wine. It had obviously knocked me out.

I put my book on the bedside table and turned off my light, falling asleep almost at once. At 2 am something jumped on my bed. It took me a few befuddled seconds to recognise Spree.

He never left Kate at night but it didn't occur to me that something might be wrong. Grumbling, I moved to the side to make room for him and fell into a coma-like sleep.

In the morning I realised why Spree had joined me. Kate was nowhere to be found and it looked as if her bed had not been slept in. My mind lurched as I recalled the prowler and the horrible message he - or she - had left us.

Now my sister was missing!

I flung on my clothes and raced round the property, my fear escalating. There was no sign of Kate.

I ran up the road and back again.

Nothing.

I checked the sheds and then did a thorough search of the house. *Oh God*. Where was she? 'Kate!' I screamed 'Kate!' There was no reply.

I rang Julia, careless of the fact that it was only six in the morning. She sounded half-dead with sleep and didn't immediately understand what I was trying to tell her.

'When did you last see her?' she asked.

'She went to bed about ten. Julia, I'm scared. I haven't had a chance to tell you but we had a prowler round here the other night.' I told her what had happened.

She gasped when I told her about the drawing.

'That's sick. Who would do such a thing?'

'Someone who doesn't want me looking into Vivien's death maybe.'

Julia was silent for a minute. Then she said: 'Philippa, you need to ring the police. This is serious.'

My heart felt like it had stopped. 'Yes. I know. I'll just have one more look outside.' I hung up the phone on Julia's pleas for me to be careful. It was a bit late for that. I ran out into the yard and looked into the sheds, scared of what I might be going to find. I found nothing.

I raced back inside.

I'd ring Stu the local cop right now. Why had I wasted time ringing Julia?

I had my hand on the phone when I noticed something. Kate's bedroom door had been open a minute ago. Now it was shut.

My heart hammering I crept down the hallway and listened. There was no sound from within. Spree leaped in front of me, scratching on the door with his front paws. He barked and I winced at the noise.

Then I opened the door. Kate was in her bed.

Apparently sound asleep.

...

Julia arrived in time to hear us shouting at one another.

Her look of relief was quickly replaced by one of amazement. She'd never heard us in full spate before. She made coffee and tried to feed us with toast while our yells reduced to a quiet bickering.

Kate had tried to tell me she'd just gone out for a walk. At 5.30 in the morning. A girl who had to be practically dragged from beneath her duvet for school most days. I wasn't buying it.

'Where were you?' I said for the fifteenth time.

'I told you.' Kate looked mutinous.

'Is Sally involved in this?' I asked.

For the first time I saw a crack in my sister's manner. She hesitated then said: 'So what if she is?'

'What are the pair of you up to now?' I asked, suddenly feeling very tired. I recalled the time they'd gone out in the middle of the night to watch the souls of the dead rising over the glacier on their way to heaven. How Kate had screamed at me that our parents' souls hadn't made an appearance, and that they must be trapped in their bodies, mouldering away in the local cemetery.

Prowlers one night. Now this. I leaned forward in my chair, elbow on the table, and pressed my fingers hard against my forehead. Kate and her tiredness. Coming home from school in the middle of the day and going straight to sleep. I'd been meaning to take her to the doctor to try and find out what was wrong with her. Now I knew. It wasn't some kind of nasty disease. She was tired because she hadn't been sleeping.

'This isn't the first night you and Sally have been out – is it Kate?'

She glared at me but said nothing.

'That's why you're tired all the time! Because you've been sneaking out after I've gone to sleep. Why, Kate?'

'All right! I'll tell you! We were doing it for you Philippa!'

'Doing what?' I put my coffee mug down on the table and stared at my sister.

'The signs.' Her voice was sulky.

For a minute I didn't know what she was talking about, and when I realised I didn't know whether to laugh or scream.

'It was *you*?'

'Well, yeah it was. I was trying to help you, can't you understand that?'

'You and Sally are the ones who have been pulling out the DOC signs. I don't believe it.'

'You go on and on about how mental they are! About how embarrassing it is explaining them to the tourists. So Sally and I decided

to do something about it for you. We had to do it at night – there
are so many people in the glacier valley during the day. So we've
been going up real late – we had to wait till Sally's parents and you
were all asleep.'

'You've been doing this on your own? Weren't you scared?'

'Not really,' Kate shrugged. 'We never saw anyone. And we usually took Spree. You know how scary he is when he barks.'

'Why didn't you take him last night?'

'He's got a sore foot – haven't you noticed?'

I hadn't. Another thing to feel guilty about.

'How on earth did you get the signs out? They are dug in really
well.'

She shrugged. 'It wasn't hard, just took a bit of time that's all.
We each had a spade and we'd just keep on digging. Sally brought
a crowbar too.'

'Wait a minute Kate,' I said recalling the appearance of some of
the signs in the village. In front of tourist businesses. In front of the
church. 'Are you telling me you got those things all the way down
the glacier valley over the handlebars of your bikes? I don't believe
it.'

'No of course not,' Kate looked impatient. 'We had the van.'

'What van? You can't drive.'

'Sally can. And it's her brother's. He never noticed it was gone.'

'Kate, Sally's twelve. It's illegal for her to drive – even if she can.'

'So?' Kate looked unimpressed.

'What about the other ones?' I asked remembering the numerous
signs that had clean disappeared.

'Chucked them in the river,' my sister said.

I stared at her for a minute and then I burst out laughing. Once
I started I couldn't stop. All the hassle this whole thing had been
causing – not just for me but for all the other guides working in the
glacier valley. The issue that was threatening to completely wreck
the fragile working relationship between DOC and the guides. All
down to my sister and her best friend. Because they wanted to help
me.

When I stopped laughing I saw that I'd only succeeded in offending Kate. 'It was really good of you to care about me so much – I can't believe that you did that for me, Kate.'

She stared at me, looking cross.

'It certainly worked. DOC are beside themselves. They would never think of it being you and Sally in a million years. But they have been blaming me – and the rest of us. Kate, you are a brilliant sister. I don't deserve you. But this has to stop now.'

'Will you tell them it was us?' For the first time Kate looked apprehensive.

'Of course I won't. But you and Sally can't tell anyone about this. If it gets back to DOC I don't know what they'd do. They might even go to the police.'

'We won't tell. It's been fun but to be honest I'm getting a bit sick of it anyway. Do I have to go to school today Philippa? I really am tired.'

I sighed. 'No, you can stay at home. I'll ring your teacher and tell her you're sick.'

After she'd gone to bed I looked at Julia, the silent witness to this revelation.

'What do you think?'

'I wish I had half their guts. I've never heard of anything like it.'

'You don't know Sally,' I said grimly. 'I don't believe this. All that angst between us and DOC – and do you know something, Julia? I had no idea who was doing it – but I've really enjoyed the whole thing. Especially the time they put the sign in front of the church.' We looked at one another and laughed.

Later I looked back on that morning as the day before things started to get serious. Up until then I'd been intrigued by the story of Vivien Revell but none of the theories about her death seemed real. Perhaps it was the prowler; perhaps it was just that I finally started to believe Julia.

For whatever reason I now believed that Vivien had been murdered.

The mystery of the signs had been solved. A much darker mystery remained.

Chapter 8

JULIA and I met the next day at Ice Rocks.

She had rung just before I left for work and told me there was something she wanted to talk to me about.

It was raining, and Sara and I got back from a less than inspiring glacier walk feeling wet, cold and over people. I felt more like going home for a hot shower than hanging out in a village café and I wasn't terribly enthusiastic about Julia and her ideas either.

'How are things with Kate?' she greeted me.

'Fine – she's back at school promising not to go out stealing signs ever again.'

Julia laughed. After a moment I joined in.

'You're not going to confess to DOC are you?' she asked.

'No. I just hope no one else tells them. It's probably all over the village by now.'

'But no one'll tell DOC,' Julia said.

I laughed. She was right. It would have been the worst kind of disloyalty for a local person to shop one of their own. Julia might have been away for years but she still knew how the Coast worked. I recalled the story about the helicopter pilot who used to fly DOC staff trying to catch illegal whitebaiters. Unbeknown to the hapless bureaucrats, the helicopter landing lights would be on – alerting everyone to get their nets out of the water and disappear before they could be spotted.

'Philippa, how would you like a few days away from Franz?'

I looked at Julia, surprised.

'There's someone in Wellington I'd like you to talk to about Vivien,' she said. 'I could have Kate and Spree to stay with me. And you could use my house in Wellington. I'd pay for your flight of course.'

'Who is it you want me to talk to?'

'Harry Lane – he was Viv's MA supervisor. She saw a lot of him just before she disappeared. He's a bit of an armchair mountaineer – he was really interested in Patrick Blake for some reason and I think he was mentoring her with her book.'

'Why don't you talk to him yourself?'

She hesitated. 'He and I had a falling out. We were friends – I got to know him through some other people after I moved to Wellington. We got talking because we had a common interest in Vivien. He – well he idolised her. Never could let go – or that's what it seemed like to me. Used to go on to me about her talent, what a loss she was. I went along with it for a while. I was homesick in Wellington and Harry was a kind of link with the past.' Julia tailed off and sipped her coffee staring at the window.

'So what went wrong?'

'I lost my temper with him one day – said some unforgivable things. Things I should have said to Vivien herself when I'd had the chance. You know how it is – if you don't get things out they fester and get worse. Well I was vitriolic about what a user she was and what fools she made of men. I included Harry in this, told him he was a sad old man clinging to the past brilliance of a girl who wouldn't have given him a second look. He didn't like it much.' Her tone was reflective.

I laughed. 'I'm not surprised. So what do you want me to do? Go and tell him I'm a friend of yours and can he please spill all those secrets about Vivien that he never told anyone else?'

'Hmmm. If you put it that way it does sound pretty bad. I was thinking more along the lines that you'd found the body, were terribly shocked and couldn't get it out of your head, that you are talking to everyone who knew Vivien to try and get a sense of who she was – that kind of thing.'

'You want me to go and talk to a guy I've never met and tell him I'm some kind of loser on a self-imposed therapy kick?'

'Well not exactly! I'm sure you can come up with a better story than that, Philippa.'

'Maybe. I'll have to think about it. I'm not happy about leaving Kate or Spree right now. You should be able to understand that'.

'Of course I do. But they'll be safe with me. I'll make sure I'm around for Kate after school and Spree will be with either my mother or me all the time. I promise you that, Philippa.'

Despite myself I was tempted. It would be great to get away from Franz for a few days and I liked Wellington. I could go to a movie, and catch up with some friends.

I probably shouldn't leave work given my unwanted managerial responsibilities but nothing much was happening right now. Angie, Matt and Sara would see to it that the business didn't fall over. One good thing about being the boss was that I didn't need to ask anyone's permission.

'Julia, how long are you planning on staying in Franz?' I asked. She shrugged. 'Probably not much longer. I wish Rose would get on and organise Vivien's memorial service. I want to be here for that. But I'm doing some work from here.'

'What do you actually do in Wellington?'

'I'm a policy analyst. As to what I do — well it's a lot of report writing and stuff — you really don't want to know.'

I shuddered. I hoped my body would serve me well because there was one thing I was sure of — I never wanted to end up in an office.

Kate, predictably, was not happy with the idea of going to stay with Julia. 'I hardly know her,' she said. 'Why can't I go to Sally's?'

'Because I need to know you're safe.' But I didn't blame her for her reaction. I wouldn't have wanted to go and stay with Julia myself.

She gave me a scornful look. 'I'm not a baby.'

'Well — okay. If Sally's mother's doesn't mind you can go there. But Julia will look after Spree. There are other dogs at Sally's place.'

Kate agreed and it was all arranged.

Before I knew it I was flying into to Wellington, peering out the plane window at the hills and houses before swooping down from above the sea onto the runway. A friend met me at the airport and we went for a coffee at a café on one of the bays. It was magic sitting in the sun, the seabirds squabbling on the strip of beach at our side. The Interislander ferry glided past as we sipped coffee and gossiped. My friend wanted to know all about my finding Vivien's body and I gave her a general rundown, not telling her that this was what had brought me to Wellington.

She in turn filled me in on the lives of friends I hadn't seen in a while. 'You need to get on Facebook, Philippa. We'd all like to keep in touch with you more than we do.'

'Maybe.' But I had no intention of getting hooked into social media networks. I'd seen enough of them second-hand looking over Matt's shoulder at work. No detail was too trivial to find its way to Facebook – or so it seemed.

Later I sat, a glass of wine to hand, as I admired the brilliant views from Julia's cliff top home. She had done well for herself. Wellington was an expensive city to live in and she owned a cottage in a spectacular place. It was weatherboard and well maintained with sun and views. It must be worth a fortune. I could have settled in here and done nothing for a few days. But I had things to do.

...

'Vivien Revell. I still can't believe she's been dead all this time. What a bloody tragedy.' Dr Harry Lane waved a hand in the air and knocked a large pile of papers off his desk onto the floor.

He had been accepting of my story. I'd essentially told him what Julia had suggested I say. It had sounded wildly unlikely to me but he seemed to have taken it at face value and had been willing for me to come and talk to him.

'Not that I can tell you much,' he'd said when I'd rung him from Julia's place the night before. He went on to give confusing directions and I eventually made it to his place, a villa that looked as if it had fallen on hard times. The roof was rusted and weatherboards at the front door were cracked.

Harry greeted me at the door, a tall stooped man with untidy longish grey hair and a beard. The house was untidy with books everywhere. I wondered how he ever found anything. He looked about seventy and was dressed in ancient corduroy trousers and an old jersey that might have once been green but was now faded to a dirty grey colour. His face was alert. I had the sudden scary feeling that amongst all the muddle and clutter was a person who wouldn't miss a damned thing.

He sat politely in the chair beside his desk and waited for me to explain myself. I did so with some difficulty.

'So you're looking for closure – is that it?' His tone was ironic and I felt myself flushing as I made a decision.

'Actually no – I'm not into that kind of rubbish,' I said. 'Look, I'm here under false pretences. One of Vivien's best friends asked me to talk to you. She thinks Vivien was murdered.'

'Does she indeed? You don't need to tell me who this friend is. As soon as you rang me I knew that Julia McLoughlin was behind this. She could have come to talk to me herself instead of sending you. Why didn't she?'

'She didn't think you'd talk to her.'

'Because of something she said to me in temper years ago? How thin skinned does she think I am?' He chuckled. 'Tell her one thing from me when you see her – to get round here for a glass of wine and a talk. I miss her. Least she can do if she wants me to bare my soul is to give an old man a bit of intelligent company once in a while.'

'I'll tell her – if I don't kill her first!'

He laughed. 'Now we've got that out of the way can I make you a coffee? Or something stronger. A whisky maybe?'

'Just a coffee will be fine.'

'Coming up. Milk?'

'Please. No sugar.'

I sat back in a dusty chair and looked around the room while I waited. A large cat flung itself onto my lap and I jumped. He stared back, managing to convey the impression that he'd seen my type before and didn't much like it. I patted him, wondering if he'd bite, but instead he broke into a loud rusty purr. He was an amazing looking animal, a rag-bag of colour, with a black and white face giving way to a grey body and a tortoiseshell tail and legs.

'That's Ferdinand,' Harry said returning with our coffee. 'Throw him off if he bothers you. He takes advantage – which is exactly what Vivien Revell used to do.'

'I've heard that from a few people now. But what makes you say that?'

'She used people. With consummate skill, I might add. Even an old man like me found himself being flattered a girl like that was interested in what I had to say. Of course that wasn't what she was interested in at all.'

'What was she interested in then?'

'Patrick Blake, that's who. Now I don't know how much you know about academics but most of us don't take kindly to having our research subjects stolen from under our noses. That's exactly what Vivien Revell did to me – and she did it so well I didn't even mind. I'd planned to write a book on him. A retirement interest you might say. I've always been interested in mountaineering even if I don't get out myself any more. He was a great mountaineer who'd had had almost nothing written about him.'

'Did Vivien get the idea from you?'

'Yes. The thing is, she didn't know all that much about him even though she had grown up in Franz Josef. I told her my plans one night and she seemed genuinely interested. I was flattered and I kept on talking. And then off she went to his widow and told her all the things I'd said as if she'd thought them up herself and the next thing I heard was that she had access to his papers and was signed up to write the book herself.'

'You must have been furious.'

'More with myself than her – but yes I was of course. Wouldn't you be? Vivien's timing was just right. Penelope Blake is a difficult woman and I wasn't expecting it to be easy to gain access to Patrick's papers. But it seems Penelope was ready for her husband's story to be told.'

'Why is everyone so interested in Patrick Blake? I know he was a good mountaineer but so are a lot of people. What made him special?'

'His flaws,' Harry said without hesitation. 'Now you do some mountaineering yourself and you know what it's like. A lot of climbers are driven and egotistical but get below the surface and they're pretty ordinary people. Patrick wasn't. He had no interest in making a name for himself yet he was one of the best mountaineers this country has seen. He did some incredible ascents, many of them solo. He broke all the rules and lived to tell the tale. Patrick Blake was a charmer but underneath it all he was cold to the bone. He is the only person I've ever known who genuinely didn't seem to care about anyone in his life. More than cold, the man was dangerous. Ordinary rules never applied. He wasn't a person I'd have wanted holding my climbing rope. What I had planned to do was write about that. The whole thing. The brilliance and the flaws. Vivien got what I was talking about. And then she decided to do it herself.'

'Somewhere along the line she must have changed her mind. Penelope told me she only gave her access to Patrick's papers for her MA on condition she stayed in Franz to write the biography once she'd submitted her thesis.'

Harry nodded. 'I never got to the bottom of that. She had the raw material for a biography that could have become a New Zealand classic. She was an opportunistic young woman but suddenly she went right off the idea of writing the book even though she could have made a name for herself with it. I never found out why. In the end all she wanted to do was write a MA thesis on women mountaineers – and the most she'd have got out of that would have been a study in sub-alpine feminism using all the same old arguments.'

I sipped my coffee, patted a snoring Ferdinand and looked at Harry. 'I came to see you with a vague idea of a motive for her death,' I said, 'but what you've said ruins my theory. I thought that perhaps she had discovered something really bad about Patrick Blake, something that could have turned a biography into a bestseller, but that Penelope had found out and killed her to prevent her doing that.'

Harry shook his head. 'I don't think so. From what Vivien did tell me I'd say the opposite was true. You've got part of the story right though – there was a scandal in Patrick's past.'

'Do you know what it was?' I stared at him.

'She told me all about it – that's when I realised that for some obscure reason she was determined to turn Patrick Blake into a hero. He'd written about all his climbs you see – it was all there in his papers. He never tried to publish anything and Vivien soon found out why. He'd collected a whole lot of other stuff, you see. Coroner's reports, that kind of thing. They'd never seen the light of day before but he went into the national archives and dug them all out. The person I'm about to tell you about wasn't the first one to die. Vivien couldn't believe what she'd found, how it was that no one ever talked about it. You can imagine. You're a guide yourself. How would you feel if one of your clients died?'

I shifted in my seat, disturbing Ferdinand who gave me an irritated look.

'It's something I dread. Harry, I live in Franz. I've never heard anyone dying when they were away climbing with Patrick.'

He grimaced. 'That's what I mean about the bloody man. Nothing stuck to him. I don't know how he did it.'

'What did Vivien make of all this?'

'She was like you – she couldn't believe it. But the facts spoke for themselves. And then she found out something else that made it all seem a lot more sinister. It happened not long before he retired. He'd been up above the Franz Josef Glacier with a young woman client doing some climbs. They were based in Almer Hut – you know it?'

I nodded.

'She fell. They were on some mountain and they weren't roped up. It happened near evening and she was badly injured. He tried to get her back to the hut but he couldn't. So he dug a snow cave, left her there and went back to the hut for a sleeping bag. According to what he told the police she was unconscious when he got back. So he got her into the sleeping bag and left her to it. Went back to the hut, made himself a meal and had a nice sleep. Pretty callous, don't you think?'

'That's for sure.' I said, shocked

'And it gets better. That's only what was in the coroner's report. The letters from the woman's father were a hell of a lot more interesting. He accused Patrick Blake of murder.'

'Really? Why?'

'He thought Patrick had staged an accident to get rid of her. Janet, Janet ... Lestrange, that was her name. Her father told Patrick he wouldn't rest till he saw him made accountable for his daughter's death but it all came to nothing. The inquest came back with a verdict of accidental death. And even supported Patrick's decision not to try and get her back to the hut. Her back was broken; he'd have only done her more harm if he'd tried to move her.'

'What did her father do then?'

'Went to the media – even they didn't think there was a story in it. So he went to Franz to talk to Patrick's mates and they froze him out. Everyone thought he was a nutter but he kept on going. Didn't seem to faze Patrick Blake at all. But then the poor man – the father I mean – died of a massive stroke and that was the end of it. Janet had been an only child and her mother was no fighter. You mean to say you have never heard of the accident yourself?'

'I might have done – but if so I'd forgotten all about it so it can't have made much of an impression. Why would Patrick have wanted to kill her though?'

'He must have been forty years older than her but he still had something going for him apparently. They were lovers, had been for a year or more. Janet had upset her parents by telling them Patrick was going to leave his wife for her. They were appalled as you might imagine – he was even older than they were. Forbade her to go anywhere near him and of course she ignored them. Next thing you know, she's unconscious on a mountain while Romeo enjoys a nice sleep down in the hut below. Not the way I'd have treated a woman I loved.'

'No guide would do a thing like that – lover or not,' I said.

'One thing is sure about Patrick Blake – he was no ordinary guide. I've seen photographs of Janet Lestrange. She was a beauty. Could've had anyone but chose an old mountaineer who was well past his prime.'

'But why would he have wanted to kill her?'

'Who knows? Maybe he didn't want to leave his wife after all. If Janet was threatening to expose their affair and wreck his marriage he might have decided he wanted to be rid of her.'

'Maybe. But no one in Franz would have thought any the less of him. He was the local hero. No one likes Penelope. *She's* the one with the motive. If she found out she could have killed Janet. Then if Vivien found out she could have killed her to keep the whole thing quiet.'

'I thought of that too,' Harry said. 'Penelope killing Janet I mean – but she can't have. Penelope was in Europe that summer. She was away for months.'

'Oh.' I was disappointed even though I knew I shouldn't be. 'What did Vivien make of it all?'

'She was shocked –which amazed me at the time because she was a permissive young woman.'

I frowned, thinking. 'Vivien wrote to Julia not long before she disappeared and said she'd discovered some secret. She seemed excited by it – pleased. But if you're right she wasn't happy about this one.'

'No she certainly wasn't – and she should have been. What a springboard for a biography that could have been.'

'She said the secret she'd discovered could be dangerous,' I said slowly. 'And it would have been. Penelope could have killed Vivien to prevent this story coming out. Come to think of it, it's strange she left those inquest reports and letter from Janet's father lying around in Patrick's archives for Vivien to find ...'

'Didn't I tell you?' Harry interrupted. 'Penelope who told her the whole story. Wanted her to put it in her book.'

...

I went back to Franz with plenty to think about.

Harry Lane was right. The story of Patrick's accidents, culminating in the death of his lover, was raw material for a great biography, especially if Vivien had investigated the whole thing more deeply and been able to come up with a reasonable hypothesis for murder. A title like *The Murderous Mountaineer* would sell a lot more copies than *Patrick Blake, Mountain Guide*.

There was something else Vivien had said in the letter to Julia, and I struggled to recall it. She had said her discovery had made her think about things she'd refused to consider, and she'd been surprised to realise how much they mattered. So how did this fit in?

Her discovery could certainly have been dangerous. I could have imagined Penelope doing anything to cover up a scandal of this kind, but obviously not if she was the one who had told Vivien the story in the first place. There was no motive for murder here.

But the more I thought about Penelope, the more I could imagine her killing someone if she needed to. Her self-containment could easily have turned into ruthlessness, and she would not lack courage.

But she hadn't killed Vivien to cover up the fact her husband had been an adulterer and possibly a murderer. She had tried to force her to write a book about it. That in itself was pretty damned weird.

No wonder Vivien had told Julia that Penelope was strange.

So what had happened that summer? Penelope had tied Vivien down with a legal contract, so she would supposedly have been forced to write Patrick's biography. Vivien had been a talented researcher and it was possible she would have overcome her reluctance in the interest of good scholarship.

But instead of that she had been killed.

There was another possibility. What if Penelope had hated her husband enough to kill him? If Vivien had found out, Penelope would have had a motive for murder after all. Even now, Penelope was fit and strong, and twenty years ago she could have easily taken Vivien up into the icefall on some pretext and killed her. Penelope had done a lot of climbing with her husband over the years and she'd have had the advantage over Vivien on the glacier. But Patrick had died of a heart attack. There had been no question of foul play at the time and I didn't see how Vivien could have found otherwise years after the event. I sighed. I didn't seem to be going anywhere with this investigation, even if I was finding out a few interesting things along the way.

...

'Patrick didn't murder Janet Lestrange,' Penelope said.

I'd called in at her house, the return of the books she had lent to Kate giving me an excuse for my visit. We'd talked about inconsequential matters while we drank coffee. Then I mentioned my meeting with Harry Lane. Penelope had seemed interested and listened to my account of what he had said without interrupting.

When I'd finished she sighed. She had every right to be angry with me for prying into her personal life but she didn't seem to care.

I leaned forward to put my cup on the table and as I did so caught the eye of Patrick Blake, framed in silver, dressed in a climbing outfit with a rope slung over his left shoulder. The photograph would have made a great book cover.

'Harry told me that Janet's father thought he had killed her,' I said.

'Yes. Poor man. Janet was his only child. He wanted someone to blame. I've always understood that. And Patrick was culpable. He didn't murder her. But he killed her.'

'What's the difference?' I asked after we'd sat in silence for a couple of minutes.

'Intent, of course.' Penelope's voice was sharp. 'He didn't mean to do it. But he was criminally careless all the same. Janet should never have been on that mountain. She wasn't experienced enough. But even so she should have made it home safely. He was the guide. He was the one who made all the bad choices. He'd done it before and he did it again – after Janet died. He was an unsafe guide.'

'And you wanted Vivien to write about all this?'

'Yes. It was a story that needed to be told.'

'Did you tell Vivien that Patrick had murdered Janet?' I asked.

She smiled but there was no warmth in her expression. 'I might have done. You have to remember this was a long time ago. I was far more upset about the whole thing than I am now. And it could have caused me to be – intemperate. Patrick had no reason to murder Janet. But I did. As you probably realise.'

'Harry said you were overseas when it happened.'

'I was. Out of the frame, as they say in detective novels. Why are you so interested in all of this, Philippa? It's ancient history.'

I hesitated. 'Julia's asked me to see what I can find out about things that were going on in Vivien's life before she died.'

Penelope looked annoyed. 'None of this has anything to do with Vivien Revell. My husband had an affair with Janet Lestrange. She was young enough to be his daughter. Looking back on it now I can see that he couldn't help himself. He always had to prove to himself that he was still attractive to women. By the time it happened I was used to his affairs. The thing that was unforgivable was that he picked Janet.'

'What do you mean?'

'Janet was my friend. In some ways she was the daughter I'd never had. I met her at an arts festival in Christchurch and we clicked. So much so that I invited her over for a visit. Patrick and I were going to take her climbing but I sprained my ankle and couldn't go. So they went off together ... and that's when it all started. It took me over a year to find out. Janet kept coming over to Franz. It made me very happy. When the three of us were together it felt like we were a family. I didn't suspect a thing.'

'How did you find out?'

'The usual way. I came home unexpectedly one afternoon and found them in bed together.'

'How awful.'

Penelope shrugged. 'It was a shock but I was angrier with myself than I was with them. For being such a sentimental fool. I needed to think and I didn't want them to know that I'd seen them. So I backed out of the house and went for a long walk on my own. I decided what I had to do with my life and did it.'

'Did they know you'd seen them?'

'No. They never found out. I came home that night and told Patrick I needed to get out of Franz for a while. I'd always wanted to go overseas but he always said the time wasn't right for him. I told him I was tired of waiting, that I was going on my own. Patrick wasn't happy about it - that was the ironic thing. He still needed me. I was his security, his comfort. His affairs were all about his ego. The women were interchangeable but I wasn't. As you can imagine, I didn't care about his feelings in the matter. I went and had a wonderful six months losing myself in Europe. After a while I stopped thinking about them. And then I came home to find that Janet was dead and Patrick was in the middle of a nervous breakdown.'

'How did the accident happen?'

'They were arguing and it made him even more careless than usual. Patrick hadn't roped them up and she wasn't concentrating on what she was doing. She slipped and fell over a rock face. Patrick rushed down to where she had fallen. She was alive but it was obvious she was badly injured. He knew he couldn't move her. He knew that she was dying and he couldn't face it. So he made her as comfortable as he could and left her to it. He was a coward,

Philippa. He told me she was unconscious when he left, that she would have died easily.'

'That's terrible.' I thought of New Zealand guide Rob Hall who had died on Mount Everest with a client who couldn't go any further. He could have gone on alone and tried to save himself but he hadn't. Patrick Blake wouldn't have died if he had stayed with Janet; all he would have faced would have been an uncomfortable night. But he had abandoned her.

Penelope shrugged. 'That was Patrick. Janet Lestrange had once meant a lot to me but to my husband she was just another woman he'd slept with. And another accident statistic. He took so many risks with the people he was supposed to be looking after. That was my real motivation for the book . The story needed to be told and I felt that Vivien Revell was the right person to tell it. I handed her an absolute gift of a subject – and she didn't want to know!'

'Why was that?'

Penelope looked thoughtful. 'I never found out, but it was a shame. She could have written a great book. She had the brains for it. She could have cut right through all the purple prose that's been written about mountaineers. It could have made her name as a writer. And it could have given me the satisfaction of seeing the truth about my husband finally being told. I hated him in the end. But I'd loved him once – with everything I had. I lived with the mystique even as every year I found out more about how different the man really was. I wasted my life. And I only have myself to blame.'

'You shouldn't be so hard on yourself,' I said. 'It's easy to get out of marriages now but I guess it wasn't so easy when you were young.'

'Actually that isn't true in my case. My parents would have welcomed me back. They were very liberal in their views. I could have slipped back into the privileged city life I'd grown up in. But I couldn't admit to them I'd made a mistake. My pride was more important to me than anything. Can you understand that?'

'I sure can,' I said grimly. 'My pride's taken me into all kinds of bad situations – and I think it always will.'

Penelope smiled. 'This was another thing. I was hurt by Patrick's affairs even while I tried to ignore them. But there was something worse than that. The knowledge that I'd spent all those years with a man who had no idea of what mattered to me, no idea of what I wanted.'

'Bloody relationships,' I said. 'Penelope – if Julia's right and Vivien was murdered, do you think it might have something to do with Callum Jackson?'

'Why should it?' Penelope looked angry.

'He was close to Vivien when she disappeared,' I said, 'and there did seem to be something wrong with their relationship. Julia certainly thought so.'

'Julia doesn't know what she's talking about. She needs to have a care and not go round making statements like that about people. It's destructive – and dangerous.'

I left soon after. There wasn't anything more to say. I was surprised that Penelope had spoken so freely to me. And more than that, she had seemed to enjoy telling me about Patrick.

Spree was pleased to see me when I joined him in Penelope's garden and we ran most of the way home.

My mind was as active as my legs. Penelope had wanted Patrick exposed for the adulterer and dangerous climber that he was. If it had been only she who had told me that, I might have thought she was lying. But Vivien Revell had told the same story to Harry Lane just before she disappeared. Penelope's life must have been hell – coping with Patrick's affairs while everyone it the village treated him like the local hero and her as the outsider. I could well understand her not going back to her family though. I knew all about pride. So instead she had tried to give her life some meaning by throwing herself into the community – and getting very little thanks for all she'd done. And then along had come the opportunity for the real story of Patrick Blake to be told. No wonder she'd been so keen for Vivien to write the book. What a vindication it would have been. Instead of that Vivien had turned down the opportunity and then disappeared.

I'd believed Penelope when she had told me she'd got to the stage that she was indifferent to her husband's infidelities, that she no longer cared what he did, that her love had been worn down to the point that she felt only indifference.

But as Spree and I pounded along the road I wondered if that was really true. It was in the way she'd looked as she'd said the words. They didn't match. There'd been more than resentment in her expression as she'd described all the wasted years. Penelope Blake had hated her husband –and still did even though he'd been dead for years.

Chapter 9

WHEN I got home Kate was nowhere to be seen. I wasn't sorry. It was great to have some time to myself for a change. Spree came rushing out of Kate's bedroom to meet me. I poured a large glass of red wine and retreated to the living room, settling in to my favourite chair with a contented sigh.

I read for an hour or so before I started to get hungry.

Spree joined me in the kitchen and we stared unenthusiastically into the fridge. There wasn't anything to get excited about in there. After giving him a large bowl of biscuits, I started assembling a stir fry, grimacing as I foretold Kate's likely reaction to this excuse for dinner.

Where was she? It was after 6. She should have been home hours ago.

I looked at my phone. There had been no text from her.

An hour later I was angry.

I rang Sally's place and that was when I started to feel afraid. Kate had left for home after school. But she wasn't here.

I put down the phone feeling sick. Why hadn't I taken heed of the warnings?

Someone had killed Vivien Revell. He or she didn't want me trying to find out what had gone on. They'd warned me. I'd ignored them. And now my sister was missing. I searched the house even though I knew it was futile. Then I started looking outside, Spree at my heels.

I went around the corner of the shed and rocked back on my heels, gasping for breath.

Kate's bike was sprawled on the ground in front of me, the front wheel twisted back on itself.

So she *had* come home. And then she had vanished.

'Kate,' I screamed. 'Kate!' There was no reply.

Beside me Spree tensed, and then he started scrabbling at the door of an old shed we no longer used. It was a long low-roofed building, once used for firewood until it became so leaky it wasn't worth storing anything there.

Spree continued scratching and started whining loudly as he did so. I noticed that the rusty old bolt on the door had been pushed home.

I hadn't locked it. I never did. So who had?

My heart hammered as I forced the bolt to open.

I opened the door and Spree pushed past me and disappeared into the dark. I followed, trying to see, and after a moment I saw a shape lying on the ground. Spree was licking it and whining.

'Kate?' My voice cracked and I bent down.

The shape moved but there was no sound. I bent down and touched it. I felt warmth I put my hand on my sister's hair. Then I stumbled backwards out of the dark, Kate in my arms and Spree leaping all over us.

She was alive. She looked terrified. And she wouldn't say a word.

...

I put her on the couch and dialled 111 with shaking fingers.

I had no idea what had happened and I needed a doctor fast. I didn't think of the police but they followed close behind the ambulance. The local paramedics were great. They talked soothingly to Kate as they examined her, and then looked at me with relief. She hadn't been sexually assaulted. They could find nothing physically wrong with her.

But it was clear she was terrified and it was equally clear that she couldn't have locked herself in the shed.

She followed me with her eyes everywhere I went and if I tried to leave the room she became agitated. But still she said nothing.

Stu Adams had got together a police team and they set up lights and went through the shed minutely. If anything was there they would find it. They also brought in a police dog but he didn't pick up anything. Stu suggested that a victim support person could come and stay the night with us but I shook my head. So long as Kate was safe I was fine. I got her into the bath and stayed with her, then got her into her pyjamas and into my bed. I wasn't going to let her out of my sight.

Spree settled in beside her and yawned. Kate reached out and patted his head. I just needed her to talk to me. But that was the thing she didn't seem able to do so I talked instead, telling her that Spree had found her, that Sally was worried about her, that I'd be lost without her, that she was going to be fine. Gradually her stiff little body began to relax and eventually she slept.

I lay beside her feeling a strange mixture of relief and anger. Anger with whoever had done this but with myself as well. If I hadn't been playing investigator this may not have happened.

In the early hours of the morning she stirred beside me. 'Philippa?' she said. And then she burst into tears. I held her small body waiting for the storm of crying to ease. Eventually she grew quieter.

'You're fine,' I whispered. 'No one can hurt you, Kate. Spree and I are right here.'

She sat up in bed and I turned the light on. Spree licked her face and she smiled slightly.

Some instinct warned me not to ask her anything but to wait and let her tell me in her own time. And eventually she did. She had come home from school and had been puzzled that Spree hadn't come out to greet her.

She was just getting off her bike when she heard someone behind her. Before she could turn they had grabbed her and put something over her face and dragged her into the shed. She had kicked and screamed. The person who had hold of her was strong and she had no hope of resisting - but she had tried and earned herself a slap on the side of the head. After that she was too scared to struggle and allowed herself to be pushed into the far corner of the shed with her face to the wall.

Her captor had spoken then – or rather whispered. In a voice that was raspy and strange. She had no idea if it had been a man or a woman. 'Tell your sister something from me. Next time it'll be her if she doesn't stop interfering,' the person had said.

'There's just one thing,' Kate said a bit later. 'When he grabbed me I saw something strange on his jersey. It was a red thing shaped like a dog's head. Right on the sleeve.'

'He,' I said. 'You think it was a man?'

'I don't know.' Kate started to cry.

And she wouldn't talk about it any more.

...

Kate and I stayed home for the day. There was no way she was up to going to school and I felt sick at the thought of letting her out of my sight. Stu Adams came to talk to us again, and I was relieved that he came on his own rather than trying to involve victim support people.

Sally was on the phone to Kate when he arrived and I was glad to hear her sounding more cheerful as they talked.

Yesterday's nightmare had become today's adventure. I only wished I was half as resilient.

I made coffee for Stu and me and as we drank it we talked about what had happened. I wasn't surprised that he was sceptical about the message Kate's attacker had passed on to her.

'You can ask her again yourself,' I said feeling exasperated. 'She didn't make it up, Stu.'

'I'm not suggesting that.' He put his mug on the table and looked at me, his expression troubled.

Kate came back into the room 'We are going to need you to make a statement about what happened,' Stu said to her. 'We can do it here and Philippa can stay with you.'

She stared at him, her expression unreadable.

'What do you want me to do?' she asked.

'Just tell me about everything that happened, every single thing you remember. Will you be okay with that?'

Kate sat down at the table and faced him. 'Will I have to go to the Police Station?'

'Not yet. I have my tape recorder with me and we can do it right here. Then I'll get your statement written up and maybe Philippa will bring it in so you can read it and sign it. Philippa will need to give a statement too but we'll start with you. You're the key witness.'

Kate looked pleased. 'Okay.'

I got up to make more coffee and to call Angie to tell her what had happened and let her know I wouldn't be in to work.

'I should hope not,' she said. 'I've kicked Matt off Facebook and told him he needs to do more work around the place. He's washing the socks and he's not happy but it won't kill him to do something menial instead of wandering round chatting up girls. Sara's gone up the glacier with ten people. Everything's under control. You don't have to worry about a thing.'

I laughed. 'Tim should have left you running the show Angie, not me.'

'You wouldn't catch me going up and down the glacier all the time,' she said. 'You're the guide not me. Kate is okay isn't she?'

'She seems a lot better today than she was yesterday. Stu's here taking her statement.'

Angie snorted. 'Lucky her.'

I went back to the kitchen and sat down to listen to Kate describe what had happened, giving a little more detail than she had the night before. She had been worried that Spree was nowhere to be seen and wasn't thinking of anything else when her attacker pulled her off her bike. She had screamed before something was pulled over her face and had heard Spree barking frantically from inside the house. It had made her feel better; she though he would come to save her. But of course he hadn't. He couldn't. He'd been shut in.

The person had bundled her into the shed without saying anything. Then he – or she – had issued the warning for me.

'He told me not to move,' Kate said with a shiver. 'He said he'd be watching me. So I stayed there for ages. Even when I heard Philippa calling I was too scared to move.'

She started to cry and I put my arms round her.

Stu had turned off his tape recorder and was looking at us with concern. 'That's all I need from you, Kate. I didn't mean to upset you but we have to know everything if we're going to catch the person who did this to you. And I promise you we will.'

'How can you be sure?' Kate asked the question I'd had in my own mind.

He hesitated. 'We can't be fully sure,' he admitted. 'But we'll do all we can.'

'What about the paint spot Kate saw on the person's jersey? Maybe you should start by searching every house in the village.'

I knew that wasn't possible and that even if it was there was a good chance nothing would be found but Stu didn't say that. He looked hassled.

'Believe me Philippa we'll do all we can,' he repeated himself.

He wasn't exactly filling me with confidence.

'What have the forensics team come up with?' I asked.

'Nothing obvious. But they haven't analysed everything from the shed yet. It takes a long time to process that kind of stuff.'

'What did they actually find?'

'Nothing significant,' Stu said with a sigh.

Kate took the opportunity to slip out of the room.

'Philippa I need to talk to you about something else. We don't think Vivien Revell's death was suspicious and believe me we've looked into it carefully. There is nothing to suggest it was anything but an accident. I know you're not going to like this but we aren't investigating Vivien's death. So why should anyone be worried about what you and Julia McLoughlin may or may not believe?'

I gave short laugh. 'Good on you for being so honest, Stu. I guess you're right. But that doesn't alter the fact – someone is.'

'I know it's a waste of time asking you, Philippa. But will you leave crime solving to us and go back to glacier guiding?'

'I don't think you realise just how sick of this whole thing I am. I'm only doing it as a favour to Julia and it's getting me nothing but grief. This threat to Kate is the last straw as far as I'm concerned.'

Stu looked surprised – as well he might. He wasn't used to me being sensible. But he didn't know how frightened I was. Not for myself – I still had the optimistic view that I could take care of myself. But since I'd agreed to look into things for Julia, both my dog and my sister had been threatened. And I wasn't up for that. No way.

...

After a day at home, Kate and I were both a little stir crazy so I was pleased when she announced that she was ready to go back to school. I was keen to get back to work as well. I had an uneventful morning on the glacier with a small fit group of tourists, then went back to the office to clean the boots. No one else was there and I enjoyed the peace.

Julia rang to tell me that Rose had decided to hold a memorial service for Vivien. She sounded stressed and I suppressed a surge of irritation. I'd told her about Kate the night before and she had seemed concerned. But now she didn't even ask how she was and that annoyed me.

The next day we closed down the Glacier Climbers for the afternoon so everyone could attend the service. Kate was at school and I was relieved that she didn't seem interested in coming along.

I went home for lunch then looked into my wardrobe for something to wear. It was a long time since I'd worn a dress and the simple blue linen shift I pulled out of my wardrobe looked new – if a little dusty. I brushed it down with my hand and slipped it over my head. I dragged a comb through my hair and pulled a mirror out of the cupboard to survey the effect. I looked awful. My face was drawn, my eyes looked tired and my long dark hair hung raggedly down around my face to my shoulders. I took a brush to my hair and lost the ragged look - though it seemed too long or too thick or something. The dress was loose. I'd been vaguely aware that I'd been losing weight but more of my flesh had dissolved than I had realised.

I rummaged in the old wooden box that housed my small collection of jewellery. There was a string of brightly coloured beads in there and I put it on. That was better. The colour helped. I dug out a pair of dress sandals, scrubbed off the dust, and slipped my feet into them.

I had another look in the mirror and couldn't believe how much better I looked. All down to tidy hair and a string of beads. I grimaced at myself, then shut the mirror away in the back of the wardrobe.

Julia picked me up a few minutes later. We didn't talk much and as we approached the church door I saw her give an involuntary shudder. I sympathised in a detached kind of a way. Maybe this would make Vivien's death seem more real. The church emanated age and peace. I looked round appreciatively. As commercialism took over the village this was one place that was unchanged. Its dark wooden pews and the blue carpet on the floor had been there forever and they still looked good. The cross at the altar was backlit by a large picture window looking out onto the mountains.

I glanced at Julia. She was wearing a dark grey suit with a string of pearls around her neck. She looked composed and sad. I was glad there was no coffin. Instead an easel stood at the front of the church, containing a large painting of Vivien. Her face glowed in the frame, the way I'd remembered her back in the days when life was easy.

Sara and Matt were sitting just across the aisle from us. The church was crowded. Most of the people I recognised, but there was a group up the front that didn't look familiar. Rose's friends? I was amused to see Jem Browne squeezed between a guy with a long blond ponytail and a large woman in a purple frock. He was right up near the front and kept turning round to see what was going on.

Penelope walked past and settled in a row on the other side of the aisle just in front of us. She was dressed in dark red trousers and a simple white blouse and carried a prayer book in her left hand. She looked composed. After a moment Callum Jackson joined her and they had a brief whispered conversation. He looked tidier than usual. He hadn't got carried away enough to wear a tie but his shirt was neat and looked recently ironed – which was more than could be said for my own ensemble. Jem turned again, his long eyebrows tangled to the point that they almost merged over his nose. His face sharpened and I turned to see what had caught his attention. Luke and Jenny Riley had just entered the church, their small daughter between them. Julia followed my gaze and stiffened.

The door to the vestry opened and the minister emerged, all robed up for the fray. I glanced at Penelope, and smiled to myself as a memory surfaced. My brother Tom and I had come here when we were children and found the vestry unlocked. Tom had arrayed himself in the minister's robes and emerged tripping over his hems as I pounded on the church organ. He had started declaiming – a sermon that owed nothing to theology but was imaginative enough to make me think uneasily of hell-fire. When his discourse abruptly halted I'd peered over the organ to see Penelope standing transfixed, a bucket of flowers in her hand. Tom hadn't waited around. I'd heard him scuffling out of his borrowed robes in the vestry but Penelope stood between me and the door. I'd waited for the inevitable scolding but instead she had laughed.

'Our minister could learn a lot from that boy,' she had said drily. 'I haven't heard anything so entertaining here in years.'

I realised I was smiling most inappropriately and tried to compose myself before anyone noticed. But all attention was on the minister as he welcomed everyone and began a speech about Vivien. He did quite a good job. He hadn't known her and it can't have been easy proclaiming like an expert when everyone in front of him had known her in varying degrees of intimacy. He seemed relieved to finish with the announcement that Vivien's mother Rose would like to say a few words.

The congregation was silent as Rose appeared at the lectern. She was dressed entirely in black and stood in front of us saying nothing for what seemed like forever. Then she began to speak, her voice intense and strong.

'Today I stand here mourning my daughter in public, as I have every day in private for many years. Some say that death is nothing at all, just a veil one steps behind, while the spirit remains with those left living. The dead can talk. Vivien talks to me. Since her body has been found she has made her way into my mind. I shut my eyes and she talks to me. She has a story I can hardly bear to hear. But I know I can follow every step she took on her last day. And I will never forgive her loss.'

Rose paused and stared at us all for a moment then looked over our heads. She shook her head, gave a half smile then continued. 'Only one who has borne children can understand the bond between mother and daughter. It challenges, it stretches and it breaks us but without it we are nothing. Nothing at all.

'Vivien was blessed. She loved her life. She was beautiful and clever. She had it all; I am left with nothing. Nothing I can do for my daughter but one last thing. As long as I live I will rejoice that she found out just before her death the thing that gave her life meaning. It's personal to her and I will not share it with anyone. But she knew. Before she died she knew!'

Rose gave a small smile. 'Today we all share our memories of Vivien Revell; tomorrow she and I take our last journey together – to Sentinel Rock where her life began. I will scatter her ashes there and think of how fortunate I am to have been able to call her my daughter.'

There was a clatter across the row, made loud by the sudden silence, and I glanced over to see Penelope scrabbling on the floor for her prayer book. When she sat up her face looked haunted. She swayed sideways and Callum put an arm round her.

Rose had given an impressive performance but as far as I was concerned Penelope had stolen the show. Pregnancy be damned. *That* had not been Vivien's secret. Rose Revell wanted to make it clear she knew what it was. And my impression of Penelope's fear had just been confirmed.

But what the hell was it? Not Patrick Blake's murky past. Concern for her friend Callum Jackson?

But he was looking totally unaffected by Rose's delivery, a supercilious expression on his face. The self-absorption of a mother whose words were mainly for herself not her dead daughter had not been lost on me – and I didn't think they had been on him either.

But he and I were outnumbered. Judging by the sniffling sounds all round me Rose had most of the congregation on side.

It was a relief when everyone started to move out of the church. Rose was in front of me, talking to Luke who had become separated from his wife and daughter. In the sunlight Rose looked scary, her long and flowing dress billowing around her. She looked like a bride who had been dipped in a vat of black dye. Luke didn't seem to be enjoying the conversation.

'We need to talk, you and me,' Rose told him.

Luke looked uneasy and she gave him a mean smile.

He fled and she turned to Julia.

'I want you to have the painting in there,' she said, smiling in a very different way. 'I am well aware that you were Vivien's only real friend in this bloody place.'

I stood beside Julia for a few minutes but there didn't seem to be much to say. There was no afternoon tea planned and people were leaving the church. I wasn't sorry to join the exodus, leaving Julia with Rose, and giving her an apologetic wave as I did so.

As I made my way back down the street towards Ice Rocks, I noticed a woman standing near the edge of the road. She saw me and smiled. It was Julia's mother, Ann. She didn't look anything like her daughter. She was much shorter and her face was pointed and small, her hair completely white and drawn back from her face with clips. Her face was lined. She looked much older than she was. It was hard to believe that she was about the same age as Rose Revell.

'Philippa, are you and Kate all right? I know it's a stupid question but I've been so worried about you.'

'We're not too bad. Kate's bounced back like nothing ever happened. I can't exactly say the same but I'm working on it. I don't want her home alone but luckily she can go to Sally's after school.'

'I shouldn't say this but I am really annoyed with Julia. She should never have put you in this position.'

'I could have said no. It's not really Julia's fault. Why didn't you go to the service?' I asked, suddenly curious.

'I just couldn't,' Ann said. 'Vivien and Rose Revell have been responsible for a lot of pain but I didn't want to witness theirs. I didn't like Vivien. I saw what she did to my own daughter. And I have never liked Rose. I have nothing to give the woman and so I stayed away. I've just seen Penelope Blake in the shop. She looks terrible.'

I told her what Rose had said and the way Penelope had reacted.

'Penelope's a difficult person to know,' Ann said. 'It's as if she's grown a hard shell all around her. But she wasn't always like that. I remember her when she was young. She had a great laugh. She was generous. And she was full of promise. Now she's disillusioned and hard and it goes a lot deeper than the failure of her marriage.'

'Why is she like that?'

'It's quite simple. You know how she adores children. She wanted her own – and she wanted them desperately. She talked to me about it once, told me that Patrick wasn't keen on a family. I told her it would all work out but it didn't. Once upon a time Penelope could have rivalled Vivien Revell with her sheer love of life. But over the years it's all been burnt away to nothing.'

'He wasn't worth it.' 'No but he did it all the same. Creative murder – murder of the spirit – the crime that there's no punishment for.'

'What do you mean? I asked.

Ann sighed. 'I hope you never have to find out,' she said.

...

It was only two o'clock and I had an hour to kill before Kate came home so I went for a walk along the side of the Waiho River. I was deep in thought, not taking much notice of my surroundings but my eye was caught by a sudden movement by the river.

It was a small child and she was dancing among the uneven rocks.

One false step and she could fall into the unforgiving glacier river. And if that happened she would die.

I didn't know what to do. If I approached her and startled her she could fall. And if I did nothing she could fall anyway. Where were her bloody parents? She spun round laughing and I recognized her. She was Luke's daughter. Emma.

'Hi,' I said and to my relief she stopped her dance and stood still looking at me.

'My name's Philippa,' I walked up to her trying not to show any trace of tension. 'You're Emma aren't you? That looks an interesting game that you're playing.'

'I was being very careful. I know not to fall in the river but that's the only place the fairies will dance.' Her face glowed. She was a gorgeous child.

'Will you come back with me now?' I asked. 'I think your daddy might be looking for you.'

She took my hand and we made our way back towards the village.

We hadn't gone far before Luke hurtled into view.

'Oh thank God,' he gasped, scooping Emma into his arms. 'I've been so worried, chicken. Why aren't you with Mummy?'

'She wanted to lie down,' Emma told him. 'And I got bored and came here to see the river fairies. Just like you showed me that time, Daddy.'

Luke's face changed from red to white in an instant.

'The careless bitch,' he said and I was shocked by the fury in his expression.

Just then Jenny came running towards us, her face stressed.

'You fucking careless bitch,' he said and Emma winced in his arms. 'Not you, chicken,' he said. 'You' – he gestured at Jenny with his free hand. While you were sleeping my daughter could have drowned. And if she had I'd have killed you with my own hands. You understand what I'm saying.'

Jenny stared at him in shock.

And I looked at the changed face of the amiable muddler I thought I knew. I believed him. He could have killed her. In this moment he looked capable of obsessive love and violent anger. Just the kind of qualities that would have been needed by Vivien Revell's killer.

Chapter 10

WE awoke to blue skies. Matt and Sara took the glacier party while I stayed in the office with Angie and Spree for company, working on my managerial paperwork. By mid-morning my head was aching.

'I think I'll go up the glacier for a while,' I told Angie. 'Do you mind if Spree stays with you?'

'No problem.' She waved me away. 'Go and get some fresh air. It's a great day.'

I didn't wait to be told twice and slung my crampons in my pack, grabbed my ice axe and headed out the door.

Jenny Riley appeared at my side as I was throwing my stuff in the car. Her usual hostile expression was missing and she was holding a bottle of wine.

'This is just a small thank you for saving Emma yesterday,' she said.

'Anyone would have done the same,' I said, edging towards the door of my car.

'I am at the end of my tether with Luke.' Jenny said, not noticing my reluctance to communicate. 'I find I'm the laughing stock of the village. It seems that everyone knew about him and Vivien Revell but me. Did you know, Philippa?'

'I've only just found out – Julia McLoughlin told me. But no one is laughing at you – it was all a long time ago.'

'So what's his problem then?" Jenny was still holding the bottle of wine. She looked angry. 'He's worried as hell about something but he won't tell me a thing.'

'Do you have any idea what it is?'

'It's all to do with her – Vivien – I know that much. He's been like a cat on hot bricks ever since her body was found. Everyone thinks Luke's such a nice guy, he's everyone's mate, but you saw another side to him yesterday, didn't you Philippa? He's got some big problems. I just hope they're all still in his head and he isn't about to do something really stupid.'

'Like what?'

'Oh I don't know! But it was Luke's fault not mine that Emma could have drowned yesterday. He's the one who told her there were fairies living in the river. He's not especially good for the people he cares about.'

It was a good exit line and she left me at that point, having thrust the wine awkwardly into my hands.

I watched her, feeling slightly bemused. I'd been so busy suspecting Callum that I'd forgotten about Luke. And I shouldn't have. He had lied to me about his whereabouts the day Vivien had disappeared. He had been upset about her relationship with Callum. Rose had all but told me she knew who Vivien's killer was – and she had something on Luke – she'd made that pretty clear after the memorial service. I drove up the glacier valley mulling it all through my mind.

According to Jenny, the discovery of Vivien's body had unsettled him quite badly. You could make a case for him killing Vivien in a crime of passion. But I could not see him sneaking round my place at night leaving that nasty sketch of Spree. And he was a loving father. I absolutely could not see him terrifying Kate.

I left the car and walked up the riverbed, reached the glacier and strapped on my crampons. I climbed fast and made for the middle of the glacier. It was a still day; the only sound the splash of water rivulets running in the crevasses. I relaxed as I breathed in the cold air and revelled in my solitude. How did people survive in cities, in situations when they could never get away from one another?

I glanced down towards the valley and saw someone moving towards me. I wasn't pleased. There's nothing that ruins a glacier walk more than the sight of another person approaching and this one was moving fast, obviously a skilled ice climber.

I cursed as I recognized Luke Riley. What did he want? Had he overheard me talking to Jenny and followed me to find out what she'd said to me?

One look at his face made me discount that idea. He looked surprised and no more pleased to see me than I was to see him. We stared at each other warily across a crevasse. I considered walking right on past him and heading down the glacier, but after hesitating a moment he called out my name. I stopped reluctantly and looked at him.

'I owe you a big thank you,' he said.

'Why?' It came out more sharply than I had intended it to.

'You saved Emma's life.'

'Actually Luke I didn't. She moved away from the river before she saw me. But it gave me a hell of a fright. I could easily have startled her and caused her to fall in.'

'Yeah – it doesn't bear thinking about. I'm sorry you had to witness that scene between Jenny and me.'

I closed my eyes and hoped he would disappear.

Luke didn't notice any hostility and turned the conversation back to himself which suited me. Even so I sped up, hoping I'd be faster on crampons than he and could get away from him. But he kept pace easily.

'I haven't been on the ice for years but it seems you never forget,' he said.

I didn't reply and we crunched along in silence for a few minutes.

'Listen Philippa,' he said. 'I'm glad I ran into you. Jenny told me she'd seen you earlier this morning. I don't know what she said to you – but surely you don't think I had anything to do with Vivien's death? On Emma's life I had nothing to do with it – I swear it to you. I hated Vivien and I hated what she did to me that summer. I've got plenty of faults but violence isn't one of them.'

'Not the way things looked to me yesterday,' I said. 'I honestly thought you were going to hit Jenny.'

'Well you're wrong.'

'You don't know anything about what's happened to Kate, do you Luke?'

'What do you mean?'

I told him what had happened and he looked shocked.

'I think it has something to do with Vivien's killer. Whoever that person is they aren't happy that I'm trying to find out what happened.'

'But even if you're right – and you have rattled someone's cage – why attack Kate?'

'To force me to lay off what I'm doing. And it's not a bad tactic. There's no place for me running round playing girl detective. I was stupid to agree when Julia asked me to do it.'

But even as I said this a treacherous thought was sliding round in my mind. Kate's attacker hadn't threatened her. He – or she – had said that if I didn't leave things alone I'd be next.

Well I could look after myself. And where was the harm in asking a few discreet questions?

'Luke, something went on that summer,' I said. 'Something that involves you. I know you lied to me about where you were the day Vivien went missing. If you weren't involved in her death are you covering for someone?'

'Not exactly.' He looked embarrassed. 'Vivien and Rose had had a fight but neither of them told me what it was about. It was over something big but Vivien wouldn't say a word and as for Rose, well …'

He didn't finish his sentence.

'What is it Luke? I'll imagine much worse things if you don't tell me.'

'Okay! But please don't spread this around. My marriage is in enough trouble. I was in a real state that summer. I went round to see Rose. I needed to have it out with her, find out what she knew about Vivien and Callum bloody Jackson. She was painting and she took me up to her studio. I won't go into any detail, you can imagine …'

I stared at him. 'You mean?'

'Yes well, Rose Revell didn't seem like anyone's mother back then. She doesn't now if it comes to that.'

'Look, I'm not judging you. I'd be the last person to cast stones given my own track record.' Even so I was amazed. This was a scenario that had never entered my head.

'I never meant it to happen. I don't know how it did. One minute we were in her studio and the next we were in her bedroom. I'd been frustrated all summer, you can't imagine. And Rose – well Rose was amazing. And then Vivien walked in on us.'

'What did she do?'

'Not a lot. She just stared at us. She didn't even seem angry.'

'Was she shocked, white-faced, shaking?'

Luke stared at me. 'How did you know?'

'That's what she was like when Julia saw her. Vivien wouldn't tell her anything but Julia worked out that something really bad had happened between Vivien and Rose. And as for Rose – she painted Vivien's reaction. She has the canvas in her studio.'

'It doesn't surprise me. Rose has no scruples whatsoever. I felt terrible. I wasn't trying to get back at Vivien, you must see that Philippa. Rose initiated the whole thing.'

'And your balls towed you along kicking and screaming,' I snapped. 'Spare me the innocent act, Luke.'

'Yes – you're right. It was awful and I brought it on myself.'

'How did Rose react to being caught out?'

'Sat up in bed and laughed at us both. And do you know something else, Philippa? The bloody awful thing was it didn't end there. There was nothing in it but sex for both of us. But I kept going back. I was there the day Vivien disappeared. I didn't kill her, Philippa. I was too busy screwing her mother.'

...

'I'm surprised at Luke.' Rose stood in her garden and lowered her secateurs. She looked amused.

'So it's true?' I'd gone round to her place with nothing in my mind apart from the need to confirm Luke's story. Belatedly I realised how intrusive I was being. But Rose didn't seem to care.

'It's true,' she said, snipping away at a vine. 'He was a lovely boy. So hurt and passionate. I must say when I saw him at Vivien's memorial service I couldn't help feeling just a tiny bit nostalgic.'

'But he was Vivien's boyfriend! She must have been really upset.'

'He was her ex boyfriend. But you're right – she wasn't happy. She was furious in fact. Vivien had been cruel to Luke and I was offering him comfort. It was good for both of us and would have harmed no one if she hadn't come in at the wrong moment.'

'Luke told me you were together the day Vivien disappeared?'

'Yes. I told you before that I was with someone that day, Philippa. But I didn't plan to tell you who I was with. Luke should be more discreet. I don't think Jenny would take too kindly to this story.'

'I think they are heading for the rocks anyway.'

'You only have to see them together for two minutes to see what a bad match they make. Luke is delightful but he has no common sense.'

'I can't argue with that,' I said as Rose moved into a particularly tangled corner of her garden.

I left soon after. There didn't seem much else to say. Luke Riley clearly had something I couldn't fathom. All those women who had loved or at least lusted after him – Julia, Vivien and Rose to name the three I knew about. And presumably Jenny once upon a time. I couldn't see the attraction at all. He was so ineffectual. I seemed to have lost two suspects. Unless Luke and Rose had conspired to kill Vivien, something I couldn't believe, they had now given each other alibis. I was left with few suspects. And no obvious motives.

...

Kate and I had pancakes for dinner. It was easy and indulgent. I washed mine down with red wine while Kate drank Coke. Spree sprawled at our feet accepting offerings from our plates. I sipped my wine watching Spree as he persuaded Kate to share half her meal with him. He had it down to a fine art.

'Philippa?'

'Mmmm?' My mind was still on Spree. He needed a bath but I didn't have the energy for it right now.

'Do you ever think about Mark?'

I stared at Kate. 'Not really. Why do you ask?'

'Sally was asking about him and I just wondered …'

'Trust Sally to be interested. Nothing's too trivial for that girl. But you can tell her from me that there's nothing doing. Mark and I are ancient history.'

Mark Nolan, a Christchurch journalist, had been my on-and-off partner for years but we had split up properly over a year ago. Then I'd got into a disastrous relationship with another guy and that had ended badly as well.

Kate's best friend Sally found my train-crash approach to relationships fascinating. Kate, on the other hand, found it unsettling and I couldn't blame her.

'Actually I did ring him up after the February earthquake,' I said pouring myself a generous new glass of wine. 'But just as a friend, nothing else.'

Christchurch had become a disaster zone over the last year as an unbelievable number of earthquakes destroyed everything from the city's landmark cathedral to walking tracks on the nearby cliffs – and thousands of houses and lives in between. Nearly 200 people had died; many more had their lives put on hold as everything that mattered to them crumbled around them.

'So you really aren't getting back together?' my sister asked.

I sighed. 'There's not a lot of point. We want very different things. I don't care enough about Mark to make any changes to my life - so I can hardly expect him to make changes to his.'

Kate seemed satisfied with this and concentrated on her pancakes while I sipped my wine, thinking about how I'd felt the day I heard that Christchurch was in ruins and many people were dead. I wasn't keen to acknowledge this to myself and I certainly wasn't going to tell Kate, but I'd felt a terrible fear for Mark. In the hours before I was able to talk to him on the phone I'd imagined what it would be like never to see him again and how I'd feel if his was one of the dead bodies being pulled out of a crushed building. And the answer was – devastated.

Where had these feelings come from? I'd honestly believed they were gone for good so why had they come creeping back? I didn't want to feel that way. Mark and I had reached the end. Nothing had changed. I hadn't suddenly turned all hormonal and decided I wanted babies and he had shown no sign of giving away any of his establishment lifestyle.

One thing was for sure – Kate didn't need to know any of this.

When I'd found Vivien's body on the glacier I had expected him to ring me but he hadn't. So that had told me something. He'd moved on and that was fair enough. Let's face it – how many single guys were there out there with good jobs and no major vices who actually wanted to settle down and have kids? He'd be snapped up.

When we had talked after the earthquake, neither of us had strayed into relationship territory. But he could be married with children by now for all that I knew. I shook myself and stopped thinking about him.

'Kate. When you were attacked – that thing you saw on the person's jersey,' I asked, trying to keep my tone casual. 'What do you reckon it was?'

My sister frowned. 'I only saw it for a second, just as he grabbed me off my bike. But it was red and it looked like a dog's head. It might have been a funny splash of paint.'

'What colour was the jersey?'

'Ummm dark I think. I don't remember. Why?'

'No real reason. I'm just thinking that it would be good if we saw someone wearing it. But it doesn't seem likely.'

Kate looked at me but she didn't reply. We returned to our pancakes in silence. But I had an idea. Even if it was a long shot.

...

'Philippa you can't just break in! What if you're caught?' Julia paced round my kitchen, patting Spree on the head in passing.

'I'll have to make sure I'm not – and if I find that jersey in his house it'll prove he's the one who attacked Kate – and the police will have to do something.'

'But it's not as if you've ever seen Callum Jackson wearing a jersey with a mark like that. You might as well suggest that Penelope did it! Or Rose.'

'I just might,' I said grimly. 'If it's not him it has to be someone. And I can't see it being Luke. Or you.'

'Oh Philippa. Why did I get you into this?'

'So you do think that Vivien's death is linked to what happened to Kate?' Suddenly it was important to have just one other person believe what I did.

Julia looked wretched. 'Yes I do.'

'Actually I forgot to tell you. I bumped into Luke on the glacier. He told me why Vivien was so upset with her mother just before she disappeared. She'd caught her in bed with him.'

Julia stared at me for a moment in silence. Then she did another restless circuit of the kitchen.

'That never even occurred to me. It should have been obvious.'

'It's not that bloody obvious. We don't, as a rule, assume our mothers are sleeping with our boyfriends.'

'Not mothers like mine, I agree. But Rose is different. It's entirely believable.'

'I see myself as pretty cynical,' I said, 'but I was shocked. It must have been awful for Vivien – and to have her mother laugh at her as well ...'

'Yes. And do you know what's plain pathetic? Here I was drifting round in the background hoping Luke would come back to me – while all the while he was screwing Rose. It's funny in a way.'

'Hilarious.'

I didn't say any more about my proposed break-in at Callum's house. But I had not changed my mind. And the next day the perfect opportunity presented itself. It would have been better to go during the day. I could have easily made an excuse to slip away from work for an hour or so, having first ascertained that Callum was safely ensconced in a meeting. But that afternoon I was in the store and saw him there deep in conversation with Penelope Blake. I hovered out of sight behind the fruit bins and listened in.

'So I'm going up to Whataroa tonight to give this bloody talk on work experience in national parks. The Lions Club organised it. I can't see there being much of a turnout but I'm stuck with it.'

'How would you feel about me coming along? I could do with a change of scene.'

'You'd be welcome. I'll pick you up about eight.'

They moved out of earshot but I'd heard enough. Kate was easily persuaded to spend a night with Sally. I went home and had dinner in an unusually quiet house.

At 8.30 pm I drove up to the village and parked my car out of sight behind the guides' office. I crept up Callum's driveway. It was dark but I didn't dare turn on a torch. His car was missing and the outside light was on.

The door was locked but years before I'd been with my Mark when he'd interviewed a retired burglar for a feature article. I'd really liked the guy. He showed Mark and me how to use a set of picklocks and because I'd proved an apt pupil he'd given them to me. I had experimented on the doors of various friends – with their consent – and had got quite good at the art of housebreaking. Callum's lock was a breeze to open. I skipped in the door feeling pleased with myself but took the precaution of locking it behind me.

Something I would soon be very grateful for.

I flicked on a pencil torch and trained it all around the room. It was his living area and looked comfortable with several big arm chairs, a coffee table covered in books, a television jammed in a far corner, and a few framed paintings of mountain scenes on the walls.

I crept upstairs and into his bedroom. He didn't seem to have many clothes and I quickly searched through his wardrobe and drawers. There was no jersey with a tell-tale red mark. I don't know what I'd expected but I wasn't prepared for the acute sense of disappointment. It wasn't here.

I walked down the stairs then froze as headlights lit the front of the house. There was no back door and no time to escape through a window so I used the seconds before he unlocked the door to insert myself into his hall cupboard among his ice axes and coats.

Praying that I wouldn't sneeze, I froze into position.

I was none too soon. The door opened almost immediately and Callum entered the room. He was talking to someone. Penelope. What the hell were they doing back so early?

There was no way I could get out the door without being seen. I was trapped like a rat until Penelope went home and Callum went upstairs.

'I'll get it for you now,' he said to her and I felt ice squeezing my heart as his footsteps approached the cupboard. He went past and his footsteps receded.

'Here you are,' he said after a moment. 'Keep it as long as you want. It's got some great pictures and some of the stories are classic. Tramping as it used to be before it was besieged by trendies in designer gear.'

'He's made some interesting choices in the places he's featured,' Penelope said after a minute. 'I haven't heard of some of these huts.'

'Yeah – it's certainly not mainstream. That's why I like it.' It sounded as if they were talking about a recently published book on tramping huts by wilderness author Mark Pickering. It was a book I'd heard about but not yet seen. I had a sudden hysterical urge to peep out from my cupboard and ask them if I could have a look. I restrained myself.

To my horror I heard him offering coffee and Penelope accepting. I could be in for a long wait and I wasn't sure my limbs were up to it. Silently I raised one foot and then another to ward off cramp.

They talked for about half an hour but it seemed a lot longer. And all about nothing. My concentration was drifting and I almost missed the moment things got interesting.

I was alerted by Penelope's tone, the lowering of her voice so that I couldn't hear what she said.

'Of course I didn't tell her,' Callum said. 'I don't trust anyone now – apart from you that is – and I certainly didn't trust anyone back then. Vivien's the last person I'd have told.'

'What if she had found out?'

'How could she have?' Callum sounded angry.

'No secret is safe. Rose knows something, I'm convinced of it.'

'Rose plays with people's minds. She doesn't have a clue. Do you think she'd have kept quiet all these years if she knew?'

'I suppose not,' Penelope said.

'You're the only person I ever told. Why are you so worried all of a sudden?'

'It's something Philippa Barnes said to me. It made me wonder if Vivien had known after all. But if so I don't think Philippa has a clue what it was.'

'There's no way that interfering little cow's going to find out.'

I winced in my cupboard.

'No. I'm sure you're right. I'd better get home,' Penelope said.

Much to my relief I heard the front door open.

'Don't worry about any of this,' Callum said. 'I know how to watch my back.'

I rubbed a cramped ankle praying that he would go upstairs. He did and as a bonus he left the door unlocked.

I slipped out into the night, gasping with relief to be free.

So Callum had a secret. Something he'd told Penelope. She was worried that Vivien might have known. Had he killed Vivien so she couldn't reveal it? But he didn't sound at all worried. And while I didn't appreciate his description of me he was right in thinking I didn't have a clue.

Callum Jackson was a mystery man who seemed to have come from nowhere. He needed no one. He had few friends. He'd left no trace of his former life for me or anyone else to follow. He wasn't going to tell me any secrets from his past. And neither was Penelope Blake.

Chapter 11

FOR the first time since the attack on Kate I fell into a deep sleep as soon as I went to bed.

I woke up and had my breakfast mulling over my activities of the night before. The jersey could be anywhere. It could be in Callum's car. Or he might have got rid of it, worried that it could be traced to him if fibres had been found by the police. Unfortunately there didn't seem to be much danger of that.

I arrived at work early. There was no sign of Matt or Sara, but Angie was already there drinking coffee with her old offsider Jem Browne. I hadn't seen him around much lately. I'd expected him to become a regular at the guides' office when Angie started working here but he hadn't.

They both looked guilty and I wondered if they'd been talking about me. They had.

'We were just saying, lass, you need to look after yourself a bit better,' Jem informed me. 'When did you last have a decent meal?'

I smiled. 'I don't really do decent meals right now. But I pick at stuff.'

'Not good enough,' he said. 'You're not on your backside in an office – you're up on that glacier and you need to feed that body of yours. You're going to make yourself ill.'

'Jem's right,' Angie told me. 'And you know something else? The sooner that Julia McLoughlin buggers off back to Wellington the better. She's got you into this mess and she's showing no sign of getting you out of it.'

'What do you mean?' I had been particularly careful not to tell Angie of the wildcat investigation I was doing. I liked her a lot but didn't really want her and Jem getting hold of it.

Well it seemed that they had. So I might as well link into Franz's answer to MI5 and find out what they knew.

'How did you find out what I'm doing?' I asked.

'It was pretty obvious,' Angie replied. 'Julia's been hanging round you a hell of a lot so I just asked her mother what was going on. She's not all that happy about it either actually. Thinks Julia needs to get back to Wellington and put the past behind her before she loses her job.'

'What do you think?' I asked.

'I honestly don't know,' Angie said. 'But do you really think that even if you're right and Vivien was murdered that the person who did it attacked Kate?'

I looked at her and sighed. 'It's possible.'

We all looked up as Matt came into the room, closely followed by Sara. The phone rang, some tourists arrived, and our day got underway.

'Did you hear about the crash last night?' Matt asked. 'Two camper vans full of tourists – crashed head on near Lake Wahapo. Blocked the road for hours.'

'Was anyone hurt?' Sara looked concerned.

'No one died – but I think some of them were quite badly injured.'

So that was why Callum and Penelope had come back unexpectedly and nearly caught me searching Callum's house.

Jem left, and Angie seemed absorbed in her work as we got ready for the glacier. But she wasn't finished with me. As I was leaving at the end of the day she jumped up from her computer and followed me out the door.

'I'm taking you for a drink,' she said. 'And I'm not taking no for an answer. I couldn't say much while Jem was there. I know everyone thinks we're soul mates and it's true we do talk about a lot of stuff. But I haven't told him this – and I don't know if I should be telling you either.'

Before she could elaborate we were joined by one of her children, Zoe, wanting to know what was for dinner. 'Your father's in charge tonight,' she told her. 'I'm having a well-earned drink.'

'Oh. Okay.' Zoe stayed in step with us as we made our way to Ice Rocks. She was a miniature version of her mother with thick dark hair and a pointed face but they differed around the eyes. Angie's were always alert and interested, while Zoe looked like she wasn't really there, her eyes dreamy and abstracted.

'Off you go then,' Angie instructed. 'Tell Dad I'll be home in an hour or so – and tell him to use his brains not the internet and get us all a meal.'

Zoe didn't argue and her mother gave her shoulder a slight push to send her on her way.

Ice Rocks was busy. I saw Matt holding forth to a couple of young women who'd been in our tourist group that morning. He was clearly enjoying himself. I gave him a wave as I followed Angie to a table on the other side of the bar. We sipped our wine for a moment in silence and then Angie leaned forward and looked at me.

'For what it's worth I think you and Julia might be right. About Vivien's being murdered I mean.'

'Stu Adams is sure we're wrong. Told me to leave this kind of stuff to the police.'

Angie snorted. 'Stu on the trail. That's a scary thought. He'd never see a thing unless it was right under his nose – he's a mate of my Alan's. That should tell you something.'

I laughed. I never really believed Angie's apparent contempt for her husband. She had plenty to say about him – and none of it was good – but when you saw them together they seemed happy enough. He seemed to enjoy her tirades and there was no real malice in them.

'Okay – here's the thing,' Angie said. 'I remember the day Vivien disappeared. It caused quite a stir – she had vanished overnight –

or so it seemed. It was the talk of the village. Penelope Blake was furious because she'd walked out on her precious book project. Rose Revell knew more than she was letting on, that much was clear. But then the story went round that Vivien had gone overseas. There was no suggestion at the time that she'd gone missing on the glacier. If there had been I'd have realised the significance of what I saw.' Angie took a sip of her wine and grimaced. 'Not very good, is it?'

'What did you see?'

'Well I was out walking that night. My mother had died that day. I didn't know where I was going, just wandered around thinking about her. I walked a way up the glacier valley. It was dark. I couldn't tell you what time it was. Anyway I saw headlights coming down the valley towards me and I suddenly felt a bit nervous out there on my own. So I stepped behind a tree but I saw who it was. Callum Jackson. Well it was his vehicle anyway. 'I didn't think anything of it then. Next day I had a funeral to organise and the whole thing went out of my mind. But now I wonder. What was he doing up the valley the night Vivien died on the glacier?'

What indeed? One thing was sure though – I'd get nowhere if I asked him. It wasn't as if he was likely to suddenly crack and tell me his secrets. I recalled without pleasure his comment about me as I'd hidden out in his cupboard. As if on cue he appeared in the bar – and to my surprise he threaded his way to our table and asked if he could join us.

'We were just talking about you,' Angie informed him.

'Really? Surely there are better things to discuss? I won't keep you long – just wanted to have a quick word with you Philippa. How's your sister?'

'She's fine.' I tried to keep my tone neutral. 'She's very brave. But whoever did this to her is a despicable coward.'

'You're right. It was a terrible thing to do. I just want you to know, if there's anything I can do to help please ask me.' I stared at him, too surprised to speak. He seemed genuine. But was he trying to cover something? Did he think I knew something that would point to him as Kate's attacker? He had nothing to worry about there.

'There's one thing you could do,' Angie said. 'Tell us what you were doing in the glacier valley the night Vivien disappeared. There's no point denying it, Callum. I saw you myself. I didn't think anything of it at the time but things are a bit different now.' He looked as if he truly regretted his uncharacteristic act of kindness and I couldn't really blame him. I didn't know what to say but Angie looked like she was about to launch into a tirade. Callum lifted a hand to ward her off.

'Okay – I'll tell you. I did go up there that night. I went to try and find Vivien. She and I had had a row a couple of nights before. I'm not going into it – it's irrelevant. But she stormed out of my place in the middle of the night telling me she never wanted to see me again.' He paused and sipped his beer, his expression grim.

'And?' said Angie after a moment's silence.

He gave us a humourless smile. 'You think I'm all kinds of bastard and you could be right – but I do have a few finer feelings at times. I was upset by our row. Surprises you, doesn't it? Well it surprised me too. Anyway then I bumped into Penelope Blake and she told me Vivien hadn't turned up for work. That worried me. So I went up the glacier valley for a look but I didn't find her.'

'Why did you think she might have gone up the glacier?' I asked.

'Something she'd said to me. She was getting bogged down in her research – felt like all she was doing was reading stuff, not experiencing it. That's part of what we fought about. I told her she was an academic not a mountaineer and she had no chance of bridging the gap. She called me an arrogant prick but I could see I'd got her thinking. As soon as Penelope told me she was missing I wondered if she had gone up the glacier to try and prove me wrong.'

'Do you still think that?' I asked.

He shrugged. 'Yeah. Why not? And it's no wonder she had an accident. That's just what I was afraid of at the time – that's why I went looking. I have to admit though I didn't expect her to get up as high onto the glacier as she did.'

'How's this for an alternative theory?' I said. 'Vivien Revell was getting to you. She was threatening your self-sufficiency. And she was pregnant with your child. So you had to deal with her and you did.'

Callum's whole body seemed to recoil in shock. '*What* did you say?'

I stared at him. Unless he was a brilliant actor this news had come as a total surprise. 'Are you saying you didn't know?' I asked.

He shook his head, seeming unable to speak.

'Rose told me,' I said. 'She also said that Vivien had no intention of telling you. That she was leaving town to get an abortion because she felt there was something strange about you.'

'Well that's great coming from her.' Callum had recovered his equilibrium.

I wasn't about to give up.

'Penelope Blake knows something about your past,' I said, 'and she's scared you might have killed Vivien to keep her quiet.'

He laughed at me. 'How mysterious. We've all got our secrets Philippa. And mine have nothing to do with you. I don't know – or care – how you've picked up that little tidbit but I'll tell you something for nothing. Penelope is a friend of mine but she has her faults. She's got an anxiety problem. She has no cause to worry about anything in my past and if she does she's on her own. I couldn't give a toss.'

'Not even if Vivien Revell's death is linked to what happened to Kate?'

Callum stared at me. 'Where the hell did you get that idea?' He looked surprised – and worried.

Chapter 12

Julia rang soon after I got home and offered to bring round take-aways for dinner. I was glad of the company and keen to tell her about my talks with Angie and Callum. I also filled her in on my housebreaking activities. She was predictably horrified at my account of the time I'd spent in Callum's cupboard.

'I don't know how you had the guts. I'd have been terrified.' She shivered.

'There wasn't a lot of time to get scared. And I was too busy stopping myself from getting cramp to think of much else. It was pretty much a waste of time – though I did find out that Callum has some secret in his past that Penelope is worried about. Problem is he isn't worried himself and I can't see any way of finding out what it is.'

'No… Look Philippa, I have to go back to Wellington for a few days for work but I think I can swing it to come back. I've got quite a lot of report writing to do and can do most of that from here.'

'There's no need for you to hang around. I'm getting precisely nowhere in case you hadn't noticed,' I said.

The next day I called in on Rose after work. She didn't seem surprised to see me and went off to get us both glasses of red wine. I told her what I'd been doing and she listened in silence.

'You know what's going on here, Rose,' I said. 'Why won't you tell the police?'

'Because I can't prove it. But I'm going to work it out somehow – I let Vivien down when she was alive but I'm not going to do it again now she's dead. I know who killed her. And that person is not going to get away with it. I promise you that.'

'What do you think of my theory – that whoever killed Vivien also attacked Kate to try and stop me looking?'

Rose put down her glass and gazed at me. 'If that's the case I'd say two things – this person doesn't know you very well – and he or she is getting desperate. But you've helped me make up my mind. I can't leave this much longer.'

'What are you going to do?'

'There's something I have to find out.'

'Are you going to talk to the person you think killed Vivien? Rose, that could be really dangerous.'

'I'm not scared of a coward who pushed a young woman into a crevasse when her back was turned. And is now getting their kicks by frightening children.'

'Won't you at least ask someone to be with you when you talk to whoever it is? You could be right about the person being a coward – but she or he is also a murderer.'

'No Philippa. I need to do this alone.' And that was all Rose would say.

I was too wound up to go home so I headed up the glacier valley instead. It was too late to go onto the ice but I loved the valley when the people had left it for the day. The river sounded louder than usual as I tramped alongside it. The evening shadows had blackened the bush and the rocks but the glacier itself was still stark and light, held in place by the dark rock walls then spilling onto the riverbed in a mass of pinnacles and ridges.

Someone had used this glacier as a murder weapon. And Rose knew who this person was. I didn't blame her not telling me – and I couldn't blame her for not telling the police. She had no proof. And they would only deal in facts. Even so she was mad to tackle it alone.

It was dark by the time I emerged from the valley. Some impulse made me walk past Rose's place on my way home. Her studio was lit up and as I watched a figure moved quickly out of the light and into the shadows. I knew it must be Rose, but something made me shiver. I went home and did nothing. I'll have to live with that fact for the rest of my life.

...

I sat up in bed next morning pushing away the tangle of limbs and black fur that was Spree. How the hell did my sister sleep with this dog? And why was he with me not her? She was welcome to him.

I had to do something. I had to stop Rose. I had to get to her place. Now. And if she wouldn't talk to me I'd go straight round to Stu Adams and tell him she was putting her life in danger. He was a policeman. He couldn't ignore me.

I was in too much of a hurry to cycle so I got out the car and took off for the village at speed. I saw the pale light spilling from her studio as I approached her house. She hadn't turned it off the night before.

My heart started hammering as I ran up the drive and banged loudly on her door.

There was no response.

The door was not looked. I ran inside, yelling Rose's name. The living area was empty.

I ran up the stairs.

The bedrooms and bathroom were also unoccupied though Rose's bed was unmade and the duvet flung back as if she'd made a hasty exit. The pillows were on the floor.

I ran upstairs to the studio.

Then stopped dead.

Someone was screaming. It took me a moment to realise it was me.

Every canvas in the room had been shredded. Mangled pieces lay on the floor or hung like strips of torn skin off the easels scattered round the room.

Blood was splashed all over them and over the white walls. So much of it. I stood on a large chunk of canvas at my feet and leaped back as I realised I was standing on Vivien's head. She lay all round the room in a crazy jigsaw of smashed portraits.

Rose lay in the middle of the carnage.

At least I supposed it was her. She lay face up but was cut up to the extent there were no facial features left to identify.

So much colour. So much madness.

I can't remember quite what I did after that.

Then I was running.

Down all those stairs and out of the house.

Back into the village.

Sobbing. Screaming. Gasping.

Angie Bennett came running towards me and other soon followed. They took me to the police station and told me everything was going to be okay.

It wasn't of course. I'd known Rose was planning a meeting with a killer.

And I'd done nothing.

Chapter 13

'I should have told you,' I said to Stu Adams. 'I knew she was going to do something stupid and I just left her to it. It's my fault she's dead.'

I kept repeating myself, feeling more and more hysterical as I did so.

Stu stared at me across the table in the tiny police interview room. He didn't know what to say. I, on the other hand, didn't know how to stop talking.

He had not allowed Angie to come in with me. It felt strange being closed in this room with the local cop.

'Philippa, don't try and talk now. I want another police officer here while you give your statement. I'll make us a coffee. Just stay there.'

He left the room and I sat staring at nothing for a long time. Eventually a woman police officer, summoned from Hokitika, arrived and we got down to business. I told them everything I knew, not bothering to add that I'd told Stu some of this before and that he hadn't believed me.

'What did you see when you walked past Rose Revell's house last night?' asked Detective Constable Wendy Munro. She was young and intense-looking with dark hair scraped off her face into a tight pony tail. Her voice was low and her expression was stern. She was looking at me as if she didn't believe a word I said. She didn't look wildly impressed with Stu either.

'Nothing really.' I hesitated. 'It was just an impression. I saw the shadow of someone in the studio. I don't know why I reacted to it. There was nothing to indicate it wasn't Rose.'

'You didn't see who it was.'

'No – it was just a shadow.'

'What was the time?'

'Just after 10.'

They then turned their questions to my discovery of the body. And I told them everything I could remember. The details were sharp in my mind and it seemed to take a long time to get to the end.

When the interview was finally over I emerged from the police station feeling drained. The shock had receded and I was left feeling as if I was missing a couple of pints of blood. It was as if there was a wall between me and what I was feeling – as if all that emotion was trapped in another room where I couldn't reach it.

Angie was waiting for me, took me home and insisted on making me coffee and toast.

'The stupid bloody woman,' I remarked after a while.

'How so?' Angie put down her coffee and, chin in her hands, leaned across the table towards me.

'She knew who killed Vivien. And she was going to tackle that person herself.'

'Well looks like it was them that did the tackling,'

Angie wasn't trying to be funny but I screeched with laughter. I felt out of control and light headed. She gave me a dubious look. I avoided her gaze and paced over to the window, giving Spree a scratch on the head as I went past.

'We might as well enjoy the peace. Franz is about to become really famous!' I said

'Philippa. I think you need to talk to someone. You can't ...'

'Don't worry,' I interrupted. 'I won't be doing anything but talking soon – just you wait.'

Angie just looked at me. 'That's not what I meant and you know it. Talking to the cops and news media isn't my idea of therapy.'

'It's not mine either. Sorry Angie. I don't really feel this flippant. I don't really feel anything.'

'You can laugh most things off. Don't get me wrong, it's one of the things I like about you – but it isn't going to help you now.' I shivered. She was right

...

The next couple of days were a nightmare. Everywhere I went there were people in my face asking questions. The police, my fellow guides, the locals and the media.

Julia arrived somewhere in the middle of it all looking worse than I felt.

'This is all my fault,' she told me. 'If I hadn't wanted to find who killed Vivien none of this would have happened.'

'Well look on the bright side,' I said. 'It proves you were right.'

'Yes. And thanks to me Rose Revell is dead.'

Neither of us said anything for a while after that. Even Spree looked depressed.

'People are saying that Rose was killed with her own ice axe,' Julia said.

'It's funny. It's never even occurred to me what a good weapon an ice axe could be,' I said. 'Maybe I should keep one under my bed. Julia, I'm every bit as much to blame as you. I pushed Rose into that confrontation.'

'Don't be stupid. She would have done it sooner or later.'

'Have you talked to the police?'

'Not yet,' Julia stood up and paced round the kitchen.

I shivered, my mind back on the scene of carnage in Rose's house.

'I keep thinking of the hatred,' I said in answer to Julia's questioning look. 'Say we are right and Rose confronted Vivien's killer. So the killer gets rid of her so she won't talk. But why smash her half to bits? Why shred all her paintings of Vivien? The killer hated Rose Revell – it's like she was the real target, not Vivien. But if so why wait all these years? Work that out if you can, Julia. I can't.

...

Stu Adams rang and asked me to come in again the next day. They wanted to ask me in more detail about Julia and what had led her to believe that Vivien Revell might have been murdered.

The little Franz Police Station had been superseded by Operation Ice. A large contingent of out-of-town police had set up their base in the local hall. The room was full of computer equipment, white-boards, and people. Stu didn't look all that comfortable with the sudden arrival of fast-lane policing and I didn't blame him.

'Who's running things here?' I asked him. '

'A detective from Christchurch – Jimmy Black. He's been on a couple of high profile murder cases and he's really sharp. He's the one you're going to have to talk to now.'

'Great,' I said without enthusiasm.

Stu took me over to the corner of the room where a middle-aged man sat frowning in front of a laptop.

'This is Philippa Barnes,' he said. 'Are you ready to talk to her now?'

'Yes, thanks.' Detective Black looked at me without smiling. He had closely cropped dark hair and the ruddy complexion of a heavy drinker. He wasn't fat but he was solid all the way through. He looked like he had packed himself into his uniform and buttoned it up so nothing could escape. A good analogy for the way he probably did his work, I thought gloomily. Nothing would escape the watchful eyes of this man. His face had a couple of shaving nicks and there were dark shadows under his eyes but there was no mistaking the sense of control.

He looked around the room and beckoned another policeman to his side.

'This is Detective Constable Greg Elliott,' he said to me. 'He and I will interview you together.'

They took me to a screened-off corner which had been set up as an interview room. DC Elliott frowned as he set up the recording equipment. He looked in much better physical shape than his boss – taller, leaner, fitter – but there was no mistaking who was in charge. I'd never met anyone with such presence as Detective Black before.

They took me through the whole thing again, but in a lot more detail than Stu had subjected me to. Their expressions were intent but they didn't react to anything I said. It was a little disconcerting.

'If Julia McLoughlin was so sure that Vivien Revell was murdered, why didn't she talk to us?' asked DC Elliott.

I leaned forward in my chair. 'That was the whole thing. She didn't have anything to go on but her own gut feelings. She asked me to see what I could find out – I live here, I know the people ...'

'I find one part of your story interesting,' DI Black said. 'Rose Revell also thought her daughter had been murdered. According to you. Unfortunately we don't have any other evidence of this.'

'Well I can't help that! I'm telling you the truth but there's nothing I can do to make you believe me. She told me she knew who had killed Vivien but she had no proof. She said she was going to deal with it her way and that she had nothing to fear from the person responsible.'

DI Black turned over a page of the sheaf of papers in front of him. He frowned.

'Do you ever remember seeing an ice axe in Rose Revell's studio?'

I thought about it for a moment. 'I can't remember seeing one when I found her body. But I saw it the previous time I was there. It was leaning against the wall near one of the windows.'

'Can you describe it?'

'It was an old fashioned wooden one – with a long shaft. And there was a smear of blue paint on the blade. Actually my axe is similar to hers.'

'The axe is missing,' DI Black told me. 'I'd like to have a look at yours if you don't mind.'

I didn't feel like I had much choice, so I offered to go and get it from the car. I noticed a lot of activity out in the street including people with cameras and a television van. The media had arrived.

'Thanks,' DC Elliott said when I handed over my axe. We'll give you a receipt. Forensics will need to look at it.'

'My axe wasn't the murder weapon! You can't take it away – I need it to do my job.'

'I'm afraid we can, Ms Barnes. This is a murder enquiry in case you'd forgotten.'

I emerged from the Operation Ice base feeling dazed. Surely they couldn't think I'd killed Rose? Well of course they could. My feelings about being a murder suspect only intensified as several reporters ran towards me waving cameras and microphones in my direction.

I glared at them and drove off as fast as I could in my clapped-out Toyota. I could have gone back to the guides' room and hung out with Angie and the others but I was in no mood for company so I headed home, picked up Spree and went out walking on the nearby riverbed.

There was no one around and the only sound was the river, rushing past over rough grey stones. Gradually I started to feel better, time on my own working its usual magic on me.

Forensics weren't going to find a damned thing on my ice axe. But if the police confiscated all our axes I wasn't sure how we were going to get tourists up and down the glacier. That was one problem Tim had never had to face in all the time he'd been running the Glacier Climbers. Trust me to take over just in time for a new kind of problem. Still it made a change from floods washing out the tracks.

I didn't have a clue what the police were thinking. They probably saw me as some kind of self-appointed girl detective with a distasteful habit for finding dead bodies. I laughed but felt more like cringing.

And as for the media ... I frowned to myself. They could be a real problem. I was a story in myself I thought without pleasure. Glacier Guide's Grim Discovery. Glacier Guide with Nose for Death. Just a couple of possible headlines they could come up with.

'Spree,' I yelled realising I hadn't seen the familiar hurtling black shape for a while. He wasn't in any hurry to return so I wandered round for another half an hour or so before he appeared, soaked and ensnared with twigs and leaves. How he'd managed to get into such a mess on an open riverbed I couldn't imagine.

I was starting to rally. There was no future in being a victim. I'd never concerned myself about what people thought before and I wasn't about to let a murder enquiry team change the habit of a lifetime. I'd told them everything I knew and they could do what they liked with the information.

I believed myself even if they didn't.

I was sure that Vivien and Rose had been killed by the same person even if the crimes were decades apart. Spree and I ran back towards home. I frowned when I saw an unfamiliar car parked outside my house. My mood did not improve when my former partner Mark Nolan stepped out and gave me a tentative wave.

...

The phone was ringing as I opened the door.

'I wouldn't answer that if I was you,' Mark said, following me inside even though I hadn't invited him in.

I turned and looked at him.

'Why not?'

'Because there's every chance it'll be a journalist.'

'Like you, then,' I said.

'Philippa, I ...'

'So you're just here by coincidence?'

I knew this was mean but I didn't care. It had been a hell day and the sudden appearance of my ex when I thought I was going to have a quiet night alone was just what I didn't need.

'I am here because of Rose Revell's death,' Mark said. 'But I haven't come to see you for that reason. You have to believe that.'

I threw my car keys on the table then opened the back door to admit Spree to the kitchen. He went crazy when he saw Mark. I couldn't believe he remembered him so fondly.

'So you're not here for an exclusive?' I asked when Spree finally calmed down and crashed on the sofa.

Mark laughed. 'I know you better than that. I wouldn't even try. But others won't be quite as considerate. You're news whether you like it or not.'

'I don't like it. But I guess you're right. I've just been pondering the headlines. Everywhere someone dies I pop up. Even I can see I have story potential,' I said with a sigh.

Mark looked good. His dark hair was a little longer than I remembered and it suited him. He'd also lost weight. He'd never been fat but he hadn't been in great condition the last time I'd seen him. Now he looked fit. He was wearing jeans and a faded blue shirt. He wasn't wearing a wedding ring. Not that I cared about that of course!

'I've been thinking about you a lot, Philippa. I'm sorry I didn't get in touch when you were on the news last time.'

'Why didn't you?' I asked before I could stop myself. I had felt resentful. After all, I'd contacted him after the earthquake. But when I'd popped up on the news after finding Vivien's body he hadn't made any effort.

'I didn't know if you'd want to hear from me.'

Lame, I thought. But I didn't pursue it.

'How's Kate?' he asked after an awkward silence.

'She's fine.'

I certainly wasn't going to tell him about the attack on Kate. But I did tell him about Julia's theory. And that Rose could have been killed by the person who had murdered Vivien.

Mark stared at me.

'How do you work that out?'

I told him and to his credit he did none of the things I expected. He didn't argue, he didn't tell me to leave it to the police – and he didn't bring out his notebook either. 'I'll see what I can find out from my police contacts,' was all he said.

'How long are you staying here?' I didn't want to talk about any of it any more. Nothing helped. No one could.

Mark walked over to the stove and plugged in the jug. 'I don't really know. Essentially as long as the story lasts. The Operation Ice base will be in town for a good while.'

'You can stay here if you want,' I said, surprising us both.

'That would be great. I won't get in your way.'

He didn't either. He spent the next hour or so on his cellphone through in the living room while I put together a pasta meal and poured myself a large glass of red wine. Eventually he reappeared to ask me if I had wireless. His laptop wasn't picking up a signal.

I laughed. 'I'm on dial-up.'

'I don't believe you!'

'I hardly use the computer. Dial-up's cheap in case you haven't noticed. Plus my computer is so old I don't think it would do wireless. Help yourself to it if you want to – the cords are behind Spree's bean bag.'

Muttering to himself Mark got the computer connected, cursing at the slow speed of the internet connection. I wasn't terribly sympathetic and left him to it, turning on the television. I immediately wished I hadn't. Rose's murder led the news and a picture of her face and a view of white-overall clad figures outside her house gave way to me emerging from the police base glaring at the cameras as I headed for my car. I hadn't even seen the bloody things but I'd scowled at them by reflex. It wasn't a pretty sight.

Kate arrived just in time to see my television appearance.

'You look awful,' she said.

'Thanks,' I replied.

She drifted out to the kitchen, giving Mark a less than friendly look as she did so. I turned my attention back to the television. A reporter, looking glamorous in designer outdoor gear, was talking live from the village.

'Glacier guide Philippa Barnes found Rose Revell's body. Ms Barnes is no stranger to death. She also found the body of Rose's daughter embedded in the ice of the Franz Josef Glacier only a few weeks ago. An ice axe, missing from the scene, is believed to have been the murder weapon.'

'They make it sound like I killed her,' I said.

Mark didn't reply. He seemed to have lost his internet connection.

Then DI Black appeared on the screen, looking tired and stonefaced.

'We would be interested in hearing from anyone who saw anyone in the vicinity of Rose Revell's house in the last few days,' he said. 'In particular we are keen to speak to a Caucausion man, aged in his late thirties, dark haired and of slim build who was seen talking to Rose Revell in the Ice Rocks Café on the night of her murder.'

'What's that all about?' I asked Mark.

He shrugged. 'I don't know. But there's a media briefing at the police base later tonight so I'll find out more then.'

He actually found out quite a lot. The police were interested in talking to some of Rose's family. I hadn't realised she had any, but apparently she had some cousins in England who had just been disinherited by an eccentric will in Rose's favour. Rose's computer had revealed some acrimonious emails between Rose and her cousins – one of whom just happened to be in New Zealand at the moment and matched the description of the dark haired man seen with Rose the night of her death.

'Surely if this is all true he'd have got rid of all the emails after he killed her.' I said. 'I can't believe the police have fallen for this.'

'They have to check. It's a viable lead.'

'There are other possibilities – they didn't know what Rose was like. If you ask me the guy in the pub is much more likely to be a casual pick up than a long-lost cousin.'

'He was half her age,' Mark said.

I laughed. 'So? I could tell you some stories about Rose that would make this one look conservative.'

There wasn't a lot more to say. I felt exhausted all of a sudden and it occurred to me that we hadn't addressed the thorny issue of Mark's sleeping arrangements.

'I'm off to bed,' I told him. 'You can have my parents' old room. There are sheets in the linen cupboard. Help yourself to a shower.'

'Great, thanks, Philippa.' He didn't sound disappointed and I was contrary enough to feel irritated.

Once in bed I couldn't sleep and I was unsettled by the phone ringing several times. Mark could field his fellow journalists. I certainly wasn't going to talk to anyone.

At about midnight he knocked on my door, phone in hand. 'You'll want to talk to this person,' he said quietly. 'It's your brother.'

When I heard Tom's voice I started crying and much to my embarrassment I couldn't stop, so Mark had to take the phone from me and tell him what had happened. Eventually I got myself together enough to take back the phone and talk to Tom.

'Why haven't you rung before?' I demanded.

'Philippa I've only just found out. I've been doing the Cornwall coastal walk. I haven't been on any media sites. And even if I had – you know what it's like here. New Zealand doesn't feature in the news in this country. I'm coming home.'

'Good,' I said. 'When?'

'I'm going back to London today – and I'll be on the flight out of Heathrow tonight. Philippa I am sorry. I'd have been home straight away if I'd known.'

It was the story of his life but I wasn't going to tell him that. For the first time in my life I really needed my brother. I wasn't sure I liked the feeling.

...

I cycled up to the guides' office that morning with plenty to think about. It was good that Tom was finally coming home. What he would do when he got here I had no idea but I was tired of dealing with everything on my own.

And I was enjoying having Mark back on the edges of my life. I didn't want to analyse that. Matt was washing the glacier bus as I cycled up. It had been a wet night but the sky was clearing now and it looked like the sun might come out before too long.

'Anyone for the glacier?' I asked him.

'Only half a dozen. Sara's getting them sorted out. I thought I'd stay and do a bit more work on the website.'

He was spending way too much time on this project and it seemed to morph into Facebook on a regular basis. I should talk to him about it but I didn't have the energy. After all, if the tourists were there, he worked hard. I made a mental note to talk to Sara about the whole thing. If she wasn't worried then neither was I. Tim could sort it out when he came back.

'There's an email from Tim,' Matt said, as if he'd read my thoughts. 'Seems like he's only just remembered that we're all out here. He's heard about Rose Revell. He tried to ring you last night but some guy intercepted the call apparently. Anything you're not telling me, Philippa?'

I laughed. 'Nothing interesting. I was trying to avoid calls from the media but I've got someone staying with me. Mark Nolan. He's actually a reporter as well.'

"And he's your ex!'

'How do you know that?' I was taken aback. I had never discussed my love life with Matt.

'Angie told me about him. Interesting – very interesting.'

'Actually it's very boring. There's nothing going on. He's here to cover Rose Revell's murder. That's all.'

'If you say so.'

'I do. Now what's Tim's news?'

'They're having a ball. I don't know what's happened to the man. Time was he couldn't handle a weekend away from his glacier. Now it's like he doesn't care if he never comes back.'

'I hope you're wrong, Matt. There's no way I want to run his business long term.'

Angie wasn't at work and I was glad of the space. She'd have been on to the Mark non-story in seconds and I wasn't up to it. Instead I read Tim's email, sent off a brief response, then spent an hour scanning Stuff and other news sites. It was all pretty depressing. I featured far too prominently even though I'd spoken to no reporters.

I made coffee and took it to the staff room out the back, putting my feet up on the table in front of me and staring up at the mountains. I kept coming back to the violence of Rose's murder and I couldn't get the things I'd seen out of my head. I was no forensic expert but it was obvious she had suffered multiple blows, many more than would have been needed to kill her. And as for what had been done to all the paintings of Vivien ... I shivered.

A wood pigeon swooped out of a nearby tree and flew over my head. I jumped and spilled some of my coffee. I got up and went back to my office work.

After a morning of this I was happy when enough tourists showed up to warrant an afternoon glacier trip. We set off in the bus and as I launched into my glacier commentary thought of murder and its associated hassles retreated. As we swung round a tight corner I told of how decades before, a woman artist had stood in the valley and persuaded the road makers to make a few extra bends in the road to avoid some rata trees, and the legacy of her intervention lived on. When in flower, the red blossoms looked amazing against the dark green bush and the blue grey rock faces. There were no flowers today but the story always interested people.

As we walked up the valley, I looked around for a clear patch of silt on the ground, eventually stopping in a suitable spot and doing a crude drawing of the glacier and snowfield with my ice axe to illustrate my talk on how a glacier was formed. Usually I was proud of my silt drawings, but today's effort looked like the work of a child.

It was another black mark against the clunky ice axe I had to use since my own one had been taken away. Several people commented on the strong smell of sulphur, and I talked about the alpine fault, the huge geological break through the earth's surface. I pointed out the impressive splinter fault line which cleaves one of the valley walls in two not far from the terminal of the glacier. You can often smell sulphur here. Sometimes you can even smell it on the glacier, issuing up through the ice from the depths of the earth.

The Waiho River had cut a deep channel in the riverbed on the far side of the valley. You could tell how dangerous it was just by looking at it, as it tore over the top of submerged boulders and burst into spray, the scattered droplets of water looking like dirty grey pearls. The blue-white cave, from which the river emerged, was a place to stay away from despite its beauty.

Today, as usual, people were ignoring the warning signs and crowding in under the gigantic roof of ice. I led my party away from this appreciating the ease of access. Last year we had aluminium ladders and ropes tied onto the glacier, now we had a staircase of ice steps. The ice rose steeply, but had enough slope to allow people to walk rather than scramble. I never tired of the sense of freedom I felt as I climbed higher on the ice, distancing myself from the real world. Even with a tourist party following behind, there was a sense of escape. For people who had never been on a glacier before it was a magical experience. We reached the top of the terminal face and paused for a view of the valley and the now ant-like people far below. The sun glittered on the pinnacles, and I led the group through the white labyrinth slowly, allowing plenty of time for photo stops. After a while we reached a relatively flat section of the glacier, and everyone could spread out more and look around. I never talked much at this point of the trip. It was better for people to experience it for themselves, uncluttered by a commentary.

I saw a movement above me. There was someone coming down from the ice fall, a climber, walking fast in crampons, his ice axe tucked under his arm. It was Callum Jackson. He nodded to me as he passed, but didn't speak. His usual look of detachment was missing. He looked tortured, grey and old.

Chapter 14

IT was midnight and I was lying in bed feeling like I'd never go to sleep again. I should have been tired. I'd had plenty of exercise, both mental and physical, but I lay there wakeful and angry with myself.

I heard a car in the driveway and sat up in bed. Mark was out with his media friends so I assumed it was him returning. Then I heard someone knocking on the door. Pulling a sweatshirt over my head I padded down the hallway. Spree, who had moved back to Kate's room, met me in her doorway and roared into life, barking like the Hound of the Baskervilles. My sister did not emerge.

Bolstered with the security of this fearsome beast at my side I opened the door and stared into the face of my brother.

As reunions went it was all pretty low key. At least I didn't start crying again. Tom had aged. He'd left home a careless boy with a head of thick wavy fair hair and returned with a much diminished crop and it was receding from his forehead. His face was lined and although he looked tanned and fit he also looked a lot older. He was dressed in ancient jeans and a t-shirt and carried a worn pack on one shoulder.

We stared at each other for a few minutes and then Spree forced himself between us to check out this stranger. Tom crouched and scratched his ears and Spree was sold. I wasn't. For once in my life I did not know what to say. And neither did Tom. I made up the bed in his old room while he prowled round the house, restless and sad. The last time he was here our parents were alive. Now they were dead. And Kate and I were rattling round with a giant schnauzer.

It must have been a hideous contrast and I felt sorry for him. We sat down and faced each other over the kitchen table.

'Tell me about Kate,' he said. I pointed towards the doorway. Our nightie-clad sister stood there staring at us.

'Who are you?' she asked Tom. He flinched as if she had hit him.

'I'm your brother – and I'm really sorry you had to ask that question. I haven't been here for you Kate. I'm sorry.'

'Philippa's looked after me.' Her tone was unfriendly.

Tom looked miserable.

'You need to sleep,' I said to him. 'You look exhausted.'

'Yeah it's a hell of a trip. 24 hours flying. I don't know if I'll ever do it again.'

'Was it good?' I was genuinely interested. Our lives had been so different. I couldn't imagine what it must have been like wandering freely all over the world.

'It's been interesting. You know what I'm like, Philippa – I can't handle being in one place too long. I was quite happy to be on the road and I liked the casual work. No ties, no career responsibilities, you know how it is.'

'So what'll you do now?'

'I'd like to stay here for a while if you and Kate'll have me.'

The days that followed were strange. Tom, Kate and I took a while to get reacquainted, Mark was trying not to get in our way, and Julia stayed on the fringes of it all white-faced and stressed. Fun? Not much.

'I'm over it all,' I told Matt and Angie in the guides' office. It was a relief to be at work away from all the undercurrents at home. 'It's awful for Tom. Staying away has only delayed things for him. He's home and our parents are dead – and he has to start dealing with that. I understand and I'm sorry for him – but there's nothing I can do to make it better.'

'You've got a lot of other stuff going on,' Angie was thoughtful. 'Having Tom home's only going to make things harder right now.' I stared at her, grateful for her understanding. Sara and Matt arrived and left soon after with a tourist party, Angie buried herself with her accounts and I cleaned boots and washed socks, enjoying having something mindless to do.

Ever since I'd found Rose's body my mind wasn't up to the task of logical thought. I still couldn't get my head round the savagery of the whole thing – and I couldn't see any of the people I'd thought capable of Vivien's murder being capable of this.

If it was any of them my money was on Callum but this was based on little more than the fact I thought he was harder than anyone else. Luke Riley could have hated Rose for his relationship with her all those years ago but it was difficult to see why it should have come to the surface after all this time. And Penelope Blake had no reason that I knew of to dislike Rose, let alone hate her. Julia had started this whole thing but it defied belief that she had would have done so if she had killed Vivien - and she also seemed to have no strong feelings either way for Rose. She thought she'd been a bad mother but that was no reason to attack her with an ice axe years after her friend's death.

There was obviously something big that I was missing and in my current frame of mind I wasn't likely to find it.

I scooped an armload of cold damp socks out of the washing machine and loaded them into the drier. Some of them were getting thin and needed replacing. I wondered idly what Tim budgeted for these things. Angie would probably know. Since I'd been in charge I hadn't bothered to use Tim's office, preferring to be out in the main room with the others, but today I decided some quiet time in there wouldn't be a bad thing. I could get some headspace and the others could stop walking on eggshells wondering if I was going to start howling again.

I plugged in the computer intending to go online to look at some outdoor clothing shops to get an idea of the cost of socks. Tim's office was little more than a cupboard and I had to squeeze to get behind his desk. In so doing I knocked something that was stacked against the far wall and it fell out with a crash.

It was a large oil painting. I picked it up and stared at it. It depicted an old wooden hotel with greying timbers and a wide front verandah, standing in the middle of a paddock of golden tussock. A study in grey and gold with mountains sketched faintly in the background. The building was dilapidated, its only colour the blood-red letters of the sign hanging above the door: The Mountaineer. I set it against the wall and stood back. It was an impressive work of art, bleak but evocative. I wondered what was inside the hotel door, what its story might be. And why Tim had it stashed away in his office.

Angie came in and joined me staring at the painting.

'What a creepy place. Where is it?'

I frowned. 'Wasn't there an old hotel near the Hermitage called The Mountaineer?'

'God knows. Let's take it out into the light for a better look.'

I was behind her as she walked out of the room, holding the painting. She placed it on the floor against a wall and we both stood back to look at it. As we did so the office door opened and Callum Jackson walked in. He stared at the painting and then at us. He looked shocked. He made some strange sound and turned on his heel, slamming the door behind him as he went.

'What the hell was that all about?' Angie was astonished.

'I have no idea,' I said.

'I wonder what he wanted.'

'Probably to hassle me about his damned reports,' I said with a sigh. 'I never seem to get round to doing them. Tim's going to kill me when he gets back.'

I went back to searching for socks on the internet but my heart wasn't in it. I'd email Tim, ask him about the painting, and tell him about Callum's reaction to it. Maybe he could explain it.

After work we all went to Ice Rocks for a drink.

Tom joined us. He had dropped Kate off at Sally's and I was pleased when he told me she had protested that she would be fine on her own at home. She was getting over what had happened. Tom was relaxed with my workmates and seemed a lot happier than he had at home. Over a few beers he and Matt talked about a trek they'd both done in South America while Angie, Sara and I had a mindless discussion about Coronation Street.

We ordered pizzas and settled in for the evening. It was fun and relaxing to be somewhere neutral talking about ordinary things. Jem Browne turned up and joined us.

'Have the police told you anything about the murder?' he asked hopefully.

'Nothing we didn't already know. But Mark tells me they're interviewing some guy who might have had a row with Rose over an inheritance. He could have visited her the night she was killed.'

'Not that young dark-haired bloke she was drinking with that night?'

'How do you know what he looked like?' Angie leaned past me to stare at her old friend.

'Saw them, didn't I?' Jem looked pleased with the attention. 'And I'll tell you something for nothing – those two weren't fighting about money. They couldn't keep their hands off one another. It was home to bed with Rosie for that young bloke.'

'I don't believe you.' Angie was incredulous.

'Just wait and see if I'm not right,' he said, not at all offended.

And as if on cue Mark came through the door, laptop under his arm.

'The cousin is out of the frame. He's in the country but he was on a flight to Auckland around the time Rose was murdered. As soon as he saw the news he got in touch with the police and his alibi checked out.'

'Told you.' Jem gave Angie a triumphant look.

'So are the police saying this casual pick-up killed her?' I asked.

'Well he hasn't come forward – that's a bit suspicious,' Mark perched his glass by his laptop and rubbed his face with his hands.

'Not necessarily,' I said. 'He could have left next day and gone into the hills tramping. Or even if he's just on the road why should he read the local news? He probably knows nothing about the murder. Look how long it took Tom to find out about everything that was happening here.'

'The police are actively looking for him, Philippa. They weren't looking for Tom.'

'True. But that doesn't mean they're going to find Rose's mystery man. Say Jem's right and he did go home with her for sex. He's going to have a hell of a time proving he didn't then kill her. So why put himself in the frame?'

'So what do you think happened?'

Mark wasn't trying to be annoying but I still felt irritated.

'Rose had other things on her mind that night. She knew who had killed Vivien and she was ready to tackle them. I don't know what she was thinking but maybe she was going stir crazy at home and decided to go out for a drink. Then she met this guy and picked him up – or he picked her up. Whatever. After that who knows what happened? The guy could have been a stray psychopath and killed her. Or she could have got rid of him then got in touch with Vivien's killer, asked him or her round to talk and ended up being killed by that person.'

Angie and Jem were both looking sceptical while Mark presented a neutral face. Tom was talking to Sara and wasn't taking any notice of the conversation.

'I find it hard to believe that Rose picked up some guy in the pub then set up a meeting with a supposed killer all on the same night,' Mark said.

'Why not? Say she had got in touch with Vivien's killer, then she went to the pub to think things over. She meets this guy and takes him home for a couple of hours. What time did you see them, Jem?'

He frowned. 'Wasn't late. Five, maybe five thirty.'

'There you are then! The guy could've been gone by seven. Plenty of time,' I said.

'It's possible I suppose,' Mark said. 'But I can't believe that a mother about to confront her daughter's killer would be interested in a sexual fling along the way.'

I laughed. 'That's because you didn't know Rose. And neither did the police. I can see why they're chasing the line of a sexual

TRISH MCCORMACK

encounter gone wrong. But I don't believe it. After all why would a complete stranger tear up all the paintings of Vivien? And what was he doing in the studio anyway? If it was the pick-up guy surely it would have happened in the bedroom.'

'The police aren't stupid, Philippa. They will be looking at every possibility.'

'Are you a journalist? Or the police's PR man?' I snapped.

'Another drink anyone,' Matt reappeared from the pool table and looked at me, taking in my anger and trying to smooth things over.

'Not for me thanks.' I stood up. 'I want to go back to the guides' office. There's something I need to check.'

I went straight to the computer and clicked onto my email. There was a reply just as I'd hoped.

'Hi Philippa,' Tim had written. 'Strange about the painting. I'd forgotten all about it but I picked it up at an art auction Helen took me along to a few months back. I actually bought it for Callum. He and I used to climb together sometimes and on one of our trips he mentioned he'd grown up at that hotel. His father was the publican. But when I tried to give it to him he refused to take it. Said something pretty weird, actually – that he had the hell in his head and he didn't need it on his wall as well.'

...

The next morning Stu's sidekick DC Wendy Munro was on the doorstep. I hadn't like DC Munro before but this time I didn't find her quite so abrasive and she further redeemed herself by giving me back my ice axe. I guessed that this job was beneath the team of Christchurch detectives running Operation Ice. It must be galling for the local cops have others running things on their patch.

I was very pleased to see my ice axe. An ice axe is an extension of yourself. No one else's is any good. The last time I'd been on the glacier my step cutting was all over the place. Now I would be able to fly again.

I wasn't all that pleased when Julia arrived half an hour or so later. It was my day off and I'd been enjoying some time to myself. Kate was at school and Tom had gone for a run with Spree.

'How much longer are you going to hang around Franz?' I asked Julia as I handed her a coffee. I tried to keep the irritation out of my voice. I was getting sick of her. She was needy and she had no sense of humour.

'Not much longer,' she said.

'Don't lose your job over all this. There's nothing any of us can do. But there is something I need to tell you, Julia. I've found out something about Callum Jackson. He grew up at Mt Cook. His family had that pub, The Mountaineer, on the outskirts of the village.'

She didn't seem all that interested. 'He has to come from somewhere.'

'Yes but that's not all.' I told her about the painting and what Callum had said to Tim about the hell inside his head.

She still didn't seem interested and I was annoyed.

'Listen Julia. We know Callum has some secret in his past and now we know something bad happened to him at when he lived at The Mountaineer. I might go over to Mount Cook and see if anyone remembers him.'

'It's a long way to go,' Julia objected. 'Do you think it's worth it?'

'It's not far by air. I'll ask Lisa Owen when she's next going over.' Lisa was a pilot with one of the local helicopter companies and she sometimes flew over to Mount Cook for the day when they needed an extra pilot to work there. She was always happy to take Franz people over for the ride.

'It must be decades since Callum lived there. Do you really think anyone's going to remember him?'

'Julia, I wish you'd stop making objections. You want me to do something don't you? Callum's childhood could be connected to his secret. And there's something else. I saw him on the glacier just after Rose's murder and he looked like death himself. There's something seriously wrong about that guy.'

'I'm not arguing with that. But I just don't think you're going to find out anything in the ruins of an old hotel.'

'Let's just see about that,' I said.

It was a week or more before I managed to arrange a trip over to Mount Cook with Lisa. I met her early one morning on the track to the helicopter port. She looked tiny in her pilot's uniform, rather like a child who had dressed up in an adult's clothes. Tourists were often disconcerted when they realised she was there to fly the helicopter not to sell them their tickets. Lisa had no ego problems. She was one of the best pilots the company had ever employed and the regular votes of no confidence from the public never seemed to upset her. I followed her into the helicopter, watching as she smoothed back her tangled blonde hair and put her earphones on. A few minutes later we were up and away, veering out over the Waiho River towards the glacier valley.

As we started climbing up over the glacier I gazed down at the chaotic tangle of pinnacles and crevasses. Years ago an elderly man on a bus tour had done a tourist flight and amused everyone when he peered out of the window and asked if the glacier was limestone. He'd been on one of those whistle-stop "see the country in ten days" tours and had completely lost track of where he was. From this vantage point you could see how he'd mistaken the glacier for limestone. It didn't really look like ice from this angle.

We cruised over the névé - the vast snowfield at the head of the glacier - and on past the Almer Hut, an insignificant bastion of humanity in this mountain world, then crossed over into the head of the rugged Callery valley and looked down on the Spencer glacier. The Minarets, the range of mountains at the head of the Franz Josef Glacier, and the beautiful sculptured shape of Mount Elie de Beaumont rose in front of us.

The helicopter bumped around for a minute as it weathered the different air flows on each side of the main divide and then we were descending into the Tasman valley. The Franz is a steep short glacier, and by contrast the Tasman looks like an enormous white highway, it's so long and flat. We flew on, sweeping over the turquoise lakes at the terminal of the glacier, and landed at the Glentanner airport, several kilometres from the Mount Cook village. The small huddle of buildings looked lost in the sea of tussock.

'Have you got much on today?' I asked Lisa.

'I doubt it. Neal's sick, and one of the other pilots is away on leave. Think they want me to be here just in case they get an unexpected rush.'

I had already talked to Lisa about hiring a car for the day, and she had offered me Neal's, brushing aside my objections.

'That's the deal,' she had said. 'He uses mine when he's at Franz, I use his over at Cook. He's not that sick. He'll be up here to meet us. Least he can do is keep me company between flights. What are you going to do, anyway?'

'I'm trying to find out about an old pub called The Mountaineer. I've got a painting of it and it made me a little curious about its history.'

My story sounded thin but fortunately Lisa didn't seem interested. She was turning on her cell phone and frowning at the screen. We climbed out of the helicopter and walked across to the flight office.

'You do know The Mountaineer is closed down?' Lisa said.

'I thought it might have. But hopefully there'll be someone here who remembers something about it. I'd like to find out who managed it and that kind of thing.'

'Neal's your man. He knows all the locals.'

Neal didn't look quite as handsome in jeans and sweatshirt as he had when I'd last seen him in his pilot's uniform, and having his voice distorted by a cold didn't help him. He seemed pleased to see Lisa, and I wondered if they were an item. Lisa never spoke of her private life. I've always distrusted men with extreme good looks, so seeing Neal at a disadvantage made me like him more. His greeting to me was friendly and he made light of my thanks for the use of his car.

'Not a problem,' he said. 'I was going to stay up here and keep Lisa company anyway. There's a bus tour due in about an hour but otherwise there's bugger all on the books for the day.'

'Philippa's researching the history of The Mountaineer,' Lisa told him. 'Wants to talk to someone who knew the people who managed it and that kind of thing. Any ideas?'

Neal shook his head. 'It's been closed down all the time I've been here. You could talk to old Bill Rogers. He's been around here for years.'

'Does he live in the village?' I asked.

'Yeah. He's retired but he used to be an odd jobs man at the Hermitage. I'm pretty sure he used to drink at The Mountaineer. Reckoned the Hermitage was too upmarket for him.'

'I'd quite like to have a look round The Mountaineer. I wonder where I could get a key,' I said.

'You won't need a key,' Neal said. 'The back door's been broken for months and no one's bothered to fix it. There's nothing in there, though.'

I hadn't really expected boxes of old papers but I was still disappointed. I asked Neal where I could find Bill Rogers, then set out, crunching the unfamiliar gears in Neal's car, and hoping he hadn't heard my departure.

As I had remembered, the Mountaineer was all on its own, close to the side of the Mount Cook road, and I stopped outside, noticing the deterioration of the old building. It had looked dilapidated in Tim's painting but it was much worse in reality. The whole façade seemed to have slumped, and much of the paint had peeled off the walls, revealing grey timber. The pub sign had come adrift from one of the wooden supports, and hung lopsidedly over the verandah, much of the lettering weathered away to nothing.

I stood for a minute enjoying the warm air flowing around me and gazed out over the dun-coloured tussocks. It was very different to the rainforest I was used to.

Turning back to the pub I noticed how filthy the cracked windows were. I tried to open the heavy front door, but it would not budge, so I headed for the back of the building, picking my way through rusty coils of barbed wire and other rubbish.

There was a hole where the back door had once been and I went inside, sneezing as I disturbed a cloud of dust, my eyes gradually adjusting to the dim light. I was surprised to see all the old black and white photographs on the walls in the public bar. It was amazing they hadn't been stolen or vandalised. They pictured happier times at The Mountaineer, the old pub freshly painted with a coach at the front door, the horses hitched to the verandah posts. There was another photograph of the interior of the pub, a big group of punters gathered round the bar and a bearded man handing someone a glass of beer.

I gazed around the empty room. Apart from the photographs, the only thing left was the bar itself, a great slab of heart rimu, battered and scarred by many years of use. I ran my fingers over the cool surface of the wood, wondering just what it was I had come here for. The deserted hotel was surprisingly free of graffiti, though someone had written 'bastard' in scarlet paint on the door.

I walked upstairs, my footsteps sounding thunderous on the uncarpeted wood. The living quarters were tiny. There were two small bedrooms with unlined wooden walls painted an unattractive shade of green, and a mustard-coloured living room and kitchen. There was no sign of a bathroom, and the only furniture left in the place was an old wire bed frame and a smashed chest of drawers. I looked in those, hoping to find papers or letters, knowing it was futile.

It was a relief to get back outside. The Mountaineer had once had character but now the only feeling it evoked was depression. It seemed amazing that so many lives could have passed through here and left nothing. Julia was right. It had been a waste of time coming here. I had hoped that visiting the old hotel would give me some kind of insight into Callum, but it hadn't. He remained as elusive as ever. No traffic moved on the road, and the only sound was the sigh of the wind in the tussocks. The Mountaineer might have had a past, but it had no future, its cracked grey weatherboard façade decaying to the point where it would no longer even make an atmospheric photograph. The rusted wire and other rubbish lying all over the place made it look even more depressing.

I sat on the verandah, clasped my arms round my knees and looked at the scene surrounding me. The browns and golds of the foothills made a striking contrast to the white and greys of the mountains. I shut my eyes for a moment and enjoyed the breeze on my face.

Mount Cook village wasn't far from here, but it was hidden around a couple of corners. It would have been easier to walk to it, but I didn't want to leave Neal's car abandoned by the side of the road so I drove the short distance past the plate glass of the Hermitage hotel and the huddle of pitched roofed buildings crammed at the foot of the mountains.

Parking outside the Department of Conservation visitor centre, I sat in the car for a few minutes, thinking. I felt depressed and it wasn't just because of the old pub I'd just visited. Flying across the Southern Alps, I hadn't been able to get my mind off my parents' accident. We hadn't flown anywhere near the place they had died, but it was the first time I'd been anywhere near the high mountains since, and I wondered just how long it had taken them to fall. It was said that fall victims had plenty of time to think as they plunged to their deaths.

I wandered into the information centre, and idly looked at the displays as I waited for the young woman at the desk to finish a conversation with a couple of mountaineers. She seemed surprised when I asked her where Bill Rogers lived, but came to the door and pointed me in the right direction. As she did so the sleeve of her tan coloured shirt fell back to reveal a tattoo of an apple on her upper arm. It seemed at odds with her professional and rather bland manner.

'He should be there,' she said. 'He never goes away.'

The cottage was painted dark brown and built on a tiny section. No attempt had been made to landscape the property and the house looked uncared for. It took a minute or two for Bill Rogers to respond to my knock. He was slightly built and crippled, his hands horribly misshapen. The copper bangle on his wrist, that mythical cure for arthritis, didn't seem to be having much of an effect. He was dressed in jeans and a red checked shirt, and his wrinkled brown face was incurious.

'My name's Philippa Barnes,' I said. 'I've come over from Franz for the day because I'm trying to find out about a man who grew up at The Mountaineer.'

'Bit extreme, isn't it?' Bill said. 'You reckon he's worth it?'

I smiled. 'Not for that reason. I'm doing some detective work.'

'You what?' I could hardly blame him for looking sceptical, but my brief explanation of what I was doing wiped the boredom from his face.

'I'd appreciate it if you didn't tell anyone what I've told you,' I said.

'No one to tell,' he said 'No one here's going to be interested in ancient history. So you've been to the pub. That won't tell you much.'

'It didn't.'

'You'd better come in.' Bill led me down a darkened hallway into a living room furnished with a tartan covered sofa, a wooden table, and a large television. I didn't notice any of this at first. The entire front wall of the room was in glass, and I gazed at a spectacular mountain views. It looked as if you would be able to reach out and touch the scarred grey rock faces.

'Pretty good, isn't it?' Bill said.

'It's amazing.'

'So who's this bloke you're tracking?'

'His name's Callum Jackson. He's lived in Franz for about twenty years, but he apparently grew up at the Mountaineer.'

'Jackson you say? There's no Jacksons lived there in my time and I've been here for getting on fifty years. How old's this bloke?'

'He'd have to be well into his fifties,' I said. 'Though he doesn't look it.'

'And you reckon he could've murdered that girl who was found on the glacier?'

'It's possible.'

'Word I heard was that it was an accident. So you're going to prove the police wrong, eh?' Bill looked sceptical.

'It's not looking all that likely right now,' I said, 'but I have to do something.'

'So this bloke, if he's in his fifties, probably lived here forty years or more ago.'

'That sounds about right.'

'There was a family there about then. Unlucky lot they were too. But their name wasn't Jackson. Can't remember what it was, but it'll come back to me.'

'Why were they unlucky?'

'The old man drank like a fish. Last person who should've been running a pub but he stayed there for years. The booze killed him in the end.'

'How many children were there?'

'Two - a boy and girl. Half-starved they used to look too, poor little buggers.'

'What about their mother?'

'She walked out. Couldn't blame her. Word was, he used to knock her around. Don't know why she didn't take the kids with her, their father was no use to them.'

'What happened to them?'

'They left when the old man got sick. Don't know where they went. Rex Callaghan, that was his name.'

'Were there any other families who ran the pub?'

'Not in my time,' Bill twisted the bangle on his wrist. 'After Callaghan left, there was a single bloke who took over. In his fifties, he was. After that, a couple. Lil, her name was. Could've sharpened a knife on her face. She ran the show. They had no kids or if they did, they never came near The Mountaineer. They left around the time I retired, about ten years ago. Since that no one's stayed long. Place was past it long before it shut down.'

Callum and Callaghan. The names weren't unalike. Could Callum have changed his name since he had grown up here, and if so why?

'What do you remember about the Callaghan boy?' I asked Bill.

'Had a massive chip on his shoulder. Not a good thing in someone as young as he was. Protective of his sister, though. She always looked a picture of misery, poor little thing.'

'Can you remember his name?'

'No. Was something common, though. Fred, Jim, don't remember.'

'What about the sister?'

'Joy. Remember that. Anything less like a Joy you couldn't imagine.'

'What happened to her?'

'Word was she died,' Bill said. 'Not long after they left the pub. An operation that went wrong, I think.'

'Did you ever hear anything else about them?'

'Well, I heard about the boy of course. Along with everyone else in the country.'

'What do you mean?'

'He ended up in prison,' Bill said. 'Killed some girl.'

...

I stared at him and he looked back, his expression nonchalant.

'What happened?'

'I don't remember the details. Some sex thing. She was sleeping around maybe. Jack! His name was Jack Callaghan.'

Bill didn't remember anything else. I made my way back to the airport with plenty to think about.

Jack Callaghan had come out of prison and changed his name, just enough to ensure that no one could easily find him. He still loved the mountains but he couldn't go back to Mount Cook where everyone would know his story. So he came to Franz instead, to the other side of the mountains, and made himself a new life. It was

audacious in a way given how geographically close the two communities were but they were also totally separate. The road trip between
the two places was huge and the convenient flight route was often
unavailable due to bad weather. The occasional shared helicopter
work did not generate all that much contact between the Franz and
Mount Cook communities. All Callum would have had to do was
to stay away from the environs of Mount Cook and he could have
a whole new life.

But he was still the same person. Someone capable of killing a
woman. His girlfriend? And then along came Vivien Revell with
her charm and her determination to have the village mystery man
all for himself. She's succeeded, presumably unaware of his past.
But she'd picked up a bad vibe off him somehow. Enough to make
her plan to abort her baby in secret. Why? What had she found
out?

I didn't know for sure that Jack Callaghan and Callum Jackson
were one and the same person, but I would put money on it that
they were.

And if so, Callum Jackson had killed a woman once. So what
was to say he hadn't done it again?

...

'I don't believe it.'

Julia put down her glass of red wine on the table between us and
stared at me, her face shocked. I'd rung her as soon as I'd got home,
and suggested that we meet at Ice Rocks.

'Do you seriously think Callum is really this Jack Callaghan?'

'According to the guy I talked to, Jack was the only boy to grow
up at The Mountaineer in living memory. So if Callum was telling
Tim the truth about living there – and why wouldn't he? – he must
be the same person.'

'But why tell Tim if it was all such a secret?' Julia frowned.

'A slip of the tongue? He didn't tell him much – I bet Tim doesn't
have a clue that Callum did time for murder. As for telling him he

grew up at The Mountaineer - you know what it's like when you're away in the hills with someone, it's easy to talk about stuff when you're stuck in a hut in bad weather with someone – even if you later wish you hadn't.'

'I don't know actually. I'd never put myself in that situation. Well Philippa – you were right. I thought your going over to Mount Cook was a total waste of time.'

'So did I really. And it would have been if I'd just gone to The Mountaineer. It was Lisa's mate Neal who put me onto Bill Rogers.'

'You didn't say anything to them?'

'No of course not – I just said I was interested in the history of The Mountaineer. It wasn't an issue – they weren't at all interested.'

Something had unsettled me though. When Lisa and I had landed on the helipad I'd seen Penelope Blake walking nearby. She'd looked into the helicopter straight at me and I hadn't enjoyed the scrutiny. She presumably knew Callum had grown up at Mount Cook. And here I was appearing in a helicopter in front of her. There was no reason for her to suspect that I'd found out – or even that I'd been over at Mount Cook. But I still wished she hadn't seen me.

'So this man – Bill – didn't remember when the murder happened?' Julia interrupted my thoughts.

'No, but it must have been decades ago.' I sipped my wine for a minute, thinking. 'Callum came to Franz a year or so before Vivien went missing. Say about 1992. How long would he have got for murder?'

'A long time – but he could have been out in 10 years, less.'

'So say it happened around 1980. Gosh that's before I was even born. No wonder I don't remember it,' I said.

Julia looked thoughtful. 'Well it should be easy enough to find out now we have his name. He should pop up in two seconds in a Google search. I've got my laptop in the car. We could check it here if this place has wifi.'

It did. Five minutes later we had it all up on screen. The name was a common one and first of all we got a million Jack Callaghans on Facebook but when we added murder to the keyword search his story emerged.

It had happened in 1981 when he was twenty two years old. His was one of the cautionary tales headlined on a website which was devoted to victims of crime. The girl he'd killed – Amanda Wells– was 18. Her father was quoted on the victims' website as having been seriously concerned about the relationship from the outset. He found Jack moody and unpredictable and was appalled by what he found out about his background. He wanted a middle class professional for his youngest daughter, not the damaged son of a working class alcoholic whose mother had abandoned the family. He was angry that a life sentence had meant only 10 years for Jack Callaghan and said that if he ever found out where he lived he wouldn't be responsible for his actions.

We clicked on to a link to a feature article on the case, published in a lifestyle magazine. If there was any doubt before there could be none now. It included a black and white photograph of Jack Callaghan leaving court. A much younger looking Callum Jackson. The likeness was obvious but there was one thing vastly different. Jack looked haunted and vulnerable. Callum had left that look far behind along with his discarded old life. The article was great, delving into all the nuances of the case.

Julia and I sat silently reading of a young man who was alone in the world after his much-loved sister died during a botched appendix operation. His father, a chronic alcoholic, had died the year before and his mother was long gone. She had abandoned the family when Jack was a child and didn't reappear in his life to support him through his trial.

The prosecution had made a case based on the innocence and unworldliness of the victim. Amanda Wells was portrayed as a kind-hearted young woman who had made the mistake of feeling sorry for Jack Callaghan – while he used the story of his tragic life to ingratiate himself into her much luckier – and much more affluent – one. Her father testified that he'd been worried from the start, horrified by everything he was told about Jack's family background.

He did not want him as a friend, let alone possible life partner, for his daughter. Amanda, as her father told it, was naïve and far too attractive for her own good. If she had been plain she would still be alive today he said, before breaking down in the witness box.

Amanda's sister Rebecca had been next in the stand, echoing her father's remarks, and adding some damning impressions of Jack Callaghan. He had been nasty about Amanda's friends, calling them spoiled rich brats, and had striven from the first to isolate her from them. Amanda was too scared to talk to boys she had gone to school with because he was so jealous. She had seen her sister lose her bright and confident personality to the point where she couldn't make decisions about the most minor things.

Other friends of Amanda were called to the stand and all spoke of Jack Callaghan's jealousy and how Amanda had changed in the months she had been going out with him, becoming withdrawn and looking unhappy.

Only two people spoke for Jack after all those who had spoken against him. Don Reynish was a farmer with a love of mountaineering. He used to drink at The Mountaineer and had noticed the look of longing on the young Jack's face when he served beer to people discussing mountains they had just climbed.

Don had taken Jack on a few climbs and given him some basic training. He admitted Jack could be moody but did not believe him capable of the bullying described by the prosecution. If he had a few problems it was no wonder given his background, Don added before being curtly told by the prosecution lawyer that the court wasn't interested in his opinions.

The defence did not call Jack to testify. His lawyer spoke for him, doing an impressive job of undermining Amanda Wells. Far from being victimised she had, the lawyer said, used his inadequacies against him. She was not the angelic victim described by her family and friends but a girl who was sexually mature long before she met Jack Callaghan.

A young man, Jim Hensen, was called, to the obvious discomfort of the family, and he claimed to have been sexually involved with

Amanda right through her relationship with Jack Callaghan. The prosecution was unable to shake this witness who revealed, damningly for Amanda, that she had been in the habit of laughing with him over Jack's sexual inadequacies.

It had all come to a head one night when Jack had come home from work early after a row with his boss and had rung Amanda and asked her to meet him in town for a drink. They had met in a bar in central Christchurch where several people remembered hearing them arguing and seeing Amanda throwing her drink in his face before storming out into the night.

Next morning a cleaner found Amanda's body in an alleyway beside a hotel. She had been strangled and Jack Callaghan was arrested the same morning.

The subsequent discovery of a letter in his flat, written by Amanda to one of her friends, provided even more motive. No one ever found out just how Jack had got his hands on it but everyone agreed that the letter alone could have led to Amanda's death. The letter was intended for a girl she'd been at school with and it painted a cruel picture of Jack and his gauche manner accompanied by a description of a sexual encounter which made him look like a bumbling schoolboy.

There was no hard evidence and the case could have gone either way but the jury found him guilty. But Amanda's reputation had tarnished sufficiently to ensure that Jack went down for manslaughter not murder.

'What a story.' Julia looked appalled.

'So I think we can safely assume that Jack – aka Callum – told Penelope the whole thing and that's the secret she is terrified of. If he's killed one girlfriend there's all the more chance he killed another one when she got too stroppy for him to handle. Or that's what the police might think.'

'What do you think?'

I frowned. 'I'm not convinced. Callum was really young then and he was also really vulnerable. But he didn't meet Vivien till he'd done a good few years in prison and he'd have learned a hard lesson. I don't see him being stupid enough to get into another crime of passion scenario, do you?'

Julia didn't answer and we sat in silence for a few minutes.

Penelope knew and she sympathised with Callum. Hell, so did I. He'd been young, vulnerable and hurt. He was a victim himself.

Yet there was another side to him, a hardness that showed itself to virtually everyone who met him. Over at Mount Cook Bill Rogers had told me Callum had a chip on his shoulder. Vivien Revell had been so uneasy about him that she had planned to abort his child without telling him she was pregnant.

No, you couldn't say he was simply a wronged victim of middle class prejudices. He had once been angry enough to kill and who could say it hadn't happened again with Vivien?

But my gut feeling was that Callum Jackson would never have let a woman get close enough to hurt him again. I'd discovered his secret. I understood why his friend Penelope Blake was so afraid he would be suspected of Vivien's murder. But I couldn't really see that he had a motive to kill Vivien – let alone Rose.

Chapter 15

MARK left the next day and I wasn't sorry to see him go.
I hadn't told him what I had discovered about Callum. It
was nothing he couldn't have found out himself after all – he was the
reporter, not me. But he hadn't and I wasn't feeling public spirited
enough to give him a great story to run with. Not until I'd finished
with it myself. I wasn't exactly sure where it was going to lead me,
if anywhere, but I had to find out for myself.

I wondered if I should go and tell Stu Adams what I'd found
out. But surely the police would have known all along who Callum
Jackson really was? A changed name wouldn't be enough to keep a
convicted killer under their radar. They'd have been onto him with
a few clicks of a mouse button. And they hadn't arrested him. There
was no way I was going to rush into the Operation Ice base like a
demented girl-detective and blurt out my story.

I was in the paddock at the back of our house scattering wheat for
the chooks. It was a flat grey day, the mountains were obliterated
and even Spree had seemed depressed.

Mark's departure had been low key. We had made no arrangements to meet again any time soon and somehow there had never
been a moment to discuss where we were at with our on and off
relationship. Off, I supposed. This made me feel empty.

I stood still and watched my brother walking towards me.

'What are you doing today?' he asked.

'Work, I guess. Unless you can suggest something better. What
about you?'

'I don't know. Is there anything you want done round the house? Painting or something?'

Spree burst into view with an azalea bush in his mouth. I'd thought his gardening days were over but apparently they were not. I'd particularly liked that plant with its distinctive orange flowers, and I wondered if it would recover from the shock.

'Why don't you start with a little gardening,' I said.

Tom wrestled the plant out of Spree's mouth and, collecting a spade from the shed, took it off for replanting.

I went inside thinking about my recent discoveries. Amanda Wells had mocked Callum's sexuality and ended up dead. What if Vivien had done the same thing? Love didn't have to be involved. Callum could have taken all the care in the world not to let himself be vulnerable to a woman ever again only to be undone by sex.

Vivien must have been an emotional wreck before she died. She had caught her mother in bed with her former lover; she was pregnant and unhappy about it. A decision to have an abortion wouldn't have been easy.

Maybe she had been trying to justify her decision in her own mind by trying to push Callum into proving he was as bad for her as she wanted him to be. Say he had sexual hang ups from his relationship with Amanda. Vivien had been worldly. What if they'd gone up the glacier together that day and she had started taunting him about his sexual performance – and thus caused him to lose his temper and kill her? Callum had been in the glacier valley late on the day she disappeared. Looking for her, he said. Or maybe trying to cover up what he'd done.

Tom joined me in the kitchen.

'Your plant doesn't look too damaged. It might survive Spree's efforts.'

I laughed. 'It's worth a try. Tom, let's do something together today. We haven't had a decent talk since you got back.'

'Sounds good. What do you want to do?'

'I don't know. Go out for brunch?'

We drove up to the village and settled in at Ice Rocks. I glanced at him mopping up the remains of an egg with a corner of toast. I'd just eaten a large helping of pancakes. We'd chatted about trivia. I'd reacquainted him with stuff that was happening in the village.

'So what is the story with you and Mark?' he asked.

'Oh you know – wanting different things, not being able to sort it out,' I said vaguely.

He didn't look satisfied with this answer so I launched into a description of the messy relationship I'd rebounded into after Mark and I had split up. With the brother of a murder victim. My brother was suitably impressed – though not in a good way.

'No wonder you and Mark are on eggshells. I'm amazed he wants to be anywhere near you,' he said.

I laughed. 'He came to Franz to cover a murder, not to hang out with me.'

'And where was the first place he went to? Ours. He must still have some feelings for you.'

'For his sake I hope that's not true. Nothing has changed. I like him – hell he's still in my system – but we want different things and that's never going to change. Mark wants a family. I don't.'

Tom sipped his coffee. 'Yeah. I understand where you're coming from there. I don't think you'll change your mind either.'

I was surprised by his perception. 'Maybe I took more notice of our parents than I realised. They were not exactly role models for family life.'

'I know you won't agree with this Philippa but I think our father did a brilliant job considering how wrong it all was for him.'

'What? Us, you mean? Well if Liam didn't want kids why have three of us? He couldn't have it both ways.'

'He stuck with us all – just escaped into his dreams every now and then.'

'Yes and really harmless that turned out to be – falling off a mountain and taking our mother with him. I'm sorry Tom but I'm not as forgiving as you.'

'No, but then you were the one who stayed home and picked up the pieces. It's been easier for me Philippa – and I want you to know I appreciate what you've done. I mean that. All I'm saying is that I understand where he was coming from. Because essentially I'm very like him.'

'Yes, well you haven't made the mistake of having three kids and then deciding you would rather have a life of adventure! Have there been any women in your life?'

'A couple, but I kept things really casual. I don't want to be tied down. I met a girl in Cornwall who was different though – she could have got under my skin and I'm glad I didn't hang around long enough to let it happen.'

'So what did happen?'

'I need more coffee if we're going to discuss this!' Tom went and ordered more flat whites, while I rested my chin in my hands and stared out the window. There were a lot of tourists around today.

'Her name's Rachel,' Tom said. 'She works in a surf shop near St Ives. She got me out on the water and we had a good time together. She's pretty unconventional. She's fun and stroppy. Doesn't know where she's going in life and reckons as long as there are good waves to ride she doesn't care. She'd probably have come back to New Zealand with me if I'd asked her but I didn't. I don't want to drag someone to the other side of the world just because of me. I didn't want to be under any sort of obligation. So I told her I might see her again one day and left.'

'What did she think of that?'

Tom shrugged. 'She didn't say a lot.'

I laughed. 'You and I are a right pair, aren't we? What are you going to do with yourself now you are home?'

'Hang around Franz for a while. I like being here. And I've got my carpentry ticket. I might pick up some work with any luck.'

'It'll be easy for you to get a job,' I said. 'There's quite a lot of building going on here right now.'

'Yes – I was wondering if it would be worth talking to Callum Jackson too. There could be some building work going on somewhere in the park. Philippa, do you seriously think he could have killed Rose Revell? And Vivien?'

I had avoided telling him about my trip to Mount Cook but there was no real reason to hold out on him. So I described what had happened that day and Julia's and my subsequent discovery of Callum's past crime.

Tom was astonished. And concerned.

'If you are right you should be a lot more careful,' he said. 'If he's killed three women already what's to stop him doing the same to you?'

...

Tom's words had got to me though I tried not to let them. Of course Callum Jackson might be dangerous, but if he was that much of a threat why hadn't he done something long ago? I could easily imagine him being the person who had left that horrible sketch of Spree on our doorstep – but try as I might, I couldn't really believe he had attacked Kate.

My brother hadn't been convinced by this argument.

'Why should what happened to Kate be connected with Rose Revell's murder? The police clearly don't think so,' he argued.

'Well there is the small detail that whoever attacked her told her it was a warning for me to lay off.'

Tom looked at me. 'Kate was terrified. She could have heard wrong.'

I shook my head but I couldn't be bothered arguing.

'I'm going for a run,' I said.

I needed to get away from him and I also needed to be moving – it didn't stop me thinking but it did help. I spun out of our driveway at a fast pace, Spree at my heels. We jogged along the road and then up onto the river bank. I gazed at the mountains as I ran along the edge of the stopbank. There was a refreshing breeze coming off the water. A wood pigeon swooped from the branches of a rimu tree and Spree jumped so wildly to avoid it that he nearly tumbled off the bank. I laughed.

Bloody Tom. Thanks to him I was starting to feel worried. I thought of Penelope's face as she had watched Lisa and me coming in to land after our trip to Mount Cook. What if she'd told Callum? He was hardly likely to have forgotten seeing me with the painting of The Mountaineer. If he'd then found out that I'd been over at Mount Cook he could easily think I'd found out about his past. And if he had, what would he do?

The appearance of a small herd of Hereford cattle took my mind off murder and I grabbed Spree by the collar and clipped his lead back on. The cattle were in good condition. I absorbed the pungent cow smell and listened to the slap of tails and click of hooves on the road.

Jem Brown was walking behind them, a rust-coloured dog at his heels. I scrambled down off the stopbank towing a reluctant Spree behind me. He didn't like big animals. Jem's cattle dog gave him a contemptuous look. As usual Jem looked as if he'd dressed from the rag bag. His old corduroy trousers were patched incongruously with some pink floral print material, and tufts of wool surrounded the many holes in his grey homespun jersey. He walked slowly, scanning the road ahead for approaching traffic, while his dog worked without instruction keeping the herd together.

'Good day for it,' I greeted Jem.

'Yep – not many cars around. Most people are pretty good though. Had a tourist stop and take a whole lot of photos last time I did this. Came here to see the glacier and ended up wasting time photographing an old man and his cows.'

I smiled. 'You could end up in a book on country life.'

Jem snorted. 'Why aren't you working today, lass?'

'There was hardly anyone for the glacier today and Sara's taken them.'

'How's young Kate?'

'She's doing really well. I think what happened to her is connected with Rose Revell's death - and the fact that Julia's talked me into trying out my amateur detective skills. But my brother doesn't agree and neither do the police. Apparently.'

'You never know – but they're playing it close to their chests. Stu Adams won't even talk to Angie's husband. Or so he says. Course he might just be telling Angie that – wouldn't blame him.'

'That's a bit hard, Jem.'

'Well Angie talks, you know.'

'And you don't?'

'I'm a bit more careful than she is,' he said.

I stared at him, amused. Angie would be furious if she heard him saying that – with good cause. There was very little to choose between the pair of them when it came to the efficient distribution of information throughout the community.

'I don't think the police believe that Vivien was murdered either,' I said. 'Jem did you notice anything strange around the time Vivien disappeared?'

'Just Penelope Blake. But she's always been a bit odd.'

'Why? What did she do?'

'What you do yourself, young Philippa – a lot of walking.'

I stared at him. 'What's so strange about that?'

'She was out at all hours and in all weathers – never looked happy either. In fact she looked like hell. I saw her doing it years before but there was a reason for it way back then. She was trapped in an unhappy marriage. But can't have been him this time – he was long dead.

'What did you think of Patrick Blake?'

'Bloody skite,' Jem said succinctly.

'What about Callum Jackson?'

'Do you think it's him? Jem looked interested.

'He and Vivien were in some kind of relationship. They'd had a row just before she disappeared. And he was seen coming out of the glacier valley late on the night she vanished.'

Jem looked at me for a moment and I could see he'd made some kind of connection.

'And you reckon Penelope might have known he'd done it? Could be. They're thick as thieves,' he said.

It was something to think about. Penelope knew about Callum's past. If he'd killed Vivien had he confided in her again? Unless he was totally callous he would have been tortured with guilt – and maybe he'd sought to ease his conscience by telling his old confidante Penelope Blake. It would have presented her with a dilemma. She liked Callum while she disliked Vivien. She had supported him and told no one of his past.

But surely if he had then confessed to another murder she wouldn't have covered that up? If she had, she must have been tortured by the knowledge. So maybe she had taken to restless walking to try and ease the burden on her conscience.

Then she would have had to stand by and watch when Rose Revell had somehow worked it out – and been killed. And Callum must have descended further into hell. Dragging Penelope down with him.

Chapter 16

Tom was cooking dinner when I got back and a bottle of red wine sat breathing on the table. I sniffed appreciatively. Lasagne. One of my favourites. Once it went into the oven he poured us each a large glass of wine and we retreated to the living room. Even if I did get irritated with him sometimes, it was still good to have him back. We had not seen each other for years and yet we'd clicked back into an easy relationship. Despite the occasional disagreement.

It's funny how you can miss the obvious things when you're close to people. I had never realised just how alike he and our father had been. What he'd said about Liam the other night made sense to me and even though I had had argued with him at the time I knew he was right. Our father had never wanted family ties. I'd never seen that – just criticised him for being so irresponsible.

I sighed.

Tom looked up from his book and put his glass on the arm of his chair.

'What's wrong?'

'Nothing really. I'm just thinking about what you said about Liam the other night – and it makes me realise I'm not as perceptive as I think I am. Maybe I should just leave everything to the police. I seem to be getting out of my depth with all of this stuff and I've no way of proving anything.'

I told him about my meeting with Jem and what he'd said about Penelope Blake. He hesitated for a moment then said.

'I don't know if I should tell you this Philippa because it probably means nothing – but Penelope may have had her own motive for murdering Vivien Revell.'

'What do you mean?'

'Maybe it's a bit far-fetched – and I can't see any reason why she would have killed Rose all these years later. But she could have found out that Vivien and Patrick once had a fling.'

'You aren't serious? How on earth do you know that?'

Tom lifted a hand. 'I don't know for sure. It's just something I saw. The two of them – together, I mean. I saw her coming out of his house one night when Liam was driving me home from somewhere. Then I saw them out walking a few times.'

'When was this?' I asked.

'Years before Vivien died. I think it was the time that Penelope was overseas. Vivien would've only been a kid herself when I think about it. She must have still been at high school.'

'No one's ever suggested anything like this. Not even Jem or Angie - and they know everything that goes on in this village. How on earth did they get away with it? I don't get it – she was what – sixteen? And he must have been in his sixties!'

Tom sipped his wine and shrugged. 'Yeah – an old man and a schoolgirl. It was pretty creepy when you think about it.'

It was more than creepy. It was unbelievable. And yet it could explain why Vivien had decided to write her thesis on mountaineering. If she really had been in love with Patrick Blake she may have wanted to understand more of the world he had lived in. Patrick had died while she was at university so she had needed Penelope's permission to look at his papers. It could have been a way of helping her deal with the loss his death had caused her.

But then she had started finding out some disturbing things about him. Like his high number of climbing accidents. And worst of all, his affair with Janet Lestrange which had ended with her death in the mountains. That had happened while Penelope was overseas – so it must have been going on while Vivien herself was involved with Patrick.

No wonder Vivien was so traumatised just before her disappearance. Patrick Blake sounded like a total bastard. It was a shame he wasn't the one who had ended up murdered.

But it was hard to believe. This was Franz Josef, a small insular world where everyone knew everyone else's secrets. And if they didn't, Jem Brown or Angie Bennett would soon fill them in. Yet here was Patrick Blake having simultaneous affairs with a local schoolgirl and a climbing client and getting away with it.

So what must it have been like for Vivien Revell, forced into daily contact with Patrick's widow while she was doing her research? He'd probably blackened Penelope's name to get her to sleep with him in the first place, using that pathetic misunderstood husband line. Given Penelope's reserved character it would have been easy for Patrick to convince a young woman who had the misfortune to be in love with him.

So Vivien hadn't liked Penelope – and she would not have liked what she was discovering about Patrick either. But maybe she had never got over her feelings for him and thus didn't want to write an exposé book about his controversial actions in the mountains.

Suppose everything had got a bit much for her one day and she had told Penelope about her affair with Patrick? She could have gloated about it if she'd been anything like her mother Rose.

How would Penelope have reacted to the news? Calmly on the surface, I suspected, but it could just have been one betrayal too many. No wonder she'd spoken so coldly of Vivien and no wonder she so bitterly regretted the wasted years of her marriage.

It would have been too late to seek any retribution from her husband. He was dead. But there was Vivien – alive and symbolising all the youth and opportunity Penelope had thrown away. Had Penelope lured Vivien up onto the glacier that day so she could kill her? She was a strong fit woman, and back then she would have been in her prime. She was experienced on ice; Vivien was not. Once she'd pushed her into a crevasse Penelope could have walked off down the glacier and left her, confident she would never get out alive.

Everything had pointed to it being Callum, especially after I'd discovered his true identity. Maybe I'd been looking at everything the wrong way round. Penelope hadn't been protecting Callum – he'd been protecting her. She'd helped him come to terms with his own past and he felt that he owed her. That could be why he had gone up the glacier valley that night. Penelope must have told him what she'd done and so he went up there to make sure Vivien hadn't escaped after all.

I shivered, imagining him despatching her with a couple of well-placed blows with his ice axe. He must have been relieved not to find her. Vivien dead from an apparent accident in the icefall was infinitely preferable to Vivien obviously murdered under everyone's nose at the glacier terminal.

It must have been a huge relief to Callum and Penelope when everyone assumed that Vivien had gone overseas. One of them must have broken into her house and taken a few of her things and her passport to make it look like she had left Franz. They must have realised that Vivien would resurface one day but they would have known it probably wouldn't happen for years and that when it did everyone would assume she had gone up on the glacier alone and had an accident.

What they hadn't factored in was Julia, the friend who was certain it couldn't have happened that way and thus jumped to the conclusion that Vivien must have been murdered. That must have caused them a few uneasy days until they realised the police weren't interested and the only person on their trail was me.

I knew just how Callum felt about that. Contemptuous.

But Penelope was still worried, scared that his previous conviction for the manslaughter of Amanda Wells would come out – and scared that this would somehow lead to the discovery of her own crime.

No wonder Penelope had sounded so convincing when she had told me that Callum hadn't killed Vivien. She was being truthful. He hadn't – but she had. And somehow Rose had worked it out. It was possible she had known about her daughter's affair with Patrick

Blake. Julia had told me that Rose and Vivien had been more like sisters than mother and daughter and if so they probably talked quite openly about their love lives – until Rose had started sleeping with Luke, Vivien's ex. That had been too much for Vivien.

You'd think a mother would have been outraged about her teenage daughter having an affair with a man in his sixties but Rose wasn't your average mother.

No wonder she hadn't been afraid to confront Penelope. She must have felt nothing but contempt for her. It wouldn't have been hard to get Penelope round to her house to talk. Then she must have told Penelope what she knew and realised too late what a dangerous thing she was doing when Penelope attacked her with her own ice axe.

Penelope wouldn't have been worried about leaving traces of herself at the crime scene. She could easily claim to have visited Rose during the day or any time, and no one could have disproved it. But she knew her fingerprints would be all over the ice axe so she'd taken it away with her. I wondered what she'd done with the axe. It was probably sitting unmolested in her shed. I wouldn't mind betting that the police didn't have the effrontery to search her place and removing offending ice axes. They'd had no problem taking mine though.

...

Angie was doing the accounts when I arrived at work next morning, frowning at a spreadsheet on her computer. Thank goodness Tim hadn't left me with that little task.

'Callum Jackson's after you,' she greeted me. 'Says you haven't submitted your report.'

I sighed. 'Yes I know. I guess I'd better do it today to get him off my case. I'll just go and get a coffee. D'you want one?'

'I could murder one,' Angie said.

As I walked to Ice Rocks I thought about Penelope Blake, wondering if my theory could be right and what I should do about it. I couldn't see the police wanting to know and I didn't feel like making an idiot of myself trying to persuade them. I had no proof. And I wasn't game to confront her myself. If the woman had killed both Vivien and Rose I'd have to have a death wish to put myself in her way.

Perhaps I should talk to Julia and get her to come with me to tackle Penelope. She couldn't attack us both. But she wasn't likely to crack and admit to anything either.

I passed Luke Riley on the road. He flushed as he caught sight of me and turned away – but not before I saw the expression on his face. He looked terrible. His eyes were red as if he'd been crying and he somehow looked older than he had just a few days before.

As I passed the church I noticed a familiar figure marching up its bush-lined path, a large bucket of flowers on one arm. Penelope Blake. I walked on after her, not sure what I was going to do. But as I turned the iron ring to open the heavy black door it occurred to me that this wouldn't be a bad place to tackle her. I left the door wide open behind me and if she turned psychotic with her bucket of flowers or a brass candlestick I could run.

Rose hadn't been prepared – but I was. And surely she wouldn't attack me in a church?

Penelope was removing dead flowers out of the vases on either side of the altar cross. She looked surprised to see me standing in the aisle. I glanced past her out the picture window to the mountains. It was an incongruous place to be thinking of murder.

'I just came in here to look at the mountains,' I lied.

'Yes – it's good that there's still somewhere in this village that hasn't been corrupted with tourism.'

Penelope put down her bucket and I looked uneasily at her strong hands. The glacier, once a centrepiece of the altar window, had slipped out of sight as it retreated but the view was still spectacular. Penelope stood beside me, seeming thoroughly at home beside the cross, chalice and other trappings of Anglican worship.

This was as good a chance as I was going to get.

'I wanted to talk to you, Penelope. I think you killed Vivien and Rose Revell.'

She turned sharply to face me. Her expression was unreadable but something flared briefly in her eyes.

'Why should you think that?' Her voice was quiet.

'I've been looking at everything the wrong way round. I thought you were protecting Callum – but he's been protecting you.'

Penelope gazed at me. Her eyes were the same grey as the river that flowed out of the glacier – and they were just as opaque.

'You tried to warn me. It was you who left that awful drawing of Spree at our house, wasn't it Penelope? I thought it was Callum.'

Penelope looked surprised and it seemed genuine. 'What on earth are you talking about? What drawing?'

I told her and she looked shocked.

'I would never have done such a thing! Kate might have found it. I would never do anything to hurt that child. She's been through enough already. Too much, Philippa, and I blame you for some of it. Do you have any idea how sensitive she actually is? You are doing your best to get her involved in something that is absolutely none of your business here in Franz. And has it occurred to you that she might have been attacked because of your activities? Has it?'

I took a step backwards from Penelope's sudden anger. It abated as quickly as it had come leaving me shaken and unsure what to do next.

'So why do you think I murdered the Revells?' she asked in a perfectly normal voice. 'Vivien's death was a major inconvenience for me. She left me with the book project undone. I was furious with her.'

'There are some things worse than inconvenience. Like the discovery that Vivien once had an affair with your husband.'

Penelope stared at me for a moment and then she did something entirely unexpected. She screamed with laughter. It sounded mad – but it also sounded genuine. She gripped the edge of a pew for support and eventually subsided, tears rolling down her cheeks.

'Poor old Patrick. He did many bad things, but to be accused of this! Oh it's too funny for words. May God forgive me for losing control in church but you, Philippa Barnes, have given me the best laugh I've had in years.'

'I wasn't trying to,' I muttered. 'But Penelope, it happened when you were in Europe. Tom – my brother – has just come home and he saw them together. Maybe you just didn't know?'

'The only thing I know is that it didn't happen,' she said. 'Now, I have a church to clean, so if you'd just let me get on with it I'd appreciate it.' Penelope shook her head and I saw laughter threatening to well up again.

I retreated down the aisle and into the sunlight feeling really stupid. Thank goodness I hadn't gone to the police. Bloody Tom. I was going to kill him. I was probably the only person in the world who had been laughed out of church, I thought gloomily.

Still, maybe this was the shock I needed. I'd been so busy enthusiastically chasing the wrong trail that I'd forgotten all about Luke Riley. If anyone had a motive he did – for both murders. Vivien had been sleeping around on him, and Rose seemed to enjoy baiting him about his affair with her. I'd seen her do it myself at Vivien's memorial service. Rose had given him an alibi for the day of Vivien's death and maybe she was about to tell the police she'd lied. She wouldn't have been scared to taunt Luke with what she was about to do. She'd been so dismissive of him. What had she said about him? That he was delightful but had no common sense. I had heard her telling him they needed to talk at Vivien's memorial service – and it hadn't sounded friendly.

Luke had looked like hell when I'd seen him just before. No wonder. If he was the one who'd hacked Rose Revell to death he must be feeling terrible. It had been so brutal and unless the killer had no heart or conscience they would have to have been badly affected by it.

Both Callum and Luke were showing signs of strain but Penelope was cleaning the church apparently completely at peace with herself. She'd been happy to air her husband's dirty linen. He was long dead while she was still alive. She'd ridiculed Tom's theory. She couldn't be the killer. I needed to put more effort in to being a good glacier guide. Because I was a hopeless amateur detective.

...

I spent the rest of the day industriously writing my report for the Department of Conservation. It was a struggle. There was a lot of stuff I'd have liked to put in there but I didn't need Angie to tell me I needed to be damned careful what I put down on paper. We were the concessionaire; DOC decided what we could and couldn't do in the glacier valley. It wasn't a relationship of equals. The very thought made me cross and blunted my prose.

A few hours later I was ready to throw Tim's computer at the wall. I glanced at Angie who was giving her terminal an equally unfriendly look.

'Time for a drink?'

'Good idea,' she said.

Once we were established in Ice Rocks, things started to look better. Angie was curious about Tom and had his life story out of me in half an hour.

'You should be leading the murder investigation, not the police,' I told her. 'You'd have a result in a week.'

She laughed. We had tried to see what was going on as we passed the Operation Ice base but there was no obvious sign of activity. There were still a lot of police there, and Rose's house was still a taped-off crime scene, but the media didn't have anything new to report.

After a while all the others began to drift in to Ice Rocks. Matt with yet another woman he'd met on the glacier. Jem with one of his farming mates. Sara on her own. She came and joined us and we had a good session on DOC and its many faults. It was a familiar theme and while complaining solved nothing it made us all feel better about things.

As I cycled home I thought about Julia, realising that she had gone awfully quiet. I wondered if she had gone back to Wellington. Surely she would have told me?

Kate and Sally were planted in front of the television when I got home, Spree sprawled in front of them like a furry black rug. I had a shower and emerged to find Sally gone and my brother and sister chatting like two old friends.

They had really taken to one another. It had amazed me to see how strong their connection was, given that they had hardly seen one another since Kate was a toddler. While Kate and I clashed, our personalities combative, her relationship with Tom was so much easier. I'd heard him suggesting things about her homework that would have had her screaming defiance at me, yet she'd quietly gone off and done what he suggested.

I'd thought our life was easier without my brother being around. How wrong I had been. After Tom, Kate and I had dinner and he disappeared for a drink in the village, I rang Julia. She didn't seem wildly thrilled to hear from me.

'I thought you might have gone back to Wellingon,' I said.

'No. Actually my mother's gone up there for a few days to stay in my house and do some shopping. So I am alone looking after things for her here.'

She listened in silence to my tale of my encounter with Penelope in the church.

'Is something wrong, Julia?' I asked after a long pause.

She sighed. 'I'm sorry – it's just that I've had an awful day and I don't know how much more I can take in. It's Luke. He came to see me today and he's in a real mess.'

'I saw him in the village,' I said. 'He looked terrible. What's wrong?'

'Jenny's left him. And she's taken Emma. Things have been bad for ages apparently but he didn't think she would actually leave. Well she has – she's gone back to her family in Dunedin.'

'What does he expect you to do about it?'

'I don't really know,' Julia said slowly. 'He's doing lots of soul searching – and he's pretty depressed about what he's finding. He kept going on about what a success I'd made of my life while all he'd done was cause trouble for everyone he'd come in contact with. He's come up with the idea that I might be able to help him get custody of Emma.'

'That's ridiculous. You're not a lawyer.'

'I know – that's what I told him. But he's got this idea that I must have all sorts of useful contacts in my great life in the city! I know he's being stupid. But he's desperate, Philippa. He really does love his daughter. She's his world.'

I couldn't argue with that.

'What else did he talk about?' I asked.

'He actually talked quite a lot about Vivien. Told me I should let the whole thing go – that she wasn't worth it, that she'd never been a real friend, that I shouldn't let her spoil my life. Stuff like that. Look Philippa, I'm too tired to think about it all now. Let's catch up tomorrow and we'll have a proper talk.'

What about? I wondered as I put down the phone. Julia was holding out on me. I was sure of it.

Her appearance next day did nothing to make me change my mind. She looked as bad as Luke had. She was pale and her eyes looked tired but there was more to it than that. She looked apathetic – and old.

'Are you going up the glacier this afternoon?' she greeted me.

'No. I've just got back. I'm going to clean the boots and wash the socks then go home.'

'Do you have time for a coffee?'

'Why not?' I carried an armload of boots through the office and dumped them on the counter. 'I'll just get this stuff out of the way and then we can go. Have you had lunch?'

Julia shrugged. 'I'm not hungry.'

'Well I am,' I said. 'Running up and down the glacier does that to you.'

Half an hour later Julia sat nursing her coffee, watching me eating a panini.

'What are you thinking about?' I asked after a long silence.

'Philippa, I don't know how to say this to you. But I want you to stop investigating Vivien's death.'

I stared at her, a forkful of panini half way to my mouth.

'You – what did you just say? Is this because I got things wrong with Penelope?'

'No! It has nothing to do with that. You're not the one who's got things wrong. I am. I should never have started interfering. If I'd kept my mouth shut none of this would have happened. Rose wouldn't have been killed. Kate wouldn't have been attacked.'

'How can you know that? The police think Rose's death has nothing to do with Vivien's. Are you telling me Vivien's death was an accident after all?'

'No.' Julia put down her coffee mug and met my angry gaze without flinching. 'Vivien was murdered. But I shouldn't have tried to play God.'

'You know who did it – don't you?'

Her eyes shied away from me and she flushed. 'Maybe. Yes, I think I do. But I'm not sure, Philippa.'

'*I'm* not sure I'm hearing things right.' I was angry and had to struggle to keep my voice down. 'You think you know who murdered Vivien – and you've decided they should get away with it. If that's not playing God I don't know what is, Julia.'

She looked wretched but she didn't reply.

'So how have you worked it all out? Did Luke confess to you when you were having your little heart-to-heart yesterday?'

'Of course not! It's me who is the problem, not him. I've caused so much damage and I have to put it right with the person who matters.'

'Julia, Vivien was your friend. Her death has caused you untold suffering. So how can you possibly sympathise with her killer? It's Luke, isn't it? This is what it's all about. He's the only person you care about enough to try and cover for. You owe him nothing Julia. He doesn't care about you - and he never will.'

She winced and I felt mean.

'It wasn't anything Luke actually said,' she said after a moment. 'It was after he left that I realised. I couldn't settle to anything so I got up into the attic to look at some of stuff that Mum had stored up there. I was looking through some old papers when it came to me. Philippa, I don't exactly sympathise with Vivien's killer. But I understand. It would have been all down to Vivien in the end, down to the way she dealt with things. I think she died because of something she said but it would have been unintentional, that's the horrible thing. An unintentional act of cruelty.'

'You're talking in riddles.'

'Yes I know – and I'm sorry. Sorry that I involved you, but it has to stop now. I had it so wrong. If the police get to Vivien's killer through Rose's murder, that's one thing. But I don't want it to be down to me.'

'So it was the same person who killed Vivien and Rose?'

'Oh yes. It had to be, didn't it? Rose was the only person who knew.'

'And now you know as well and you've decided it's all okay? So are you going to talk to a killer pledging your undying understanding? Get real, Julia.'

She stood up. 'I don't know what I'm going to do. I'll talk to you later, Philippa.'

It took far too long for the sense of déjà vu to kick in. Like I said I'm a lousy amateur detective.

...

Rose Revell had made a date with the killer and she hadn't lived to tell the tale. What if Julia tried the same approach, thinking it was all going to be fine because she understood and sympathised with the killer's motive? How bloody naïve was she?

It was nearly ten o'clock at night and Tom had gone to bed early while I, wide awake, tried to concentrate on reading a book. Kate was in her room but I was pretty sure she wouldn't be sleeping. Now that her sign-stealing career was over she was back to her life as a night owl, reading till all hours.

What was Julia up to?

I picked up the phone and called her number. There was no reply though I let it ring for a long time.

I pictured the old farmhouse, set well back from the road and screened by a tall hedge of trees. It was a lonely place.

My mind started to race as I grabbed my car keys and let myself out into the night. Surely Julia hadn't been stupid enough to invite the killer round there for an evening chat? I flooded the engine in my haste to get started, only succeeded in waking Tom who appeared at the doorway looking bewildered.

'What the hell are you doing, Philippa?'

'Julia's in trouble,' I yelled and he ran across the yard in his shorts, pulling a tshirt over his head.

'What are you talking about?' Tom got into the passenger seat.

The car started and I tried to tell him what I was thinking as we took off into the night.

'You're not making any sense,' my brother told me.

I ignored him, leaning forward over the steering wheel and willing myself to be wrong.

But as I turned into Julia's driveway a car appeared from behind the hedge and swerved to get past us, its headlights on high beam.

Tom swore and I hit the brakes and leaped out of the car, grabbing the torch as I went.

'Julia! Julia!' I yelled.

There was no reply.

I shone the light around and froze as I saw what lay in front of me.

Julia was sprawled on the ground just outside the front door. She was not moving and there was a large pool of blood under her head. I felt her pulse. She was still alive.

But she didn't look like she was going to stay that way for much longer.

Chapter 17

I don't recall much about what happened after that. The night was a blur of light. Headlights of police cars, headlights of the ambulance. And the screaming of sirens. And questions. So many questions.

'So here you are at another crime scene, Ms Barnes.'

Detective Inspector Jimmy Black did not sound pleased to see me, but I was past caring. Julia was going to die. I hadn't been smart enough to save her. I wondered dully if hell could be much worse than this.

The Operation Ice base was buzzing. Lights blared, computer keys clicked, and multiple phone conversations were going on. DI Black and DC Elliott were facing me across the interview room table and I felt like a possum in the headlights.

'Is Julia still alive?' I asked.

DI Black looked tired. 'Yes as far as we know. She's on the way to Christchurch Hospital. You saved her life getting to her when you did. If she'd been left lying there all night she would certainly be dead. Are you able to tell me what happened?'

I told him everything.

'So Julia McLoughlin told you she knew who had killed Rose Revell? And Vivien Revell?'

This was the first time anyone from the police had acknowledged the possibility that Vivien's death might not have been accidental. I should have felt vindicated but I didn't feel anything much.

'Yes,' I said, 'but she wouldn't tell me who it was. Just like Rose – and it took me too bloody long to realise what was going to happen.'

'Why didn't you come to us when you did?' DI Black asked.

'I panicked. I didn't think of anything except the need to get to Julia's place fast.'

'Can you recall exactly what Julia said when she told you she knew who this killer was?'

I told him and he listened in silence.

'I was going to talk to you before Julia was attacked. I'd found out about Callum Jackson but I thought you'd know all that anyway.'

'What did you find out?' His voice was sharp.

I told him of my trip to Mount Cook and my discovery of Callum's identity. As I finished he was shaking his head slightly, but he was smiling slightly. 'We underestimated you,' he said.

DI Black stood up then and escorted me to the door.

'You've given us a lot to think about. And you've saved your friend's life. You've done well, Philippa – but leave it to us now, okay?'

I stared at him without replying. Leave it now? No bloody way!

...

I drove over to Christchurch the next day, insisting to Tom that I was fine to do this on my own. I needed the space even if he didn't. Tom could look after Kate and Spree. And I needed to see Julia for myself.

I hadn't been to the city since the devastating earthquake a month or so before and at first the place seemed just the same. It wasn't until I'd driven down some of the streets and seen collapsed fences, houses missing walls or roofs, and the liquefaction in the streets that I gained some appreciation of the scale of it all. This impression was enhanced as I drove closer to the central city and saw all the rubble-filled sections where tall buildings had once stood.

So many people had died while we'd had an ordinary day in Franz taking tourists up the glacier.

Soon after this my discovery of Vivien's body had driven all thoughts of Christchurch out of my mind. Seeing the after effects was a shock. Christchurch had been nothing if not stable and now it was a different place.

Hospitals are the same wherever you find them though. The same bustle, the same smell, the same look of fear in people's eyes. I slowed down as I got closer to intensive care. I didn't really want to see Julia but I had to do it.

Ann McLoughlin met me by the nurse's station. She looked older. Her eyes were red, her face tightly drawn, her hair untidy. She hugged me.

'Has she …?' I couldn't finish my sentence.

'No. She's still unconscious.' Ann took my hand and led me through a curtain wall to Julia's bed.

I tried not to flinch as I looked at her dead-looking face, at the tubes and monitors, at the white nothingness of the cubicle she was in.

'What do the doctors say?' I whispered.

'They're telling me not to lose hope but they don't know how long she'll be in a coma. It's hard, just waiting.' Ann's voice faltered but she braced herself and when she next spoke her voice was steady. 'The police are not far away. They want to talk to her, of course.'

'At least she's safe here,' I said, thinking about the fact that there was someone in Franz who wanted to kill her, someone who must be feeling very worried right now.

Oh God – if she died. My mind closed on the thought and I swayed slightly. Ann touched my arm and led me to a chair. We sat side by side for a while looking at Julia. Nothing changed.

'So tell me what happened, Philippa.' Ann said. 'The police have told me the basics but I need to hear the whole story.'

I told Ann everything, keeping my voice low so Julia wouldn't be able to hear if, by some remote chance, she was still with us. She certainly didn't look as if she was. I shivered. Death would be infinitely preferable to living with brain damage. My intervention could prove to be an abomination.

'Would you mind if I had a look in your attic when I get home?' I asked Ann. 'Julia said she made the connection after going through some of her old stuff there.'

Ann looked concerned. 'Don't you think you should leave that to the police?'

'Probably – but they didn't know Julia and I do. I have to do something Ann. I feel so responsible.'

'Well you're not. Get that idea right out of your head. I don't blame you, and Julia wouldn't either. She made her own decisions – unfortunately. The police will have scoured the place but you're welcome to have a look if they have finished their investigations. But please be careful. We don't want any more attacks.'

I left soon after, giving Julia a scared final glance as I went. If she died... But I wasn't going to think about that. I rang Mark instead, not sure what kind of reception I'd get, but he sounded pleased to hear from me and invited me to stay with him. As I didn't feel like jumping back in the car for a five hour drive to Franz I was happy to agree.

We arranged to meet at an Italian café in one of the suburbs. There was nowhere to go in the central city any more. The more I saw of Christchurch the worse it seemed to get. After visiting Julia in intensive car, driving round the shattered city didn't exactly cheer me up

Mark was late and I was glad to have some time to collect my thoughts over a glass of red wine. I was starving and got stuck into pizza bread as I waited. The café was noisy and it felt good after the antiseptic silence of the hospital.

Mark arrived looking hassled and I nudged the wine bottle in his direction. He poured a large glass and leaned back in his chair with a sigh. He hadn't tried to touch me and I was glad and annoyed at the same time.

'Are you okay?' he asked.

I laughed. 'Yes, I'm feeling on top of the world. How about you?'

He grimaced. 'Okay – stupid question. But I don't know what to say to you, Philippa.'

'There's not a lot to say. Things are about as bad as they could be and there's no point talking about it. I've just been to see Julia, Mark. She looks bloody awful.' I filled him in on everything over our meal and then we went back to his place.

I hadn't seen his house for a long time and I was impressed. It was an old weatherboard cottage in a section of well-established shrubs. There was a big magnolia tree at the back of the garden, a cluster of azaleas near his patio and two lancewoods and a few other natives near the back door. He'd painted the house grey and restored its wooden window frames which were painted a dark shade of crimson.

Inside was pleasant – comfortable old furniture, polished wood floors, lots of book shelves and a new-looking computer and printer set up in the corner of the lounge.

'You were really slumming it at my place,' I remarked as he handed me a glass of wine.

'Only with your internet connection. Otherwise your place is brilliant.' Mark smiled at me. 'I can't compete.'

He was right. I looked out at mountains; he looked out at the neighbour's fence. I maintained a tactful silence. It felt unnatural. Mark glanced at me, then got up from the couch and disappeared into the kitchen. I was left to look around his living room. It had a pleasant lived-in feel and I stretched out in my chair and relaxed, fingers curled round the stem of my wine glass.

'Tell me about what you've been up to,' I said when he came back into the room. 'I am seriously over my own life. Tell me about yours.'

He walked to the window and looked out, giving me the chance to admire his back view. He was actually damned good to look at – tall with broad shoulders and an athletic stride. It was hard to believe he earned his living at a computer terminal. He had the build of a mountaineer even though he did nothing more physical than the occasional run round the park.

'My life's been all about the earthquake.' He turned to face me. 'It wrecked our offices and gave us more stories than we'd dreamed of – right here in our own back yard.'

'Did you know anyone who died?'

'Yeah a few – no one close – just people I knew through work. And one of my mother's oldest friends.'

I hadn't asked him any of this stuff when he'd been at Franz and I felt ashamed of my former self-absorption.

'It must have been terrible. It's hard to appreciate how bad everything is here until you actually see all the carnage, I said'

'Yes it was – still is, really. The streets are an unbelievable mess – detours everywhere. A real pain when you're in a hurry to get to a job. But you just get up in the morning, do your next lot of stories and try not to analyse anything too much.'

'Your house seems okay.'

He smiled. 'You'll find yourself walking downhill if you sleep in my spare bed tonight. The floor's on a strange angle. There are a few other cracks to the house but nothing too serious.'

Where else did he think I was going to sleep? I looked at him for a minute.

'Mark, is there anyone special in your life these days?'

'No. There was for a while last year but it didn't work out. I don't seem good at relationships.'

I laughed. 'You're not as bad as me.' The relationship I'd had the previous year had ended spectacularly and with great finality. There was no way Mark could compete with that.

'So what went wrong?' I asked.

He sighed. 'It was my fault. I thought I wanted a whole lot of things but turns out I didn't. You know, kids and all that. She'd have been keen. I went right off the idea.'

'And you tell me I'm contrary.'

'Yeah, I know. None of that stuff seems to matter any more.'

He sat down on the floor and leaned his back against the wall. We smiled at one another. My God. I still liked him. Where had that come from all of a sudden?

'You know something, Philippa? You were right to end things between us when you did. We were going in different directions back then. I was so sure of what I wanted and so were you.'

'And now?'

Mark sipped his wine. 'Now I have no bloody idea what I want. Maybe it was the earthquake, maybe it's just me – I don't know. What about you?'

I grimaced. 'Hell, Mark, I don't really know. I have everything I thought I wanted. But I'm bored and I don't know what to do about it. I'm not unhappy, just wondering: "is this it?"'

He reached out and stroked my bare foot. I stared at him. How could a simple touch to the foot make my body feel the way it did?

He grinned at me. 'Now Philippa – what's it to be? The spare bed? Or my bed?'

'I'm surprised you need to ask,' I said quietly.

And that was all it took. The best route to oblivion in the world. I woke up a few hours later wondering where I was. It wasn't pitch dark as it gets in Franz. There was a street light not far away and I could see Mark's sleeping shape beside me. I snuggled into him and let my mind drift. How could I have let this go? We were good together. I'd forgotten.

This dream-like state lasted until we were having our breakfast in the morning and he asked me what my plans were.

'I'll go back to the hospital and see how Julia is. Then I have to go home. She found something in her mother's attic and that was how she worked out who the killer was. I need to have a look myself.'

Mark put down his coffee mug and stared at me. 'You're not serious! There's a killer on the loose in Franz and you're off on some wildcat investigation of your own. Philippa don't be so reckless.'

'It's not reckless – how's the killer going to know what I'm doing?'

'Maybe he or she is watching Julia's house. And anyway the police will have been all over the place. They'll have found anything that's there.'

'I'm not talking about physical clues. I think it'll be something a lot more subtle than that. They haven't a hope of finding it.'

'And you have? I don't believe you, Philippa Barnes – I really don't.'

'Well I can't help that! I have to do something.'

'You're trying to do too much.'

'And not achieving anything. I can't just sit back and wait for the Operation Ice team and Stu Adams to come up with the answers. They haven't got a bloody clue what's going on.'

'I don't know Stu – but I've dealt with Jimmy Black lots of times over the years. He's a smart cop. Don't underestimate him.'

'Well he hasn't worked out who's doing all this killing. How hard can it be? Franz is small; there are not that many people it could be.'

'These things take forever – you know that. The police work quietly away making their case and then one day it's all on and they have someone for it. It's frustrating for we journos too you know. But I've met a lot of cops over the years and trust me – Jimmy Black is one of the good guys.'

'Is the lecture over yet?' I snapped.

'Philippa, I love you. I don't want you putting yourself in danger.'

'Don't be so ridiculous! We've hardly seen each other for the last two years. It's far too soon to be talking about love. I'm not living my life waiting for someone else to make all the decisions, Mark. And you'd better get used to that.'

I was fuming as I drove across town to the hospital. Mad with Mark, mad with myself. A visit to Julia didn't help. She looked terrible still and there'd been no change in her condition. Ann looked a wreck.

I left Christchurch as soon as I left the hospital, not even pausing for a coffee. A couple of hours later I pulled in at the alpine village of Arthurs Pass and had some lunch at one of the cafés. I took out my cellphone and texted one word to Mark: 'Friends?'

A few minutes later the phone pinged and a new message appeared. 'So long as you let me see you really soon.'

I grinned at my phone like a stupid teenager. Suddenly the day seemed much brighter. I was still in this hormonally challenged state when I pulled up at Ann McLoughlin's house. It was deserted. The police had been and gone. I looked round the place uneasily before unlocking the door and going inside.

I wasn't quite as reckless as Mark thought. In fact I was scared. I locked myself in and did a careful search of the house to make sure I was alone. I'd parked the car round the other side of the house out of sight of anyone on the road. By my standards I was being careful.

The attic had me stumped for a while. There was a trapdoor in the hall ceiling with no apparent means of getting up to it but eventually I noticed a metal ring set into it and found a pole in the hall cupboard with a hook on it. I reached up with the pole, connected with the ring and pulled. As If by magic the trapdoor swung open and a tug of the pole produced a neat set of stairs.

I pulled them down to floor level then looked round again, uneasy at the thought of being trapped like a rat up there on my own. I was relieved when I got to the top that I was able to pull the ladder up behind me. I'd brought the pole up with me and could relax knowing that no one could get to me. I groped around in the ceiling space for a light switch. I found it almost straight away and lit up the small attic.

There wasn't much to see – a broken wooden chair, an old bird cage, a roll of carpet. And a couple of cardboard boxes. I picked my way across the roof joists and squatted down in front of them.

Piece by piece I exhumed Julia's childhood. A velvet bag with three baby teeth inside. Homemade Christmas cards with drawings of teetering pine trees and lumpy reindeer. 'To Mummy love from Julia.' An old toy elephant. School reports. A decayed blue swimming cap.

The next box was full of university notes, a plastic folder of writing paper and a packet of old stamps. A student ID card. Julia stared out at me, young, with her thin face framed by long red hair. She wasn't smiling. Nothing new about that.

An envelope with something inside. A photocopy of her birth certificate: Julia Mary, McLoughlin daughter of Ann, a housewife and Leonard Brian, a farm hand. No great surprises here. I was about to shove it all back into the box when I noticed something different amongst all the university notes. A spiral-bound note-book.

I opened it, rocked back on my heels, and like the ultimate nosy neighbour began to read:

January 3 – I'm not really writing a diary, my life's not interesting enough to record day-by-day, but I am going to write about the important things that happen. Not that I'll need a diary to remember last night. Luke and I made love. It was the first time for me. We went out to the lake for a picnic. It was a perfect day. We swam, lay in the sun, slept for a bit and woke up looking at one another. He took me to a beach no one ever goes to. We just talked, then he touched me, then it happened. I thought it would hurt but he was so gentle with me. I can't believe what's happening to me. I saw my parents' marriage and what it did to my mother. I used to lie awake listening to my father shouting. Mum never said anything but she couldn't hide all the bruises. I didn't plan to fall in love – I'd seen how it ends – but with Luke it could be so different. I think he was as awed by what happened as I was.

January 10 – We've made love often since that first time. I can't get enough of him. What if I get pregnant? He's using condoms and I guess that's safe but sometimes I imagine what would happen if we did make a baby. I love him. It's that simple. Luke's child – my child. It has more meaning than my study, more meaning than my books. I love him so much.

May 15 – My father is dead. I came home to find Mum talking on the phone and when she got off she said: 'Len's dead.' Just like that. He'd had a heart attack and died out on a paddock on his farm. Mum and I had a brandy together and we talked about him for a bit. But there wasn't a lot to say. He'd been gone from our lives for a very long time and none of my memories of him were happy. But I can't sleep which is why I'm up writing this at midnight. It was a relief when we left him and for years I looked over my shoulder, scared he would find us and that the shouting would begin all over again. That my mother would get that haunted look in her eyes again. But maybe my father was more important than we thought. Will there be a time when I regret not knowing him?

October 17 A dream, that's all it ever was. Luke is sleeping with Vivien. I want to die.

And that was it. I'd read so much crime fiction. It was what private investigators did – they snooped into peoples' lives, into every secret place until they found what they were looking for. There was no room for scruples, no need for guilt. It was what they did to get the job done. I felt like hell. I'd exposed Julia's deepest feelings and it had all been for nothing.

I still had no idea who the killer was.

Chapter 18

WHAT had Julia realised? Why couldn't I see it?

I sighed with frustration as I drove home, passing Matt coming back in the glacier bus on my way. He flicked his lights and grinned at me and I smiled back, feeling a sudden urge for my life to be normal again. It would be good just to be doing glacier-related things and hanging out with the other guides, not running round trying to second-guess the police.

Spree was home alone and leaped from the couch to greet me with great enthusiasm. It was good to see this bad old dog of mine. I looked around but couldn't see any evidence of Spree-related chaos.

'Hasn't Tom taken you for a walk, old boy?' I asked him just as Tom appeared in the doorway.

'I have actually. That dog is lazy. He wanted to come home and I'm willing to bet he's been on that couch ever since.' My brother carried two bags of groceries and set about stashing them away while I watched.

'What have you been up to?' I asked.

'Getting myself a job,' he said. 'DOC needs some work done on their houses. I've just been up sorting it all out with Callum Jackson. I don't see what your problem is with that guy, Philippa. He seems pretty decent to me.'

'Even though he murdered someone?'

'That was years ago. He's paid for it and frankly I don't think it's any of our business.'

'Whatever.' I couldn't be bothered arguing and got up to make coffee. As we drank it I filled him in on my trip to Christchurch –

omitting my renewed relationship with Mark. That was something I definitely didn't want to discuss. Murder was a much easier topic and I wondered what that said about me. I told Tom about Julia's diary and what a heel I'd felt like reading it.

'You could have stopped if you were feeling that bad,' he pointed out. 'I don't understand why Julia would lie to protect a person who'd killed two people.'

'Unless it's Luke. She really cared for him.'

'Do you think it's him?'

I hesitated. 'He's the only person I can imagine Julia wanting to protect – and I'm sure she thought it was him at first. But now – I'm not so sure. The hatred around Rose's murder – I don't know, I can't see why Luke would have felt that way. Not all these years later. And attacking Julia? Maybe I'm being naïve but I can't see that either.'

I cooked dinner that night. It was a nice mindless task and I tried to forget about everything as I chopped garlic and tomatoes.

'Do you have a passport?' Tom asked me we ate our meal.

'No. Why?'

'I was just thinking that maybe it's your turn to do some travelling. I could stay with Kate. What do you think?'

And then I knew.

I stared at him as my mind finally made the connection. The realisation was so strong that it pushed away the amazing chance he had just offered me.

I was back in Rose's house listening to her tell me of the day Vivien had got her passport. Remembering the ironic smile on her face, the way she hesitated as if about to say more but changed her mind and said nothing.

I was in the church listening to Penelope's wild laughter.

I was in the attic reading Julia's diary.

Yes! There it was. The motive for murder. I saw how Julia had worked it out. I'd bloody well helped her, all unknowingly. And I could understand her empathy with the killer.

Julia had said that it was possible Vivien had been killed because of an unintentional act of cruelty. But there had been nothing unintentional about what Rose Revell had done. She'd been playing a game for years and when the killer finally came to her door she had reaped a hatred she had nurtured for decades.

If it wasn't for what had happened to Julia I too would have felt sympathy. There were some crimes the law couldn't touch. Things that could drive a person to madness.

...

This time I was going to the police. I had no proof of what I had discovered but it was something for them to deal with, not me. There was no point my trying to tackle the killer in the hope of a confession. I wouldn't get one.

I'd thought I had solved the mystery before and had been disappointed. But this time all the pieces fitted. I'd made the mistake of thinking I knew everyone well enough to gauge their likely actions. It was galling to admit how wrong I had been, but I wasn't going to compound my mistakes by tackling the killer and risking death myself. I'm not really a hero.

It was early morning and the glacier valley was still cold. There was no one else around but me and I was glad of it. I wanted to think about what I had discovered, make sure I really had something to tell DI Black. I didn't want to talk to him until I'd thought things through properly.

I left the track to the glacier, walking instead along the side of the river, leaping from boulder to boulder and feeling the usual satisfaction of a body in tune with the environment. Good rock walking has an almost poetical rhythm. The glacier was moving backwards now, retreating in to itself fast, but it was a bit like trying to see the hands of a watch moving. You never saw the ice receding but you knew it was happening all the time and would keep doing so.

After bending to strap my crampons onto my boots I glanced up at the terminal face. A new route onto the ice was opening up, slightly to the left of the one the guides had been using. The glacier had receded so much that it was becoming really difficult to find a safe route onto the ice.

I cut a few steps as I climbed, but my crampons were adequate to tackle the ice unaided in most places. Pausing at the top of the ice face, I looked down into the valley and saw one person walking up the track. There was no sign of the glacier party. It was too early. Apart from the ant-like lone tourist down below I had the whole place to myself.

I turned and began my climb up to the icefall, the only sound the crunch of my crampons as they bit into the ice. I jumped off the glacier and scrambled over the moraine until I reached a rocky ledge. It made a perfect resting place with a sweeping view of the glacier and valley. No one ever came here. It was too far off the route to the mountains for climbers to bother with. I pulled off my jersey and stuffed it into my pack, broke open a bar of chocolate, and sat enjoying the purity of the mountain breeze.

I let my mind drift. It was good to be here with no real destination in mind. After a while I climbed back onto the glacier. The pinnacles seemed particularly dense and after a few abortive attempts to get into the maze I paused, rammed the shaft of my ice axe into the crystalline glacier and leaned back against the blade. I was glad I wasn't trying to get up to the névé. It would take hours.

I gazed at three pinnacles. They crouched like witches with their heads together, sharing secrets. The profile of one of them was perfect, a parody of a tall forehead, large hooked nose and jutting chin. Sinister white witches.

To their left I could see a figure far below, moving fast, heading in my direction. The person I'd spotted earlier must be a climber.

I had no premonition of trouble, just a feeling of annoyance that my space was being invaded. I wandered round a bit more, half-heartedly trying to get into the icefall but more often stopping to gaze up at pinnacles or stare down into crevasses.

I didn't hear anything so I didn't even have time to feel frightened as something shoved me in the back and sent me tumbling down into a deep blue crevasse.

This time there was no snow. And I wasn't dreaming.

Chapter 19

I felt the abrasions as I fell and moisture on my cheek as I struck a razor-like ridge of blue ice. I put my hand to the sore spot and it came away covered with blood. It wasn't until then that I started to feel scared.

I looked up. To the slit of blue sky and the face peering over the rim of the crevasse. Then I looked around, flinching as the movement made my head ache. It wasn't a really deep crevasse but the glassy blue walls were so straight it would be hard to climb up out of it.

And even if I could, Penelope Blake wasn't going to let me past. Her face moved above me, strangely disembodied.

I stood up but my legs were shaky and I was forced to sit down again. How was I going to get out? A swift blow from Penelope's ice axe would stop my ascent before it even began.

'If you kill me you'll be in worse trouble,' I said, struggling to stay calm. 'Julia knows what you did. She won't keep quiet now.'

Penelope smiled down at me. 'Julia's dead. She died early this morning.'

I said nothing, absorbing the shock of her words.

'I thought you would have heard,' Penelope said, 'and it was a bit of luck finding you up here. You'd have never thought it, would you Philippa? You think I'm a feeble old woman.'

'You forget. I found Rose's body. That wasn't the work of a feeble old woman.'

I knew I must get her to talk. Somehow, there's a way out of this, I told myself. I just need time. Julia. Don't think of her.

'Julia sympathised with you,' I told Penelope. 'She wanted me to stop looking once she realised why Vivien had been murdered. Yet you had to kill her too. Why, for God's sake?'

'Because it was quixotic nonsense. I didn't want her sympathy. Eventually she'd have told someone. I couldn't risk that.'

Penelope's head disappeared from view and for a moment I thought she had gone. Then I knew she wouldn't leave me this way. What would be worse, I wondered. A blow with an ice axe or a boulder smashing down on my head? There were quite a few rocks littered on the glacier, it wouldn't be hard for Penelope to find one that was suitable.

I was relieved when it was only her head that reappeared.

'So Julia's sympathy was worth nothing?'

'I've gone well past needing that kind of emotion in my life. All I want is to be free of the past.'

'You never will be,' I said, 'no matter how many people you kill.'

'That's for me to judge.'

'How did you find out?' I asked. The situation I was in no longer felt real. It was as if the cold seeping into my body was also freezing my fear, leaving nothing but curiosity. Bravery wasn't involved. My sensibilities had just shut down.

'Looking through Patrick's papers after he died. There was no shortage of evidence. Photographs, the occasional letter.'

'So that's why you chose Vivien to write a book on Patrick,' I said. 'You knew the kind of book it was going to be.'

Penelope laughed. 'It appealed to my sense of justice. Patrick was a cheat and I was planning to manoeuvre his illegitimate daughter into writing a book which would have discredited him. What a revenge it would have been. But then it all went wrong.'

'Vivien needed her full birth certificate for her passport,' I said. 'That's how she found out.'

'Yes,' Penelope said. 'She wasn't the least bit concerned about my feelings. All she could talk about was how exciting it was for *her* to have a father who was so famous. And how she couldn't wait to tell the world about it. Rose had told her that her father was unnamed on her birth certificate. But she had lied.'

'Julia told me Vivien's father had left Rose when she was a young child. But they can't have lived together. Patrick was married to you.'

'He was a mountaineer who went off on expeditions.' Penelope's voice was sarcastic. 'Not to the Antarctic for the summer as I thought, not climbing in the Himalayas for three months. To a love nest instead.'

'You never suspected anything?'

'Why should I have? There were never any letters even when he went on genuine expeditions. He would go away for months and I'd get on with my life here. That's how our marriage was.'

'This was obviously before Rose and Vivien came to live in Franz?'

'Yes. They lived like nomads. Patrick had to chase them all over the country. Poor man.' Penelope's tone was scornful. 'Eventually Rose Revell decided she didn't want him any more. The *expeditions* stopped then.'

'So why did Rose come to live in Franz?' I asked.

'Because she liked playing games with people. She'd have enjoyed seeing Patrick watching his daughter, knowing he could have no contact with her. Vivien was only a toddler when he was banished from her life. She didn't recognise him when they came to live here years later.'

'And there was you as well, Penelope.'

'Yes. Patrick Blake's naive wife. Rose must have enjoyed watching me, knowing I had no idea. I hated her when I found out. Far more than I ever did Vivien.'

'How did Rose meet Patrick?'

'God knows. She probably came here as a tourist and went on the glacier with him. It must have been here, I know that.'

'Yes,' I forgot my cramped feet as a memory resurfaced. 'She all but told you at Vivien's memorial service, didn't she? I thought it was her reference to Vivien's secret that made you drop your prayer book. But it wasn't, was it?'

'No. God but I'm pleased I killed that woman. "I'm scattering Vivien's ashes on Sentinel Rock. The place where her life began." That was for me.'

'But what did it mean?'

'You know there's a place beyond where the tourists go? You've got to push through thick bush to get there, but once you've done that your privacy's all but guaranteed. That's where Patrick took me while we were courting. And that's where Vivien was conceived. Rose told me that after Vivien's funeral.'

'Patrick never left you, though.'

'And surely you've guessed why,' Penelope said. 'Rose didn't want him. She let him into her life for just long enough to get attached to his daughter and then she cut off the contact for ever.'

'Why did he agree to it?'

'You're not being very clever, Philippa. He was in no position to argue. I've told you before, Patrick was weak. He was no match for Rose. And he couldn't have coped without me either. He must have dreaded me finding out because he'd have known I'd have left him. And he'd have known just as surely that Rose Revell wouldn't have taken him in.'

I was silent as I tried to picture the whole thing.

'Rose had Patrick right where she wanted him.' Penelope's voice sounded distant. She must have got tired of peering down at me as she had withdrawn from the edge of the crevasse and I could no longer see her. The disembodied voice created a sense of unreality.

'Didn't you notice anything in those early years? I asked. 'After all, he was living a double life.'

'I remember how he was when he came back. He was always depressed. I thought it was because he loved the mountains so much he found it hard to cope with ordinary life. It was one of the reasons I didn't push him when he told me he didn't want a family. Amusing, isn't it?'

'And of course that's why Patrick hung round Vivien when she was a teenager,' I said. 'Not because he was having an affair with her, but because he wanted to get to know his daughter.'

'Yes. You can understand how amused I was when you came up with the theory that they were lovers.'

'Mmmm.' I looked at the icy channel at my feet, measuring the distance to the far end of the crevasse. A few steps would be enough and if I could get down there, I had more chance of escaping as it was shallower at that end.

'Vivien must have liked Patrick without knowing who he was. But when she came back to Franz to write her thesis things started to go out of control for her. Her relationship with Callum wasn't working out and she was pregnant. You were forcing her to write a book when she didn't want to,' I said.

'Yes. Even before she found out Patrick was her father she was reluctant about that.'

'Julia was Vivien's friend but there were a lot of things she couldn't discuss with her,' I continued. 'Things were going from bad to worse for her and then she came home and caught Luke Riley in bed with her mother.'

'Is that true? That woman was worse than I thought,' Penelope said.

'You can understand why everyone thought she'd decided to escape from it all and go overseas. She needed to get her birth certificate for her passport. That's when she found out the thing that was more important to her than anything else that had happened in her life. No wonder she was so angry with Rose that summer. Thanks to her, Vivien didn't find out who her father was until it was too late.'

'The only problem was, she'd been finding out a lot of things she didn't like about him.' Penelope sounded amused. 'His high number of accidents. And his affair with Janet Lestrange.'

'So what was it like for you?' I asked.

'Finding out Patrick was Vivien's father, you mean? It made me realise that I'd wasted my life. I loved Patrick for all those years, yet he'd never given me what I really wanted.'

'What was that?'

'I wanted children. Wanted them so much. Patrick didn't. I thought it was because he was too selfish for the sacrifice, or that he wanted me all to himself. And all that time, he had a child. He was paying Rose for her upkeep at a time when we had no spare money. There were times when he was away on his so-called expeditions when I didn't have enough food, when I couldn't pay the bills. Patrick's money would have made all the difference to me and there it was sitting in Rose Revell's bank account. My parents would have helped but I was too proud to ask. After they died, I had money all of a sudden. I could go to Europe when I found out Patrick had been cheating on me with Janet Lestrange. It gave me options again.'

'Not the option you wanted though.'

'No. You know about loss, Philippa. What happened to your family was terrible, but people understand that kind of sorrow. I've lived with loss all my life, the loss of never having had. Your sister Kate has lost her parents, the worst thing that could happen to a child. Yet no one sees that other kind of loss. A child that never was.'

I didn't say anything. I could understand Julia's sympathy for Penelope Blake. Though knowing that she'd killed Julia and was about to try to kill me didn't encourage me to share the view.

'It was bad enough that my husband betrayed me,' the voice floated down to me and I had to strain my ears to catch it, she was talking so quietly, 'but to do so with Rose Revell... For years I've felt her condescension, but until I found out that Patrick was Vivien's father I didn't know why.'

'Were you planning to kill Vivien from the time you found out?'

'Not really. I did think about it. I'd never been given the chance to have my own child. Killing Vivien seemed like the only truly just punishment for Rose. Unfortunately it was too late to punish Patrick. He was dead and beyond my reach. But I soon realised there was no real closeness between Vivien and her mother. I didn't think Vivien was anywhere near as bad as Rose. She was self obsessed but she wasn't nasty and manipulative. I never seriously planned to kill her.'

'So why did you change your mind? Because she found out that Patrick was her father?'

'I asked her to come up the glacier with me. I wanted to talk through the issue with her, and I was foolish enough to hope for some kind of understanding from the girl.'

'But you didn't get it?'

'No. Vivien had one thing in common with her mother. She was used to doing exactly what she wanted in life. We had a picnic lunch up here. I can see her as clearly as if it happened yesterday, sitting on a coat on the edge of a crevasse, an attractive young woman with her whole life in front of her. She reminded me of how I'd once been. You'd have thought she could have showed a bit of compassion.'

'What did she say?' I asked after a silence that seemed to last for minutes.

'She told me I'd been a fool, that we all make our own destinies and that it wasn't her fault I'd chosen pointless self sacrifice.' Penelope sounded ironic. 'She said that Patrick was her father whether I liked it or not, and that she was proud of the fact. I asked her to keep quiet about it for my sake and she laughed at me. Then she said: "You've wasted your life and all you can think of is your reputation, Penelope. I pity you." That was what did it. One moment she was mocking me and the next minute I was looking down on her body in the bottom of the crevasse. I don't remember pushing her though I know I must have done.'

'Was she dead?'

'I don't know. She landed face up and she was certainly unconscious. I knew she wouldn't be able to get out. She was in deeper than you are – and she was not an experienced climber. I hadn't planned to murder her, as I've said. But once I thought of it I knew I had a good chance of covering up what I had done. Everyone knew she was planning an overseas trip. She was having relationship problems and had signed a legal contract to write a book when she didn't want to. I saw Rose Revell in the village later that day so I went straight round to her house, found Vivien's passport and took some of her clothes to make it look like she had gone away.. I hid it all when I got home. But I needn't have worried. No one came looking.'

'You must have known her body would come down the glacier, though.'

'Yes. But I thought the police would assume exactly what they did, that it was an accident. And that's where the matter would have ended if it hadn't been for Julia's interference.'

'Julia told me Vivien could have been murdered for an unintentional act of cruelty, that she said and did things she didn't mean.'

'That's rubbish, Philippa. We're all responsible for what we do.'

'You obviously didn't see anyone else on the glacier that day?'

'No. I was lucky. I stayed up in the icefall till evening and managed to get down without anyone seeing me. But when I got home I got worried. What if I'd been wrong and she was still alive after all?'

Penelope hadn't looked over the edge for quite a few minutes and judging from the distance of her voice, she must have sat down somewhere. Slowly, I started to work my way down to the shallow end of the crevasse.

'So that's why Callum was in the valley the night Vivien died, I said'

'Yes. I didn't intend to tell him. I had no plans beyond getting my hands on Vivien's clothes and passport so it would look like she had left the village. But I was worried. Callum turned up for something and he realised there was something wrong.'

'So you told him.'

'Yes. Callum had good reason to understand.'

'You'd helped him come to terms with his past.'

'There was a good deal more to it than that. Callum knew Vivien and me well and he could understand how the whole thing had happened. He went straight up the glacier.

'What would he have done if he had found her?'

'Talked to her. That's all. Persuaded her not to say anything. But it wasn't necessary – she hadn't miraculously made her way down the glacier – and we knew she must be dead.'

'Weren't you worried that Callum would be a prime suspect if Vivien was found? The police would have soon dug out his background.'

'We didn't think there was much danger of her being found. You know how quickly the glacier changes. Vivien would have been covered in ice in no time and once she was, I was safe.'

'So how did you feel when the body was recovered and Julia asked me to try and find who'd killed her?'

Penelope was silent for a moment. 'My only fear was that you'd find out about Callum. I wasn't the slightest bit worried that you'd discover my motive. Callum was more concerned.'

'Callum! He treated me with contempt. I didn't think he was the least bit fazed by what I was doing.'

'You were wrong. He was worried about me and he was concerned about your persistence. Rightly, I have to admit.'

'I can understand how you killed Vivien – and Rose. But I'll never understand how you could kill Julia.'

'That was necessary. I didn't like doing it. I don't really want to kill you either, Philippa, but I have no alternative.'

I felt cold - in more ways than one. Keep her talking, I told myself, edging a few inches further down the crevasse. I knew I'd be able to get out under ordinary circumstances, but with Penelope poised with an ice axe I didn't like my chances. My cramped legs weren't going to aid my escape either.

'Weren't you worried Rose would point the finger at you once Vivien's body was found?' I asked. 'After all, she knew the truth about Patrick.'

'Not really. I knew it would seem like an accident. Vivien was a perfectionist, she was writing about women mountaineers, so she wanted to be one. She could have easily decided to go up on the glacier alone so no one could see just how bad she was on her feet.

Do you want to hear the biggest irony of all, Philippa Barnes? I actually saved Vivien from death earlier on the same day.'

'How?'

'She slipped. If I hadn't arrested her fall she'd have gone right over the terminal and fallen a hundred feet or more onto the rocks. If I'd been a bit slower on my feet that day I wouldn't have become a murderer.'

'And what about Rose? Was that murder planned?'

'Not exactly. I thought the loss of her only child was punishment enough, that every day she would wonder where Vivien was until she was eaten away with it all. Then she rang me and asked me round for coffee. Said she had something she wanted to talk to me about.'

I didn't answer. I had finally managed to wriggle to the end of the crevasse.

'When I got there she started talking about Vivien's death. How she was starting to realise it wasn't an accident. Asked me what I thought. I didn't say anything. She watched me like a cat stalking a bird. Then she took me up to the studio. I looked from the paintings of Vivien to the calculating look on her mother's face and I couldn't hide my hatred. Rose Revell told me Patrick had said I was frigid, told me the intimate details of her relationship with him. She was goading me to admit I'd killed Vivien, but there was more to it than that. She seemed to be able to tell what his deception had done to me; I could see the enjoyment she was getting out of my suffering. Patrick was a fool but she was evil. Then I noticed the ice axe.'

Penelope didn't say anything for a couple of minutes and I was startled when she looked into the crevasse at me. After everything she had told me I expected her to be changed, expected that genteel mask to be gone, but her face was the same as it always was. Somehow that made the situation all the more frightening.

'It was the most satisfying thing I've ever done in my life. Once I started hitting her I didn't want to stop. I smashed up all the paintings of my husband's bastard too. I knew the axe would be covered in fingerprints so I took it home and hid it. The next day when the police came to talk to me my arms were so stiff I could hardly carry the tray of coffee through to the lounge. They didn't have a clue. They were embarrassed at having to take my other ice axes and kept apologising for the inconvenience.'

'Well they didn't apologise to me when they took mine.'

Penelope smiled. 'It was obvious I was never a suspect. Rose's promiscuity made sure of that. That was the other thing she'd told me that night, you see. About the young man she'd just had sex with. "You're never too old for it, Penelope," she said, "but then you wouldn't understand that would you?" I don't like swearing but that woman was a bitch.'

'You don't mind killing but you don't like swearing,' I said.

'I don't actually like killing people, Philippa. I don't want to kill you but I have to do it. You know too much – even if you can't prove it. But more importantly, with you dead I will get to keep your sister.'

I lurched in my ice prison. '*What* did you say?'

'Your sister didn't make it to school this morning, Philippa. Kate is with me. She's had a lot of insecurity in her short life but I'm going to be here for her now. With you dead there'll be no one to look after her. I will treat her as my own, you can be sure of that.'

This was hardly reassuring.

'I don't believe you.' I said.

'Why would I lie?'

'You won't keep Kate,' I said with a lot more confidence than I felt. 'Tom's home now. She will live with him – unless you plan to kill him too.'

She laughed. 'Tom! He won't stay around. He'll be glad of the offer of a home for his little sister.'

'You won't have a hope. You abducted her – no one's going to let you adopt her. You'll go to prison for that alone.'

Penelope squatted down at the edge of the crevasse. She was laughing. I stared at her, seriously frightened. I had to do something or I'd be dead and Kate would end up living with this mad woman! I could imagine how plausible she would sound to Tom. What could I do?

'The glacier party will be up here soon, I said.

'They won't come this far.'

But as I had hoped Penelope was distracted for half a minute as she looked down the valley – and I lurched to my feet, reached over the lip of the crevasse and grabbed her by the ankles. She came crashing in on top of me and I tried to dodge her crampon clad feet, wincing as I felt one point dig into my shoulder and another into my arm.

My legs were stiff, I moved as if I'd been drugged, and it took me a few minutes to realise that there was no real hurry any more. Penelope had struck her head on the blade of my ice axe as she fell and she was unconscious.

I checked her airways and placed my jersey under her head, then covered her with a coat before running down the glacier. Eventually I saw the glacier party approaching.

Matt and Sara stared up at me as I came plummeting out from behind a pinnacle.

'She's got Kate,' I screamed at them.

Chapter 20

A hastily assembled search team went up the glacier and got Penelope Blake out of the crevasse. She had a broken leg and sore head but no other apparent injuries. Matt, who had been one of the rescue team, said she had been quiet and calm. She had thanked them all as they lifted her into the helicopter.

She was a lot calmer than me. I had fairly flown off the glacier in my haste to get back to the village to find Kate.

I ran up Penelope's driveway, Tom close behind me. The door was locked so we smashed a pane in her French door and rushed inside yelling Kate's name. There was no one there.

Stu arrived in his squad car, his face grim.

'She tells us she has Kate somewhere we won't find her,' he told us.

'Oh God.' My voice was shaking. 'She's mad, you know Stu. Everything she said was rational – in a crazy kind of way - till she started talking about Kate. She thought she'd be able to keep her even though she had abducted her. That's when I realised she was truly mad.'

We went back home then, hoping against hope that Penelope had been lying and that Kate would be home from school as she usually was. There was no one there.

I paced round our living room and looked out the window. 'This is useless. We need to go up to the village and see what the police are doing. We can't just sit and wait for something to happen.'

'Yes – you're right,' Tom looked drawn and worried.

Stu came out to meet us at the police station. 'We've got the Operation Ice team searching all empty houses,' he told us. 'It's lucky there are still so many police here. They're sending a local team and a search dog and handler down from Greymouth – I'm expecting them any time. We'll find her – I promise you both.'

Tom and I looked at him without replying.

'We're going to help,' I said after an awkward pause. 'Sure,' he said. 'That's good.'

'Where have you looked so far?' Tom asked.

'The guys are working their way south from Whataroa. You know what the farm roads are like round there – there are a lot of places she could be. When the local team arrive I'll get them started at the bottom of the Fox Hills and work their way back towards the village. Kate must be here somewhere. Penelope didn't have time to get her out of the village.'

It sounded good. This would cover everything within a thirty kilometre radius of the village in the north and about ten in the south. It should be possible to look everywhere before dark.

'We'll work south from our place,' I said, thinking of a side road that stretched for kilometres off the main road. It had once been home to scattered farms but lifestylers had moved in over the last ten years or so buying blocks of land and building baches and holiday homes.

Tom and I set off, not talking as we drove down the narrow gravel road. There were more houses down here than I'd remembered and I couldn't help being pleased that a team of police would be joining us soon.

Starting at the far end of the road we slowly worked our way back, exploring every unoccupied house along the way. It was nerve-wracking and depressing. My heart hammered each time we walked up to a house. I was past caring about legalities and liberally used my picklocks to gain entry wherever I could but it was no use. Many of the places were neglected, with grass growing long and unkempt, and moss creeping over the driveways. The holiday dreams seemed to have turned into yesterday's toys for many of these absentee owners.

My cellphone rang in my pocket, making me jump.

'Philippa? It's Stu. I think we've found the place. We're going in now.'

My heart froze.

'Where are you?'

'Just up the road from you – I can see your car from where I'm standing. It's a dark stained two-storey place with a lot of trees around it. You can't see it from the road and I don't know who owns it. The curtains are pulled and it's all locked up but there are fresh tyre tracks on the driveway. Someone's been here pretty recently.'

'We're on our way.' Tom and I ran for the car. We got there as Stu and another cop forced open the door. I was too stressed to offer them my picklocks. We peered into a living room full of old mismatched furniture. It was the kind of stuff you found in peoples' baches – an uninspiring Formica table and chairs, a battered brown corduroy couch and a couple of cracked black vinyl-covered armchairs. There were books all over the coffee table and I recognised some of Kate's favourites.

Then I was pushing past the police to run upstairs to the bedrooms. The bed in the first room was unmade, the sheets and duvet thrown back as if someone had exited it in a hurry. I gasped as I recognised my sister's red polar fleece jacket slung over a chair at the bottom of the bed.

She had been here. But she wasn't here any longer. She had vanished.

And a thorough search of the rest of the house and the grounds revealed no sign of her.

'Why don't you go home and wait?' Stu said to us. 'We'll be combing every inch of the area around here. There's a dog handler who'll be here any minute and the rest of the searchers will be concentrated round here. It could be that she's hiding somewhere. After all she doesn't know we've got Penelope.'

'She could have got out of the house easily,' Tom said. 'But if so, where is she?'

Maybe – just maybe – Penelope had killed her.

No one voiced the thought but it was on all of our minds.

'I'm not going anywhere.' I said.

And so we stayed until the search was called off for the night. Not that it did us any good. The dog had picked up a trail leading away from the house and out onto the road but lost it a kilometre or so later. The search of the whole area around the house was extensive. But it yielded nothing.

I'd have kept on going all through the night if there had been anywhere else to search. But there wasn't.

'She can't be dead,' I said to the weary search team. 'Penelope wanted to keep her. She would never have killed her.'

No one stated the obvious – that if this was true we would have found her. We were standing round outside the house when Stu's phone rang.

'Yes? How did you find out about this? Where is he now?' he asked.

After a minute he clicked his phone shut and turned to Tom and me, his face grim. 'There's been a sighting of Kate.'

'Where?' I could hardly get the word out.

'Early this morning – about nine o'clock. Someone saw her running down the track to the helicopter base. A boy on holiday with his family. Seems that he'd struck up an acquaintance with Kate and Sally the day before.'

'Where is he now?'

'At the Operation Ice Base. Wendy is taking his statement now.'

'Can we talk to him?' Tom asked.

Stu shrugged. 'Once Wendy has finished, yeah.'

Tom and I raced back to the village. We walked into a busy scene at the Operation Ice base. There were police search and rescue people everywhere. It was a shock being in a brightly-lit building after the semi-dark of the area round the search scene.

After a while a boy emerged from the interview room, DC Wendy Munro at his side. He had a thick head of dark red hair and an alert expression. He was looking about, obviously interested in the police operation going on all around him. Wendy introduced him to Tom and me.

His name was Will and he told us he wanted to be a police prosecutor one day. I liked him. If I hadn't been so upset I'd have liked to ask him where that idea came from and why he wanted to be a prosecutor rather than a defence lawyer, but for now my focus was entirely on what he had seen of my sister.

He frowned as he spoke, taking care to get things clear in his head before he said anything.

'She was in a hurry but she didn't look scared,' he told us.

'How could you tell?'

'I suppose I can't be sure – but I had a good look at her face and she didn't look upset. Just intent, like she was in a hurry to do something.'

'The police told me you met Kate and Sally yesterday,' I said.

He smiled. 'Yep. My parents and sisters were having coffee and I was bored. So I went for a walk and saw your sister with that cool dog. We got talking. So when I saw her today I was curious. I wondered what she was up to. I nearly went after her. I wish I had now.'

I wished he had too. Tom and I went home soon afterwards. I had no idea what we were going to do when we got there. I was past all logical thought.

As we pulled up at the house the door opened.

A familiar face looked out.

Kate had come home.

...

Tom and I leaped out of the car and ran and threw our arms round our little sister.

I stared at my family and couldn't believe how lucky I was. I thought of the loneliness of Penelope Blake and almost felt sorry for her. Despite everything she had done.

'She told me you'd asked her to come and get me, Philippa.'

We were sitting at the table eating fruit toast and it seemed like the best meal in the world. Stu and a whole lot of other searchers were there with us. Kate had been explaining about how she had decided to do a bit of detective work on her own the day she went missing. So she'd bunked school and taken herself off to Callum Jackson's place to have a look round. He had come home – fortunately before she'd managed to get herself into his house – and she'd run off - headlong into Penelope Blake.

Penelope, it seemed, had just seized the opportunity presented to her. She had no trouble encouraging Kate to tell her story. When she had finished Penelope had told her that I had sent her to find her, that I had to go away for a few days, that the investigation had put us both in danger.

Penelope had offered to hide Kate and she told her that I had agreed to this. Kate believed her. Why wouldn't she? She'd thought it strange when they didn't go to Penelope's house but Penelope just said that they'd be too easy to find there. So they'd gone to the house of a friend of Penelope's. It was empty and located well out of the village down an infrequently used farm road. The friend was overseas. It had been as easy as that.

'She said she was going to be gone for a few hours and told me to stay inside.'

But something about her manner had made my sister uneasy.

'I never really liked her, you know,' Kate said. 'She used to come to school a lot and she lent me some cool books and stuff, but there was something a bit creepy about her. So after she'd gone I started to get worried. You know what this road is like, there's nowhere to hide, and I thought if I started walking home she might catch me. So I headed for the creek and followed that to the road. It was cold but I had to leave my jacket behind – it's so bright I thought she might have seen me. Then I came home through the paddocks on the other side of the road. I figured she wouldn't find me that way. But it took me a long time to get home and when I did you were both gone.'

While Penelope had been on the glacier trying to kill me my sister had been walking home.

'Weren't you scared to be here on your own?' I asked.

My sister shrugged. 'What was there to be scared of? I had the door locked – I wouldn't have let Penelope in. And I had Spree. You're often out at night, Philippa. I wasn't worried.'

She had been abducted but she had come home apparently un-traumatised. Just a little cross with herself for being taken in by Penelope Blake.

We were so lucky.

I suddenly remembered Julia and felt sick.

'What is it, Philippa?' Tom noticed my expression and looked concerned.

'I'm just thinking of Julia. I can't believe she's dead.'

He stared at me. 'She isn't dead. She has come out of her coma. She's going to be fine.'

Chapter 21

THE house was full of people. Spree was not impressed. He was not a party dog. He wandered round the room eyeing our guests with disbelief. He unbent somewhat when offered food but his general demeanour was one of outrage.

'Isn't he funny?' Kate knelt down and put her arms round him and I caught my breath as I looked at them. I was more traumatised at the thought of Penelope abducting Kate than I had been about Rose's murder.

It had been a strange week. Kate, Tom and I had been pretty absorbed in our own affairs and none of us had been out much. I was still intrigued at the connection between Kate and Tom. They weren't really alike and their experiences were worlds apart but it was as if they knew each other. It was uncanny.

It was only now it was all over that I truly felt the emotion of it all. Most nights I woke up several times, my heart racing, and had to tell myself that Kate was back, that everything was okay. I lost count of the times I crept to her room and peeped in, just to see her sleeping in her own bed.

We had talked a lot about our parents, the life they had given us in Franz and the way they'd left us. As I listened to Kate I realised how much she had moved on from their deaths, how it no longer threw a huge shadow over all that we did.

Yes, it was the right time for a party. We needed to get back into our ordinary lives again and this was a good way to start.

'What are you doing in the kitchen all on your own, Philippa?' Matt stood in the doorway, glass in hand.

'Just thinking,' I said. 'But it's all good. Matt, I had an email from Tim today. He and Helen are married – and they're coming home a bit earlier than planned. So you'll have a real boss again in a few months' time.'

He sighed. 'I don't want a real boss. You suit me just fine.'

'That's because I don't make you do anything. I can't wait to have him back. He can do Callum Jackson's bloody reports for one thing!'

Matt laughed. 'Callum's actually here tonight. Did you ask him? I couldn't believe it when he turned up.'

'I did ask him – I asked the whole village – but I didn't think he'd come.'

'Well he's sitting out there yarning away to Tom looking quite at home.'

I laughed and followed Matt out to the living room, picking up a glass of red wine on the way. Angie and her husband Alan were here, as was Jem Browne. Sara sat in a corner talking to Kate and her friend Sally, Spree in attendance. Other people I hadn't seen in ages filled the space. The room was full of talk and laughter.

I was surprised to see Stu Adams standing over by the window, glass of beer in hand. I joined him.

'Thanks for everything you've done for us Stu,' I said. 'I haven't been very gracious to you.'

'I was hardly besieging you with good news,' he said.

'No. But I gave you no credit for finding out what was going on – and that wasn't fair.'

'The reality is we didn't really find out what was going on. We'd have got there because once Julia McLoughlin had been attacked she would have changed her mind about keeping Penelope Blake's identity secret. But if Julia had died – and she would have if you hadn't come along – it would have been much harder.'

'What's happening with Penelope?'

'She's in custody and has shown no interest in applying for bail. But she is denying everything apart from taking Kate. She's arguing that she was doing Kate a favour, rescuing her from an unstable home.'

'So it'll go to court?'

'Probably. There is no way she is going to confess. She's saying that everything she told you was lies. That you wanted a story – and so she told you one.'

I shivered and noticed Callum Jackson standing close by listening to our conversation. He looked stricken and I felt sorry for him. Penelope had been his friend.

Before I had the chance to talk to him Angie appeared at my side.

'There's one person I don't see here tonight, Philippa. Mark Nolan.'

'Why would he be here?' I could feel my face getting hot.

'Most people ask their boyfriends to their parties,' she retorted.

'He's not my boyfriend.'

'According to my sister he is – she saw the pair of you getting really cosy at an Italian café in Christchurch not so long ago.'

'But nothing had happened then.'

She was on it in a flash. 'Not then. So it did happen later? What's going on Philippa?'

'You and Jem are the limit. Can't you keep your intelligence work confined to Franz Josef!'

'Hey,' Jem protested. 'This is nothing to do with me.'

'If it's not one of you it's the other,' I said laughing and avoiding my brother's eye. I did not want to talk about Mark and now I'd been outed at my own party in front of half the village.

The talk moved on as it does at parties. It was a fun night and I tumbled into bed late having drunk far too much red wine and did not awaken until nearly 10 o'clock next morning.

There were a couple more things I had to do. And then I would go back to being a glacier guide.

I would not get involved in another murder. Ever again.

...

It took me a few days to make the phone call to Callum Jackson. We needed to clear the air and it helped that he'd come to my party. It seemed that he too was keen to make a move.

Matt, Sara and I had spent an idle morning in the office after our small glacier party decided they didn't want to go out in the rain. We talked about Penelope and how she had come to do the things she had. Matt couldn't understand any of it. Sara could though.

'I don't see how you can go around making excuses for her,' he said. 'She was a raving bloody pyscho. You can't go round chopping up people you don't like with ice axes. And then abducting children. None of it makes sense.'

'And it never will to you,' Sara snapped. 'You don't have the imagination to see anything. Or the empathy.'

'If that's where empathy gets you, you're welcome to it. I'm happy to be an ordinary guy.'

'You're that all right.' Sara's voice was grim.

I gave them a distracted smile. I needed to get on and do it.

Callum didn't seem surprised when he heard my voice on the phone. 'I've been meaning to get in touch with you, Philippa. Do you want to meet for a coffee at Ice Rocks?'

'Yes – that sounds great.'

I hadn't been keen on running the gauntlet of the DOC office. I was sure that Callum's colleagues would have an opinion on what I'd been up to and I didn't expect it to be a good one.

Ice Rocks was busy but I managed to secure a table tucked away in the far corner. I ordered a coffee and read the local paper as I waited. He joined me, looking hassled.

'Sorry I'm late. I've had head office on the phone. They're not happy with all the publicity DOC's getting with all of this.'

'They need to get over themselves. This isn't about a whole lot of Wellington bureaucrats for God's sake!'

'My thoughts entirely,' he said.

Our coffee arrived. I stuck my spoon into the froth of my flat white, making patterns on the surface.

Callum looked at me for a moment in silence then he gave a kind of grimace. 'Philippa, the first thing I need to say is that I am really sorry about leaving that drawing on your front doorstep. It was crude and it was cruel. I was trying to scare you into stopping your investigations. And then, when you didn't stop, I scared Kate by dragging her into the woodshed. It was unforgiveable. And I felt terrible afterwards, I was worried I'd permanently traumatised her. I still can't believe I did those things. There's no excuse.'

'I thought it might be you,' I said. 'And it only made me more determined, I'm afraid.'

'I guess I didn't know you very well. I was desperate to stop you. I'm sorry.'

'I understand why you did it. Penelope was your friend and you were trying to protect her. I just hope she realised what a good friend you actually were.'

'Believe me it was nothing compared to what she did for me. You know, don't you? When I saw you and Angie with that painting that day I thought you were trying to pay me back for what I'd done – and I didn't blame you. I still don't understand how the hell you found out.'

'Well I hadn't found out then. I found the painting in Tim's office and wondered what it was doing there. But it did lead to my trip over to Mount Cook and that's where I found out about your past. It kind of went from there, taking me off in all the wrong directions.'

Callum was silent for a moment then gave me a sad smile. 'She saved my sanity. When I came out of prison I came to Franz because I needed to be near the mountains. But I couldn't forget what I'd done. I never will. Penelope became my friend. I told her everything and she helped me get my mind back together. And now I have to sit back and watch her lose her own. She was a fine woman until Vivien …'

'You helped her too,' I said. 'You were there for her all the way. I saw you on the glacier just after Rose's murder. You looked terrible.

You knew what she had done – and you didn't know how to stop it.'

He gave a short laugh. 'I underestimated you Philippa. I thought your mind was as sloppy as your report writing. I know differently now.'

'Yes, well that's one of the things I need to talk to you about. Tim's coming back early so you won't be subjected to me for much longer. I'm going back to being one of the peasants and I can't wait. Management isn't for me.'

'It's not really for me either – but it's better to be in charge than being told what to do.'

I forbore to mention that he wasn't actually in charge, given that he had Wellington bureaucrats watching his every move.

'I'll never talk about it around her,' I told him. 'Your past, I mean. The media don't know anything about it and the police certainly won't tell them. Callum, I don't usually give people advice but one thing I've learned since my parents died is that there comes a point when you've got to let go. You can't keep analysing things.'

He looked at me for a moment before he replied. 'Thanks, Philippa. I've been very wrong about you.'

'And I have about you. When Tim gets home he'll get a hell of a shock to find that we're friends.'

Callum laughed. 'While we're on the subject of secrets – I've always wondered why the sign vandal suddenly ceased operating in the glacier valley. I'm sure you know?'

'It wasn't me,' I said. 'But let's just say I've dealt with it and it won't be happening again.'

'You won't tell me?'

'Okay then – so long as it goes no further. It was Kate and her friend Sally. They were trying to help me.'

He shook his head. 'Unbelievable. Your parents taught you both to be strong, didn't they?'

'I like to think we've taught ourselves that.'

Callum smiled. 'And I liked the time they put the *extreme danger* one outside the church. I thought it was a brilliant touch even if

I had to disapprove officially. Between you and me those signs are ridiculous.'

We laughed together but even as we did so I thought of Rose Revell and felt sad. She'd thought it was funny as well. There were no happy endings for her and somehow I thought it would be no easy matter for Callum Jackson to shed his past.

Julia came home from hospital a few days later. I had been surprised that she had come back to Franz instead of just returning to her life in Wellington. But it was good because I needed to see her.

Ann McLoughlin was apologetic when I rang. Julia was sleeping, she told me. She was fragile and not keen to see anyone. I was irritated but tried not to show it. After all she had been grievously injured and rendered unconscious for several days. It was hardly surprising if it took her a while to get over it.

In the end it was Julia who made the next move. She rang me at work just as I was about to leave with a glacier party.

'Philippa, can you come and see me sometime soon? I don't feel like coming into the village yet but I do want to talk to you.'

I agreed to go to her place after work and went up the glacier with my mind a million miles away from the job. It poured with rain that afternoon and I got drenched cycling home. Tom was nowhere to be seen but Kate was home from school sprawled in front of the television with Spree. They were eating crumpets and dripping maple syrup everywhere, but I couldn't find it in me to be annoyed.

Kate was walking on water as far as Tom and I were concerned and she'd been quick to see the advantage in the situation. Well she might as well enjoy it while it lasted.

'I need to go and see Julia,' I told her. 'Will you be okay here on your own?'

She gave me a contemptuous look and I laughed. 'Okay, silly question – see you later.'

I parked my car as close to the house as I could get and stepped out only to be drenched by a dripping tree. Ann met me at the door.

She looked ten years younger than the woman I'd seen keeping vigil at her daughter's bedside.

'It's good of you to come, Philippa,' she said. 'Julia is so keen to see you.'

'How is she?'

'Better now she's out of hospital. She won't be back at work for some time and she still gets very tired. But there's no lasting brain damage. She's been very lucky.'

Julia was sitting in the lounge. She was paler and thinner than she'd been but she still looked good. Amazingly so. We talked about the whole thing. Or I did. She wanted the whole story, every detail.

After I told her I looked at her thoughtfully. She looked back with a slightly defensive expression.

'But how did you work it out?' she asked me

I read your diary, Julia – and I'm ashamed of myself for doing it – but it didn't help.'

'You would have had to be inside my head and believe me that's not a place I'd have recommended to my worst enemy. I found that old copy of my birth certificate – and then I read the stuff I'd written about Dad and I just knew what the secret was that Vivien had been going to tell me. She'd found out who her father was – that he was Patrick Blake. You'd told me about Penelope laughing at you when you said that Patrick and Vivien had been having an affair and I suddenly realised why.'

I sat back in my chair and looked out the window. Rain was sheeting across the paddock and the trees swayed in the wind.

'I knew what Vivien was like. I knew she'd have shown no empathy to Penelope. It's what I said before, she could be so cruel – even if it wasn't intentional. That's why I tried to protect Penelope and do you know something Philippa? To the day I die I'll never forgive myself for exposing this whole thing. Rose would still be alive if I hadn't had this pathetic need to find out the truth. And Penelope wouldn't be mad.'

'That's debatable,' I said with a shiver, recalling Penelope's cavalier attitude towards my sister's future – not to mention the small matter of her shoving me down a crevasse. 'Well next time you decide to utilise my dubious detective skills try and remember this conversation Julia!'

She winced. 'You don't have to remind me. It's a nightmare.'

'And to think this whole thing started because of your feelings for Luke Riley.' It was a cheap shot but I was getting a little sick of Julia's attitude. She had been bashed over the head but she didn't need to be so bloody miserable about everything.

She flushed. 'That makes it worse. It was all over nothing. I looked at him when he came to see me that day and I wondered what planet I've been on for all these years. I was obsessed with him – but there's nothing to obsess about! He's so damned ordinary.'

'You said it. But at least it's over. You can get on with your life again Julia. And you should.'

'What are you going to do?' she asked.

I thought of Tom's brilliant offer and I suddenly decided I was going to accept it.

'I'm going overseas,' I said. 'Just like Vivien Revell should have done.'

Epilogue

'How do you find the accused – guilty or not guilty?'
'Guilty.'

Penelope Blake swayed slightly but showed no other reaction.

She stood listening to the judge as he spoke the formal words. When they were finished she walked out of the dock for the last time. She did not look round as she was taken out the side door and down to the cells.

Penelope had not spoken during the trial but her lawyer had done a good job on her behalf. I had been a witness so was not able to spend any time in the public gallery until my evidence was complete. Angie had been there for the whole thing and filled me in as the trial went along. Julia had given her evidence but unlike me she hadn't waited around for the verdict. She had seemed to have endless time off in Franz the previous year but suddenly she was apparently needed in Wellington and couldn't spare any time to see the end of the story she had started.

Penelope had admitted to the attack on Julia. She could hardly do anything else. But she had staunchly denied the murders of Vivien and Rose. Most of the case was circumstantial but there was one damning piece of forensic evidence. There was nothing the defence lawyer could do to mitigate the fact that the police had found an ice-axe, covered in Penelope Blake's fingerprints, when they had searched her house. Traces of Rose's blood and brain matter were still all over the axe which – unbelievably – Penelope had not disposed of. She had put it under her bed!

It was over.

The jury had reached the right verdict but it didn't make me feel happy. The whole thing was tragic. If only Julia – and I – had left things alone. No good had come of our efforts. I hadn't been able to contact Penelope during the trial, given that I was a witness, but now I could go and see her – if she would agree.

I didn't know if I would. Penelope's life was ruined and I felt partially responsible.

As I walked out of the court I saw Callum Jackson. He had been there right to the end. I was pleased for Penelope but I didn't want to talk to him. Not now.

Things had changed in the last year. Kate was at high school in Hokitika. Tom was working there as a builder and had rented a house for Kate, Spree and him to live in.

I was free for the first time since my parents had died. It was time for a change. We had shut up our house in Franz. I was taking a year off being a glacier guide.

I got into my car and sat for a minute, thinking about life. The places we started were so random and some of us were luckier than others in the hand we were given. But in the end it came down to choice, just as Vivien Revell had told our school class all those years before. I would always love Franz and one day I'd come back, but it was time to go and see some different places.

Author's Note

WITH two exceptions none of the characters in Glacier Murder are based on real people or animals. But conflict between conservation and tourism interests in the Franz Josef Glacier valley is all too real.

It has never been easy to balance public safety and wilderness experience and it probably never will be. The Department of Conservation (DOC) came under intense criticism in the wake of the 1995 Cave Creek tragedy. The country was traumatised by the deaths of 13 students and a DOC worker when a viewing platform collapsed in Paparoa National Park. As a result it seemed that every structure and track within its DOC's jurisdiction suddenly gained a danger warning. As far as I know no one has been driven to physically remove warning signs from the Franz Josef Glacier valley as Kate does in this novel, but it is easy to see how such a thing might have happened.

Today the balance seems about right. No warnings mar the spectacular riverbed route to the glacier but once you get there graphic signs leave you in no doubt as to the death that awaits those unwary enough to clamber under the ice.

The two real characters in Glacier Murder are Spree (aka Pete) the giant schnauzer and my nephew Will Shaw who makes a cameo appearance near the end.

And the dynamics of the landscape and people of the glacier country are as real as I can make them, my tribute to a unique way of life.

Other books by Trish McCormack

Assigned to Murder

Trish McCormack

Philippa Barnes mystery 1

Available in print and ebook editions

Philippa Barnes, a young West Coast glacier guide, is getting over her parents' death in a climbing accident, when Kirsten, her journalist friend, is murdered beside a nearby lake. Philippa teams up with Kirsten's brother Jack to try and find out what Kirsten was investigating, while a diarist tries to understand the emotion behind a betrayal that has poisoned at least one life.

Philippa's search will take her from the secretive people of the lake to the home of High Court judge, Loraine Latimer, a powerful woman who has a strange relationship with her family.

Philippa finds that the murder of Kirsten is linked to a decades-old mystery, but not in time to prevent another tragedy.

Past and present finally come together in a late-night confrontation at Lake Kaniere when two very different people face the consequences of choices they made many years before. It all comes down to what people mistake for love, and the destructive nature of some friendships. The novel's characters reflect the contradictions of their environment – where life can thrive, even in the ice, and where things that inspire can kill.

Cold Hard Murder

Trish McCormack

Philippa Barnes mystery 3

Available in print and ebook editions

The darkness felt tangible. Like it was pressing against my blind eyes ... We were going to die here. Slowly, slowly.

Two people struggle on a ledge high above the surge pool at Punakaiki's Pancake Rocks. One falls to their death, beginning a sequence of violence as Department of Conservation ranger Matt Grey announces plans for a commercial tourism venture bitterly opposed by the local community. More people die, and it seems their murders are motivated by something more personal than a threat to the integrity of the national park. But the trail is as cold and twisted as some of the park's most labyrinthine caves. Philippa Barnes is asked to do some unofficial sleuthing, which is not welcomed by the police. She delves into the lives of some strong-willed individuals, many of whom have secrets, uncovering a dark story that resonates with events in her own life. But caught in a desperate struggle deep underground, has she run out of time to stop a determined killer?

Find out the latest on Trish's writing on her Facebook page

Assigned to Murder - Trish McCormack - Community

www.trishmccormack.com